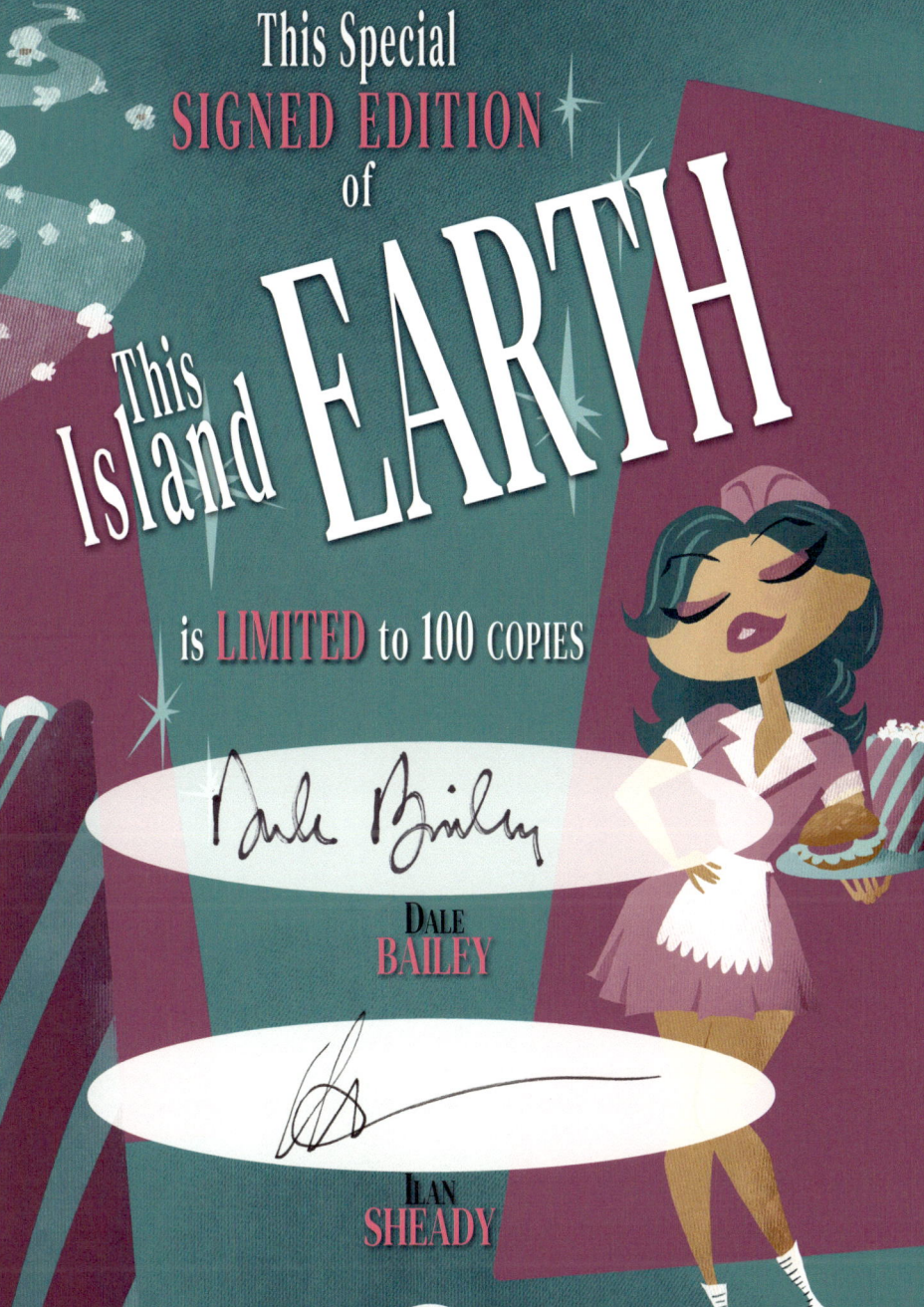

Praise for THIS ISLAND EARTH

"A love letter to sci-fi and horror movies, this is a must-read for all fans of the classic era. With a master's precision and a longing for those cherished moments of cinema that made us who we are, Bailey brings heartache, honesty and humour to films that never existed—but you will wish they did."

—Stephen Volk

"Dale Bailey is the schlock-film host of your dreams. Again and again, he finds the beating heart within the most lurid titles in Hollywood history and demonstrates they're really home movies. You may be too moved even to finish your popcorn."

—Andy Duncan, Nebula and World Fantasy Award-winning author of *An Agent of Utopia* and *The Pottawatomie Giant and Other Stories*

"Dale Bailey has long been one of the greatest undersung writers in the fantasy genre. If you don't know him, this book is an ideal introduction. On display is a full range of humor, depth, horror, sweetness, heartbreak, and wonder. If there is any justice left in the world, *This Island Earth* will be recognized as a classic."

—Nathan Ballingrud, Shirley Jackson Award-winning author of *The Strange and North American Lake Monsters*

Praise for Dale Bailey's Short Fiction

"*The End of the End of Everything* . . . features nine fantasy, dark fantasy, and horror stories that are as beautifully written as they are startling, with some of them reminiscent of Bradbury at his best. Even his apocalypses bring joy the reader."

—Ellen Datlow, World Fantasy Award-winning editor of *The Best Horror of the Year*

"Throughout all these fictions, however varied their subject matter or atmosphere, Bailey exhibits his compassion for and comprehension of his characters, his inerrant sense of choosing just the right words, and his determination to make all the matter of fantastika over afresh. Such a book makes one hope that our genre still has a future."

—Locus

"Every story . . . is a leap off the cliff. Bailey chooses his cliffs with care, reimagining standard science fiction, fantasy, and horror themes with marvelous physicality, quiet compassion for his characters, and language whose sharpness we barely feel till we look to see blood flowing from the cut."

—The Magazine of Fantasy and Science Fiction

THIS ISLAND EARTH

8 FEATURES FROM THE **DRIVE-IN**

THIS ISLAND EARTH

8 FEATURES FROM THE DRIVE-IN

by DALE BAILEY

This Island Earth
Collection & Introduction
Copyright © Dale Bailey 2023

Cover, Interior and Endpaper Art
Copyright © Ilan Sheady 2023

This hardcover edition is published in April 2023 by Electric Dreamhouse, an imprint of PS Publishing by arrangement with the Author. All rights reserved. The right of Dale Bailey to be identified as the Author of this Work has been asserted by him in accordance with the Copyright, Designs and Patents Act 1988.

This book is a work of fiction. Names, characters, places and incidents either are products of the author's imagination or are used fictitiously. Any resemblance to actual events or locales or persons, living or dead, is entirely coincidental.

First Edition

ISBN
978-1-78636-897-3
978-1-78636-896-6 [signed edition]

Design & Layout by Michael Smith
Printed & bound in England by T.J. Books

PS PUBLISHING LTD
Grosvenor House, 1 New Road
Hornsea HU18 1PG, England

editor@pspublishing.co.uk
www.pspublishing.co.uk

CONTENTS

PREFACE IX

I MARRIED A MONSTER FROM OUTER SPACE
    The Bride Wore Terror! 7

I WAS A TEENAGE WEREWOLF
    Driving this boy is a savage lust...to kill! 41

THE HORROR OF PARTY BEACH
    Weird atomic beasts who live off human blood! 61

NIGHT CALLER FROM OUTER SPACE
    Space creatures snatch girls to mysterious planet! 91

CREATURE FROM THE BLACK LAGOON
    Centuries of passion pent up in his savage heart! 137

INVASION OF THE SAUCER-MEN
    Creeping horror from the depths of time and space! . . 155

TEENAGERS FROM OUTER SPACE
    Teenage hoodlums from another world on a
    horrendous ray-gun rampage! 175

THE GHOUL GOES WEST
    But now, since I play Dracula, I am the bogeyman! . . 209

ACKNOWLEDGEMENTS 249

PREFACE

WHEN I SAT DOWN A DECADE AGO to write the first of these stories, "Creature from the Black Lagoon," I did not know that it would turn into a larger project that would culminate in the publication of this book. What I *did* know was that I had wanted to write a story about the Creature from the Black Lagoon for a long time. I don't recall precisely when or where I first saw the film. It debuted in theaters in 1954, well before I made my own debut fourteen years later. I might have caught it on television in the late '70s or early '80s, just before the VCR came along and drove a stake through the heart of the Friday Night Creature Feature.

Horror films were a catch-as-catch-can affair in those days. You watched whatever you were lucky enough to stumble across on TV, a chancy business, and even more so if you lived in the mountains of southern West Virginia, where you could depend on the rooftop antenna to catch only two of the three networks with any reliability. The third—ABC, home of *Battlestar Galactica*, the show I most wanted to watch as a ten-year-old—came in only on clear nights, if the wind was right and you had made sufficient propitiations to the gods of the airwaves. Even then it required more skill in adjusting the rabbit-ears on top of the TV than I could usually marshal. Compounding these difficulties, my father refused to *buy* a television set. Instead, we endured a series of wheezing black-and-white hand-me-downs from family members who had upgraded to color.

This Island Earth

Pictures flickered and dissolved into snow. Vertical hold was an issue. During one memorable era, we could not change channels without the judicious application of pliers. We often went without a TV altogether.

As a consequence, my education in the genre was spotty. I was more likely to read about a film—in the pages of *Fangoria* or in some fervid account of the Universal pantheon I ran across in the local library—than actually see it. And when I *did* see it, I rarely saw the whole thing. I caught a scant few minutes of Christopher Lee in 1966's *Dracula: Prince of Darkness* years before I tracked down his first turn in the role, 1958's *Horror of Dracula*. It didn't matter. Those few minutes were enough. Lee's Dracula—or, more accurately, my imagined version of Lee's Dracula—took up residence in my dreams and remains there to this day. The same was probably true of *Creature*. Long before I saw the film, I imagined it into being.

At the time, this seemed like a vast injustice; in retrospect, it was an enormous gift.

The deprivation gave me room to dream, drawing on what little I knew of the films and what I imagined about them. What I knew of them were mostly the titles. And what lurid titles they are! Brazen appeals to the developing teen culture of the '50s, they shrug off logic and risk—indeed embrace—absurdity. Consider *Robot Monster* (1953), *The Amazing Colossal Man* and *I Was a Teenage Frankenstein* (both 1957), and *Attack of the Giant Leeches* (1959). There is a kind of unhinged poetry here, a conceptual purity that is breathtaking. A film called *I Married a Monster from Outer Space* (1958) can *only* be a film about marrying a monster from outer space. The title is the thing itself.

This is the ideal I sought to honor when I took up *Creature from the Black Lagoon*. My Creature, whatever else he might be, had to be an actual Creature from an actual Black Lagoon. And the story's conceit—which is established in the first paragraph—grew out of that rule. What if the Creature had been captured, I wondered, and had wound up in Hollywood—playing the Creature from the Black

Preface

Lagoon, of course, and keeping company with Bela Lugosi and Boris Karloff? The resulting story was embedded in the arcana of *Creature*'s making, but it took an entirely different direction than the film's plot, or the plots of its sequels, *Revenge of the Creature* (1955) and *The Creature Walks Among Us* (1956), in both of which the Creature *is* captured. These sequels are significantly weaker than the first movie, an acknowledged classic, and the last in Universal's unprecedented run of iconic horror movies, which had begun in 1931 with Bela Lugosi's seminal performance in the lead role of *Dracula*.

The other decision I made in writing that first story was that I would handle the material with as much emotional honesty as I could muster. The story is not without humor, but my intent was to take the Creature and his plight seriously. We have all, at one time or another, found ourselves in the Creature's existential condition, ostracized and alone, torn between sorrow and desire. The mark of the great monsters of cinematic history is that they are not truly monsters. They are us, filtered through the tropes of cinematic horror. When we look into the funhouse mirror of the best creature features, we see ourselves as we are. King Kong died for love. Who among us hasn't?

These are the rules that governed the series of stories that followed—a series that I did not then know that I would have to write. Each story draws its premise from the title of a movie that might have shown up as a late-night creature feature on one of the flickering black-and-white TVs that passed through my boyhood home. Most of them—apart from *Creature* and, to a much lesser degree, *I Married a Monster from Outer Space*—are virtually unwatchable today. They probably were then, as well. The teenagers occupying the cars at the drive-in theaters where they were shown had other things on their minds, anyway.

In many ways I did, too. I have seen bits and pieces of these movies over the years, but I will not pretend that I have watched them in any real sense. *Creature* and *I Married a Monster* aside, I abandoned them all well before the final credits rolled, and I have consistently made choices here that served my own ends—for example, John

This Island Earth

Gilling's 1965 adaptation of Frank Crisp's 1960 novel *The Night Callers* is better known as *Blood Beast from Outer Space*. But its alternate title, *Night Caller from Outer Space*, was infinitely more evocative for me, and so that is the title that appears here.

I have largely avoided the classic films of the '50s. They cast shadows too large for the imagination to illuminate. *Invasion of the Body Snatchers* (1956) and *The Blob* (1958) are indelible expressions of cold-war paranoia, as is *The Thing from Another World*, Christian Nyby's 1951 adaptation of John W. Campbell's 1938 novella *Who Goes There?* (though I prefer John Carpenter's more faithful rendering of the source material in 1982's *The Thing*). George Pal's 1951 version of *The War of the Worlds* situates H.G. Wells's 1898 classic in the same context. The giant ants that colonize LA's sewers in 1954's *Them!* are, like Godzilla (who first stomped Tokyo in the same year), irradiated mutations of the world's nuclear nightmare. Nor did I wish to take on *Forbidden Planet* (1956), which brilliantly reimagines *The Tempest* as a pulp-era space opera—though I have risked drawing this book's title from 1955's *This Island Earth*, another good space opera, this one based on Raymond F. Jones's 1952 novel of the same name.

In short, these stories should not be seen as homages to the movies they draw their premises from. They are, if anything, homages to the movies I summoned into being as a boy—movies that never truly existed outside the theater in my head. For whatever reason, these titles spoke to me. Absent the movies they were attached to, I found the space to speak them into being. Imagination works best not in a void, but in the lacuna where something is supposed to be. And so this book ends with a story about such lacunae—a story about films that only halfway exist, that were never completed or were lost or only imagined. It draws its title from a movie that lived entirely in the mind of Ed Wood, the aspiring auteur responsible for *Plan 9 from Outer Space* (1957), often cited as the worst film ever made. *The Ghoul Goes West* was to star Bela Lugosi, but Lugosi died before Wood could raise sufficient funds for the production. Aside from a

Preface

few minutes of test footage, nothing remains. Lugosi's last years were tragic. These stories are often tragic, as well, in the small way that tragedy too often attaches to the lives of those like Ed Wood, who aspire to dreams beyond their power to fulfill, or Bela Lugosi, who achieve their dreams only to see them slip away. Insofar as the stories are nostalgic, they are nostalgic of my own youth and the world I constructed from the potsherds available to me on the Friday Night Creature Feature. Memory is not an accurate index of the past. Loss is indiscriminate. It is also possible to ache for the passing of an era that never truly existed in the first place.

THIS ISLAND EARTH

8 FEATURES FROM THE DRIVE-IN
by DALE BAILY

for Durant Haire

I BRING YOU A WARNING: EVERY ONE OF YOU LISTENING TO MY VOICE, TELL THE WORLD, TELL THIS TO EVERYBODY, WHEREVER THEY ARE. WATCH THE SKIES. EVERYWHERE. KEEP LOOKING.
> *The Thing from Another World*

WHAT WILL SURVIVE OF US IS LOVE.
> *"An Arundel Tomb," Philip Larkin*

I MARRIED A MONSTER FROM OUTER SPACE

THE BRIDE WORE TERROR

THIRD SHIFT, THREE IN THE MORNING, even the Walmart in Crittenden, Pennsylvania, is quiet. Just the soothing hum of the buffer over in Grocery and a few zombies cruising the aisles looking for something they'll never find, because there's some things even Walmart doesn't carry and never will. Margo is busy at the customer service counter, so I'm alone in my chute, stealing a chance to lounge against my register, and here comes this alien rolling down the alley that runs between Housewares on one side and Hardware on the other.

First thing I think is, it's the best Halloween costume I've ever seen. It's just turned October, after all, and the hotspot front and center of the store is packed with your skull-shaped candles and plastic witches' cauldrons and dozens of cheap Halloween costumes, ranging from super-hero duds for the tots to sexy Vampirella get-ups for their moms. I reckon there's got to be an alien costume or two in the mix, but it's hard to believe this guy is actually wearing one of them. Sure, his silvery foil jumpsuit looks the part, but he has these giant pincers for hands—think crabs and you'll get the idea. And his head—well,

This Island Earth

if it's a mask, it's the best mask I've ever seen. Imagine a colossal Brussels sprout, only the Brussels sprout is really an exposed brain surmounting these black goggle eyes that give absolutely nothing away, and I mean nothing. He doesn't have a nose to speak of, just a pair of slits beneath those googly eyes, and his mouth, underneath all this ugliness, is a thin, lipless scar. Plus, he's seven feet tall if he's an inch. What I'm trying to say is that he was an alien and after that first fleeting thought, there was never any doubt about it in my mind. He was clutching this blue Walmart shopping basket with one set of those pincers, too.

Me, I didn't bat an eye. If there's one thing you come to appreciate working the third shift at Walmart, it's just how inconceivably weird the world can be. I've had a guy dressed like the Pope come through my lane (he was buying Marlboro Lights) and I've had Elvis, too (a twelve pack of condoms, ammunition, and a bag of tangelos).

So when the alien glides into my lane, it's not like I'm not prepared. Nor am I surprised by all the weird stuff he's piled into his basket: a box of tampons, a sewing kit, and a crescent wrench the size of a baseball bat. A can of Fix-A-Flat (which Donny says never to use—but more about Donny later). And a Blu-ray disc from the bargain bin in Electronics—*National Treasure*, which isn't much of a movie, though Donny likes it. And there I am with my blue vest and my nametag that says Ruth and this seven-foot alien standing in front of me. I say, "Find everything okay?" and start dragging his selections across the scanner and slipping them into the bags on the whirligig at the end of my lane. I was always careful about that. You don't want your Tide and your milk in the same bag because it makes your milk taste like laundry detergent. But this alien just stares at me with his big bug-eyes and if he appreciates my efforts, he doesn't say. He doesn't say anything at all actually, and I don't take that to heart either. To most people, a Walmart clerk just fades into the background, and that's how I felt most days, Ruth Sheldon, the invisible woman. Sometimes even Donny, sweet as he could be, made me feel that way, like his eyes were just sliding right past me.

I Married a Monster from Outer Space

That's what I'm thinking as I'm dragging old Bug-Eyes' last purchases across the scanner. "That's sixty-one ninety-three," I say, smiling, and the whole time I can feel Margo's eyes drilling right into the back of my head, like twin laser beams. It's not the alien either. It's me she's looking at. Maybe it's just the old animosity between salary and benefits and $7.25 an hour and hope you stay healthy, and maybe it's not.

Last week, my register came up $7 short, which precipitated a sit-down with the shift manager. No, I didn't steal it, if that's what you're thinking. You try running a few hundred transactions every night, and see if you don't make a mistake or two counting back change. I'm sure Margo had her own sit-down with management. It had happened on her watch. I'm sure she wasn't happy about that, either—which is a roundabout way of saying that as this is all going down I'm barely paying any attention at all to the big galoot standing in my lane.

What I'm focused on is bagging every item just so. And all the time, Margo's making my skull smoke with those laser beams of hers. So when Bug-Eyes just stands there, I'm not a happy camper.

"Forget your wallet?" I say.

Bug-Eyes just stands there.

"I'm sorry, sir," says Margo, who has somehow closed the distance between the customer service counter and my chute at the speed of light. "We'll have to void your order."

So that's what I have to do. Drag each item out of its bag, scan it, and dump it back into his empty basket, like a time-lapse film run in reverse. The whole time the two of them stand there staring at me, Margo with this thin-lipped sneer and the alien with no expression that you can discern. Who knows what he's thinking? He's an alien. But in that moment, I could have clawed that smug expression right off Margo's face and peed on Sam Walton's grave. What I'm saying is that I feel a certain sympathy for this big heap of ugly because it wasn't too long ago that I'd come up short at the grocery store and had to look on as the cashier fished stuff out of *my* bags and voided them one by one, until we got down to what I could afford, which was exactly $57.30. I ask you: is it too much to ask to have a pint of Ben and Jerry's Boom Chocolatta once in a while?

The whole thing was humiliating, so I feel some sympathy, or empathy, or whatever's the right word, for old Pincers here. Which is why what happened after my shift happened at all, I suppose.

The alien, it walks out of the Walmart, and into the night. Four hours later, I punch out and follow it, zipping through the sliding doors and into a morning so beautiful that I almost forgot how much my feet hurt and how tired I felt.

The sky was all streaky with different shades of pearl and gray, and low in the east, just where the sun was breaking, it looked like some careless artist had smeared these swathes of red and orange and gold and half a dozen other colors I didn't have a name for. It almost took my breath away it was so pretty. I stood there and took it all in, letting the rays of light shooting over the Hooters just burn Walmart right off of my skin.

Then I noticed all the buggies that people had left standing in the lot right where they had unloaded them—I mean, is it really too much trouble to walk them over to the cart corral?—and I noticed the spindly trees that looked so sad standing there on their little islands and the discarded Coke bottles and the crushed beer cans and this pile of cigarette butts where someone had dumped their ashtray. I even saw a seeping diaper lying right out there on the blacktop where someone had changed their baby in the backseat. I knew what kind of life that baby would face. I turned away from it all, and trudged toward my car at the far end of the lot. It wasn't much to look at, that car—it was a sun-blasted Oldsmobile '88, it must have been older than I was—but it ran like a tick. When it comes to engines Donny's a genius with his hands.

I slid in, started her up, and swung the big wheel toward the access road that ran next to the highway, and that's when I saw the alien. It was sitting on a curb under one of those spindly trees. It had its head between its knees and six or seven of those crushed beer cans

I Married a Monster from Outer Space

from the lot between its feet. It must have been sucking out the backwash, and I could have sworn it was eating year-old mulch.

I've never quite figured out why I did what I did next, but what I think is that it all came crashing down on me. The sneer on Margo's face as she watched me unwind the alien's order and the bitter taste in my mouth when that grocery store clerk ran my own Boom Chocolatta backward over her scanner. I think it was those rays of light like you see in Bible pictures shooting over the Hooters and lighting up acres of gray pavement littered with stuff people didn't want anymore. Maybe it was the Hooters itself, where I could have gotten a job even if I didn't have a diploma, only I don't look anything like a Hooters girl, and can't lean over and push my boob up against Donny's shoulder when I deliver a fresh pitcher of Coors Light. Donny always over-tips at Hooters, and afterwards, when we get home, he tastes of beer when he kisses me, and he always turns off the light.

So maybe that was it, and maybe it wasn't.

But what I did was cut across the lot and brake right there in front of the alien. I wound down the window and said, "Come on and get in, if you want to." The alien looked at me out of those big googly eyes. Then it climbed to its feet, pincered open the door, and folded itself into the passenger seat. It had to bend its head over to keep its brain from rubbing the tattered upholstery of the roof, and it smelled like stale beer and dead mulch and something else, a dry alien odor that prickled your nostrils.

It said something in a language like no language I'd ever heard before. Its voice sounded like a locust trapped in a jar. I pretended I understood it.

"I don't know where we're going," I said, but where we went was home.

About halfway there it occurs to me that it's a pretty dumb thing I've done, picking up an alien. I'm not even sure what planet it's from for one thing, and for another I don't have the first clue about its intentions and whether they're honorable.

This Island Earth

"Just don't get any ideas in your head, okay?" I say to the alien, though given the size of that brain, I reckon that it must be all over ideas. It buzzes at me in that locust voice and I pretend I know what it's saying. Thanks for the ride, it says, and I say "You're welcome." I feel a little better after that. It's always chancy picking up someone you don't know—you want to set the ground rules right away—and I wonder why I've risked it in the first place.

Except I don't really wonder. Not really. You don't have to be Sigmund Freud to figure it out.

It started with Scrap. Every morning I drove home from work, I see this mutt tied up outside this rotting trailer. Half the time it had flipped over its water bowl and the other half it didn't have a water bowl in the first place. I figured it must be halfway dead with thirst, so one day—I still don't know what came over me—I pull over and march straight up the stairs of that old mobile home and start hammering on the door. You pound on the door of a trailer—it's nothing but flimsy metal—you make a lot of noise, so I've barely gotten started when there's suddenly this wiry, shirtless guy with washboard abs standing in front of me.

This is what I'm thinking about as I make the turn onto Zion Road with Brainiac from Planet X here in tow: I'm thinking about this boy who can't be more than nineteen years old, sloe eyed with a scraggly beard and hair like Jesus. He props himself in the doorway, a joint smoldering between his fingers, and he says, "Well, I'm up. What do you want?"

"I want that dog," I said, and he just looks at me like he didn't even know he had a dog. Then I hear this girl from inside the trailer. Her voice is good looking the way a DJ's voice is good looking. You know how you can just see them inside your head.

"What do they want, Aaron?"

Aaron takes a hit off the joint, exhales, and sucks the smoke back up through his nostrils. "She wants the dog," he says.

"Then give her the fucking dog, and come back to bed."

Aaron shrugs. "You heard her. Take the fucking dog."

I Married a Monster from Outer Space

So that's what I do. When I showed up back home with it lolling out the window of the Olds, Donny says, "You're gonna get us shot, Ruth, stealing people's dogs," and I say, "They don't care about that dog," and I guess I'm right because the boy with the Jesus hair and his girlfriend with the good-looking voice never have shown up to claim it.

After that, I'm all over animals. I make Donny stop the truck so I can move turtles out of the road. And when someone drops a couple of kittens in the woods across from our trailer, I take them in, too. Thing 1 and Thing 2, Donny dubbed the kittens.

So it's Scrap that greets us the morning I bring the alien home. He comes tearing out from under the trailer, yapping his head off the minute we pull into the driveway. I reckon that he'll calm down once he gets a chance to snuff my hands and lick my face, the same as he always does, but I forget about the alien climbing out of the passenger seat. *Thunk*, goes the alien's door and the dog falls silent for maybe a second squared and then he rips into another tirade.

I'm starting to get him settled down—the whole time the alien is just standing beside me—when the door opens and there's Donny in sweats and a wife-beater, leaning against the doorway of our trailer, in the exact same position as the boy with Jesus hair, only Donny's hair is a lank no-color brown and he doesn't have washboard abs. Donny's built more like the Pillsbury Doughboy, and he's yawning and scratching lazily at his big, soft belly as he watches us. When Scrap finally calms down enough for him to get a word in edgewise, he says, "You've really outdone yourself this time, Ruth."

"Klaatu barada nikto."

That's what Donny ends up saying to the alien, and believe it or not, the alien chirrups something back at him in that locust voice. Donny grins this big loony grin, and I feel something break inside me for this sad, stupid man and the situation we've gotten ourselves into. We're just barely old enough to drink and between us we've already acquired one dead baby, one dog, two cats, an alien, more in the way of medical bills than we can ever hope to pay, and grief enough to last two people a lifetime. We live in a rundown firetrap of a rental trailer and work crap jobs and a big night on the town is twenty wings and two pitchers of Coors Light at Hooters, after which Donny fucks me in as many ways as he can think of—which is a lot—in a room as dark as he can make it. And here he is spitting gobbledy-gook at our alien who is spitting it right back at him. I love him a little bit, I guess, and I vow that I will love him even more—or try—as he waves us grandly inside.

Which is hardly fit for company. Here I have an alien in tow and Hurricane Donny has blown right through the place. Six empty cans of Milwaukee's Best on the coffee table, a bag of crushed Doritos on the sofa, and the congealing remains of a TV dinner, presently being investigated by Thing 1, on the counter. Thing 2, meanwhile, is clawing at the sofa, and Scrap, who has followed us inside, has his front paws on the alien's thigh and is rooting around in its crotch. This is my house—dirty dishes in the sink, the TV blaring, and the ammonia stink of cat pee in the air, because Donny always forgets to clean the box—and this is my husband, slipping out a morning fart, his face tattooed with lines from the sheets.

Donny says, "Why don't you rustle us up some grub, Ruth? I'm gonna go shower for work," and just like that we slip into our morning routine, and I have the same thought I always have, which is, why bother showering in the first place? Donny works in the pit at the Quicky Lube out on Route 70, staring up at the underside of one car after another for eight hours straight. By the time he comes home, he'll be filthy: black gunk caked under his nails and in his hair. Sometimes it takes me two or three washes to get his coveralls clean enough to read the name stitched over his right breast.

"It's a waste of his talents," I tell the alien, muting the TV. I sweep up the beer cans and dump them into the trash, ditto the Doritos bag and the TV dinner, much to the distress of Thing 1. I set the coffee going and stir up some eggs. The alien sits down on the sagging sofa. Donny found it by the curb in some swanky neighborhood and loaded it up in the bed of his F-150. It's beginning to pill and I hate that because it has such a pretty pattern.

The alien buzzes its locust buzz.

I pretend I know what it says.

"He's a genius with his hands, leastways around an engine. Give him a day or two with a clunker and he'll have it running like a tick. If he had his certificate he could be pulling down eighteen dollars an hour easy, but he dropped out of school to take care of me. My dad put me out soon as he knew I was pregnant."

An interrogative buzz.

"He's supposed to be studying for his GED so he can take a few classes over the community college." Emphasis on supposed to be. What Donny does with his off hours is mostly watch old movies and guzzle beer. But before I can go on, Donny comes scooting out of the bedroom in his clean coveralls. I slap down a plate of scrambled eggs and a cup of Maxwell House for him, same deal with the alien, right there on the beat-up coffee table. Donny starts wolfing it down like he's starving to death and couldn't live off his fat for six months straight. All the alien does is sit there looking at me.

Donny says, "It ain't gonna eat, I'll take it."

That's when I remember. I head outside with a plate. When I get back, Donny has helped himself to the alien's eggs. "Gort here didn't seem to mind," Donny says.

"Gort?" I say.

"Well, we got to call him something," he says. "What you got there, Ruth?"

What I've got is a plate of old mulch from last spring, when I insisted Donny try to dress the place up a bit, and what I do is set it down in front of the alien. Gort. I open it a can of Milwaukee's Best and Gort digs right in.

Donny whistles. "Least he's going to be cheap to feed. What is it you plan to do with him, Ruth?"

"Put him up for a while, I suppose."

"You can't just keep an alien, Ruth. It's not like he's a dog."

This Island Earth

"I didn't say I was keeping him. I said I was putting him up. Why don't you listen for once?" And then: "You want to go up to the Hooters Saturday night? I'm off."

Donny's stumped. He knows he wants to go to Hooters, but we can't really afford it. This is just about my only card, and I don't play it often, but sometimes you do what you have to do.

Finally—you can practically see the wheels turning—Donny says, "Well, I guess it couldn't hurt to put him up a little while, anyway. Long as he eats mulch, I guess we can afford to feed him."

"Thank you, Donny," I say, and what I do next is I kiss him on the crown of his head, which smells of Pantene.

He just shrugs and climbs to his feet, saying, "I better get moving or I'm going to be late for work."

"Have a good day," I say, but how you could have a good day in the pit of a Quicky Lube, I do not know. I don't say this to Donny, of course. I just endure his coffee breath when he leans over to kiss me and watch him out the door. A moment later, the F-150 rumbles to life. I listen to its engine noise fade down the road. In the silence that follows, I put my elbow on the counter, prop my chin on the heel of my hand and gaze across the room at the alien.

"I guess it's just you and me now, Gort," I say.

Sometimes I think that was at the bottom of all the trouble that followed, Donny giving the alien a name. Once a thing has a name, it starts to acquire other things you might not want it to have. Gort was clearly a boy's name, for instance, so the alien acquired a sex. It's not like we ever actually had him sexed, you understand, the way they'd sexed Thing 1 and Thing 2 at the vet when they were kittens. It's just that with a name like Gort, you'd never check the little F box on those forms you fill out at the urgent care. And that's just the start of it. Before you knew it Gort had his own place at the table and his own spot in front of the TV and his own square of countertop to keep his Tupperware containers of mulch on, which I put there so I wouldn't have to go out and fetch it in the rain. But I guess I'm getting ahead of myself because none of that had happened yet. All, I'm saying is, you give a thing a name, it'll take everything you ever had if you're not careful.

That's what I'm thinking as I stand there staring at Gort—not consciously, exactly, but in that way you chew things over in the back of your mind without quite realizing you're doing it. Meanwhile, Gort's just sitting there with his pincers in his lap, staring at the TV. *The Today Show*'s on and Matt Lauer's watching some TV chef whip something up in the kitchen. You can tell Matt's wisecracking by the deadpan expression on his face.

"You want the sound up?" I ask.

Gort buzzes back at me, which is how I end up sitting there on the sofa beside him, fumbling with the remote. You'd think he'd put me off, with his weird alien funk and those big bug-eyes of his, but I keep thinking about dragging the stuff in his basket backward across the scanner. The whole thing makes me so sad somehow that I wind up teary-eyed and shivery inside. It's all I can do to turn up the sound.

Gort buzzes at me.

"I'm okay," I say. "Don't worry about me."

After that, it's quiet except for the TV, which is probably the nicest thing we own. Except it's not ours, not technically. We got it from Aaron's Rent-To-Own and who knows when it'll ever really be ours to keep, if it ever is. Which makes me want to cry all over again. Thing 2 plops down beside me on the sofa, curls up, and starts to purr. Over by the door, Scrap yawns and lowers his head, looking mournful, the way dogs do. On the TV, Matt's taking a break while Natalie Morales reads off the news. And the whole time me and Gort are just sitting there.

After a while—I don't know how long—he buzzes at me again, and I say, "It's nothing, really." And then, because that's obviously a lie, I say, "It just made me sad, having to drag all that stuff in your basket back across the scanner. Don't you have any money?" I ask, which is kind of a stupid question. He's an alien, after all.

Gort buzzes.

I pretend I know what he's saying, and I say, "We get by, I guess."

But we didn't, hardly. There was always something. I was seventeen when I got pregnant, and here we are five years later. It might have turned out different, I guess, but everything went wrong at once. First the doctor put me on bed rest. Then I was too sick for homebound, and then the baby and all that.

Blah, blah, blah. Everybody's got trouble. Mine is nothing special, and I know it, but here I am on the verge of tears all over again. Gort buzzes at me, and this time I can't help it, I start to cry a little. "It's nothing," I say. "I just get weepy when I'm tired."

Gort buzzes, and I pretend I know what he's saying.

I tell him he can stay as long as he wants, it won't be any trouble, and I tell him this and I tell him that and I tell him the other. It was blah and it was blah and it was blah until I flat ran out of blahs. He buzzed once in a while, but that alien was mainly a bear for listening, Gort, even though he didn't have any ears as far as I could see. He was all brain, that alien, all the way down to his shoulders. Those goggle eyes and the twin slits of his nose and his lipless little mouth seemed to have been stuck on as an afterthought, the way you stuck on Mr. Potato Head's features when you were a kid.

By then, Matt was long gone and Judge Judy was nearly over. I nip into the bathroom to use the can, and when I come back Gort's standing in the hall, staring into the spare bedroom. We always keep that door shut, but here's Gort, his first day in the place, he's gone and opened it right up, like the whole place belongs to him. I feel something kind of loosen inside me, and I say, very firm but gentle, too, the way you'd talk to a toddler, "Gort, that door stays shut. House rule, you understand?"

He only stands there, staring into the room. And what I do is I walk down the hall and lean past him into the bedroom. It's half-lit up, but I contrive not to see anything as I get hold of the doorknob—it's cool in my hand—and swing the door shut.

"It's late, and I have to work tonight," I say. "I'm going to bed."

Which is what I do. I leave the door cracked in case Scrap wants to join me, and he does after a while. So I lay there in the gloom with Thing 1 and Thing 2 in a heap at my feet, and the dog curled up on Donny's side of the bed, smelling all doggy. But none of it helped any. I couldn't sleep and I wanted Donny, even though he was dumb and I didn't love him but only a little, and I wasn't even sure of that.

It was quiet then, except for the sound of the TV. Gort was watching some soap opera and everyone had secret identical twins and was having an affair and someone had gotten himself murdered, and so on, all this crazy stuff, and when it lulled me to sleep at last I dreamed this crazy dream in which *I* had a secret identical twin who'd never gotten pregnant in high school, and had a whole different life that should have been mine.

Turns out Gort's spaceship had come down on Jim Hastings' old Christmas tree farm across the road from the Walmart. When I was a kid, Jim had had fields of pine trees to either side of the road for what seemed like miles. But Jim had gone bust somewhere along the way, and his farm got parceled out commercial. What used to be Hasting's Lane became Hasting's Highway, lined on either side with your fast food chains, your Applebee's, and your standard big-box stores, a Best Buy and an Office Depot, even a SuperTarget for the people who were looking for something a step up from Walmart when it came to discount retail. Then the economy tanked and you couldn't move real estate even down on Hasting's Highway.

Which is a long way of telling you how Donny found Gort's ship when he got off from the Quicky Lube that afternoon. "Wasn't much to it," he says over TV dinners and mulch that night. "Anywhere else people would have seen it. And he couldn't have walked far, could you, Gort?"

Gort buzzed and Donny forked up a big bite of Salisbury steak and shoveled it in. "Hard landing, wasn't it, Gort?" Donny says, and Gort buzzed again, and Donny says, "Ship's intact, but you can see where he came in. Trees are all torn up. Must have lost an engine, or something. You oughta see it, Ruthie. It's something to look at."

This Island Earth

He was right about that, though I didn't see it for myself until the next morning, when I hiked across the road after work and ducked into the trees. I found it four or five hundred yards in, totally invisible from the road. Branches slapped at my face the whole way, and my hands got gummy with all the sap, but it was worth the trouble. Sure, it looked exactly like every flying saucer you ever saw—just a disc of silver metal—but it was big. Really big, is what I'm saying. If you lined up three or four buses and drew a perfect circle around them, you'll get a sense of just how big I mean. Plus, the sun shooting down through the trees made it seem all shimmery and strange, and I couldn't help thinking that it had been to places so far away that I couldn't begin to imagine what they must be like—other planets, I mean, circling other stars. Which kind of put our own sun into perspective. It's funny to consider the sun just another star, because we don't really think of it that way, do we? For us it's the center of everything, and we take it for granted. But peel back that complacency, and what you have is nothing but mystery and more mystery, all the way down. Standing there, I understood how small I really was. I guess none of us really matter in the long run, not when you think about how big and strange the universe is. Even Gort's gigantic ship seemed like a brittle, tiny thing, zooming from star to star through all the endless black space in between. It *was* fragile, too. It had crashed, hadn't it, plowing this long divot in the ground and scattering pine trees like toothpicks, and as the sun rose higher, I could see that it wasn't quite as smooth and bright as I had thought it was. Sooty black streaks ran the length of it, and it had been pretty dinged up by the trees. I wondered if there might be dead Gorts inside it. The thought made me awful sad somehow, and I felt selfish for being all weepy the other morning like I was.

Who could say what Gort had been through, and what it might have done to him?

I stood there a long time, just wondering.

I Married a Monster from Outer Space

So all this, and I'm home late, and here's Donny standing in the doorway, trying not to look angry as I barge past him. Inside, the TV is blasting. Gort's sitting on the sofa with Thing 2 curled up in his lap. He's petting her with one pincer and clutching a can of beer with the other. I never saw an alien who could put away such whopping quantities of beer.

"Where have *you* been?" Donny says. He has to shout over the TV. Donny tends to jealousy, but as far as he's concerned it only runs one way. Take the Hooters girls, for example. Especially Star. Donny always asks to be seated in Star's section. The service is better, he says, by which he means that Star always gives him a nice long close-up of the beauties jiggling around in her little Hooters t-shirt when she leans over the table to deliver our wings. The service, by the way, is inadequate, I'm pretty sure that Star isn't her real name, and even if it was, she wouldn't be giving a guy like Donny the time of day if he wasn't paying her for it.

All of which passes through my head in an instant as I dump my purse and reach for the remote, silencing Savannah Guthrie midsentence. "I went to see the ship, Donny, that's all."

At that his whole face lights up.

"Gosh, isn't it something?" he says.

"It is." By this time, I've shrugged off my coat, and I'm reaching into the refrigerator for the eggs. "Too bad it's wrecked. We could all fly off to the stars and live happily ever after. Wouldn't that be nice?"

And it would, too, but Donny, who's a homebody at heart, says, "I don't think I'd like that, Ruth."

"What would you like, Donny?"

"I think I'd like to fix it," he says.

"Fix it?" I look up from where I'm cracking eggs into a pan.

"So Gort can go home."

"Donny, you can't fix that ship."

"Why not?"

"It's not like it's an old car."

"Sure it is. It's just a machine."

This Island Earth

"It's a machine designed by aliens for traveling in space, Donny. No way you can fix that."

To which he says, kind of put out, "Give me enough time, Ruthie, I think I could fix just about anything." I look up at him, then, and what I see is that light in his face all over again. Just looking at it I could see there was more to Donny than I'd ever given him credit for. Maybe people weren't so different from the universe itself: maybe you never really got to the bottom of them. Peel back the surface a little and it's just mystery and more mystery, all the way down.

"What are you looking at?" Donny says.

"Nothing," I say, and that's when I realize that I've left the eggs on too long. Donny likes his yolks runny, but it's two or three minutes too late for that, and the whites are going to be rubbery, too. To be honest, the eggs are practically inedible, but Donny—the Donny I was married to who wouldn't stand for rubbery eggs for even a minute—Donny just sits down and starts forking them in.

I dump some mulch in a bowl, pour a can of Milwaukee's Best over it, and hand Gort a spoon. Once I'd got them both started, I sat down at the little table between them, no appetite at all, I felt so strange. I'm thinking again that maybe there's dead Gorts inside, but I can't bring myself to say it, not in front of Gort, so we sit there in silence except for the piggy little grunts Donny makes when he eats and the clink of Gort's spoon against his bowl.

"I'm gonna have a look at it when I get off work today," Donny says, pushing his plate away, and a minute after that he's off to brush his teeth, and a minute after that he's gone. I missed him when I woke up that evening, too. Usually we get an hour or two in the evening over TV dinners. Donny always eats the value-sized portions and I stick to the Weight Watcher's Smart Ones, even though they always leave me feeling hungry and they don't help any anyway. You could say I'm big boned, the way my mother did, or you could say I'm fat. Either way it comes to the same thing. But that night it was just me and Gort staring at the TV while Donny was out messing around with Gort's ship.

"I think I'm gonna have some ice cream," I say. "You want a little mulch?"

And Gort, he buzzes. I act like I know what he's saying, so I serve us up and we sit there in front of the TV, feeding our faces and watching reruns of *Law and Order*. Then it's time for me to go to work. I'm already out the door when Donny's truck comes rattling into the yard. He climbs down and we stand there for a minute, talking in the cold October air. I want to ask him if there are dead Gorts inside the spaceship, but I can't bring myself to do it. Somehow I don't want to know the answer at the same time as I do, and for sure I don't want to know it this way, passing in the yard, and having to work through whatever he tells me while I'm running a register at Walmart. Donny's got other things on his mind, anyway. He's practically breathless with excitement, and I can see right away that it's going to be this way for a while yet. Donny's love for Gort's spaceship trumps his love for me, at least for now, and at the thought of it, something breaks inside me, and is still.

After that it seemed like I spent more time with Gort than I did with Donny. Half the time I didn't see Donny except at breakfast; the other half I passed him in the yard as he came in from tinkering on the flying saucer and I slipped out to the Olds for my shift at the Walmart.

Gort was always there, though. Mornings, we watched *The Wheel of Fortune* and *The Price is Right*. Evenings it was *Law and Order* reruns or *The Big Bang Theory*, while Gort snacked on mulch and drank beer and I ate a Smart One and then treated myself to a big bowl of ice cream with Hershey's syrup on top. Even though I know it doesn't make any sense to do that, I couldn't help myself. I never could. And sometimes I passed Donny on the lawn as I left for work and sometimes I didn't.

And we talked, Gort and I. Buzz buzz, he would say, and I would say, Lord, my feet hurt, and I would soak them for a while in Epsom salts and warm water. They would feel better then, but only a little.

This Island Earth

My feet always hurt. You try standing in front of a register for eight hours at a time and see how your feet feel. I'm not complaining. I'm lucky to have a job at all, and I know it. I'm just saying.

Or my phone would ring and Gort would buzz and buzz when I didn't answer it. I always checked the number on its screen and it was nobody I wanted to talk to. I didn't have any girlfriends, and Donny—well, Donny used to call me on his lunch break, but he didn't do that very often anymore. Mostly it was just those weird mystery calls you get from out of state—people wanting to sell you something or take a poll or whatever—and I didn't want to talk to them, anyway.

But Gort buzzed and buzzed every time it happened.

That's how I ended up telling him how it used to be the hospital that called us all the time, hounding us about their money. Turned out they had charged us more than a hundred thousand dollars to let our baby die. I ignored them to start with—where was I going to get that kind of money?—but finally they sent somebody out to knock on our door, so we set up what they called a hardship payment plan, which is why the hospital takes $40 out of our checking account at the end of every month. I did the math one morning and figured out that we'll be almost two hundred years old before Donny and I pay them off, and that without interest.

Just telling it I start to cry. I can't help myself. Gort buzzes, and I say, "It's nothing. Don't worry about me," and what I do is, I lean my head up against his arm. I don't know why. It's nothing I think about. I just do it, the way you do things sometimes. His foil jumpsuit is softer than you'd think and cool against my cheek. He doesn't say anything, so I just lay up against him and cry. Maybe I even doze a little, because when I lean my head against Gort like that we're watching *Friends*, the one where Chandler gets locked in an ATM with a supermodel, and when I open my eyes it's *Seinfeld*, the one where Jerry starts getting those tiny little checks for twelve cents from Japan and doesn't know what to do with them.

I knew what I'd do with them. I'd cash every one of them. And that starts me crying all over again. My face is all snotty and I can't breathe good. "Let's turn off the TV for a while," I say, but Gort just sits there staring at the screen. He takes a slug of beer. After a while, still wiping at my eyes, I get up and go to bed.

Then one day I had to get out of the house, so we went to see this dumb sci-fi movie. It was your standard stuff, aliens invading the earth because they wanted our water or our women or whatever. The whole thing embarrassed me, because Gort wasn't anything like those aliens at all. It got worse when we had to move to the back row because some creep behind us kept complaining that he couldn't see over Gort's brain.

I was mortified, which was my mother's word, so it's her I'm thinking of when we stop by Mickey Dee's to get something to eat. I scoop up a handful of pine needles from under the shrubbery outside and set him up with them on a napkin while I order a double quarter-pounder with cheese, a large fry, and one of those fancy coffee drinks, even though I can't afford it. When I sit down to eat, Gort buzzes at me, and the funny thing is I'm still thinking of my mother, and that's exactly what he asks me about.

So I start to tell him about how nice she always was to me. She really was. I was the kind of kid nobody cared enough about even to be mean to—and it's better to be bullied than not even noticed in the first place, right? But Mom always promised me that things would get better for me. She said I was a wallflower and that the thing about flowers is, they always bloom. I let myself hope that maybe I would, too. Then Mom died, and I couldn't lie to myself anymore. The truth was, I wasn't a flower at all. I was just a wall, and the thing about being a wall is anyone can hang up any old picture they want on it, and from then on that's what they see. Dad hung Mom's picture up no sooner than she was cold in the grave, and right away I went to packing his lunch for him and cooking his dinner and getting him another beer when he wanted one. The teachers at school hung up a picture of a plain girl with a bad complexion who walked the line between overweight and

This Island Earth

obese, and because she always managed a C, didn't cut up in class, and didn't mess with drugs, they didn't waste their time ever looking at her again. As for the other kids, well, they didn't even bother hanging up a picture in the first place. To them I wasn't a wall, I was a window, and they walked the halls of Crittenden Senior High and looked right through it without even smudging the glass.

Except for Donny, I say, pushing my tray aside, and Gort, he buzzes, and I say, "Donny, he really saw me, if you know what I mean," and at the time I thought he did, leaning up against my locker and chatting and looking me right in the face, like he didn't care that I was fat and had a lot of pimples. Not that he was anything to look at himself—even then he was built like the Pillsbury Doughboy—but he had friends. Anybody who has hands as talented as Donny's are, he's gonna have friends in Auto Shop and Wood Shop and classes like that. Me, I was college-prep and people mostly didn't date across that line, but here's Donny leaning beside my locker. One day he's asking me for help on his English homework—which is really easy, barely English at all—the next he's asking me out to the movies, and the first thing you know, he's asking me to go to prom with him, only we couldn't, because Dad wouldn't spring for a dress. Who cared anyway? That was what Donny said when he heard it.

Which is how we ended up at Mount Horeb, parked behind an abandoned church where you could look out over town, which from up there looks almost pretty, like a handful of fallen stars glittering in the dark valley below. Donnie had gotten a pint of Old Crow somewhere and he had a six-pack of Sprite, too. We sat on the tailgate of his truck drinking whiskey and Sprite. It was better than prom, didn't I think so? he said. It would be all crowded and hot in the Elks Club, and nobody really wanted to wear those ridiculous clothes anyway. Wasn't this better?

I allowed that it was, though secretly I was sorry I wouldn't have a prom picture to look at later, or any of the favors, like a napkin and a fancy glass with the prom's theme etched on it, which that year was Moonlight Serenade.

I Married a Monster from Outer Space

But it really *was* nice up there with the spring breeze and the trees smelling green and fresh and I liked the bite of the whiskey among all those bubbles. So I took another drink and then another one after that, and the next thing I know I'm flat on my back in the bed of Donny's truck, with my jeans hanging off one ankle and my bra rucked up around my shoulders. Donny's kneading one of my breasts and probing around with his thing between my legs until he finally hits the spot and pushes it right up inside me. From then on, that's all I can feel, that and the ribs of the truck bed digging into my back. I can smell the sting of Donny's aftershave, too, and over the curve of his shoulder I can see an ocean of stars, it's so clear. I let my mind rise up there into the stars until what Donny is doing to me is happening a million miles away, and what I'm thinking is does anyone really live up there in all that sky? Then Donny lets go with a little grunt, and bam, I'm right there in the bed of the truck again, pounding on his back, saying, Get off me, Donny, get off me!, until he finally pulls away. I'm crying a little as I put myself back together. My bra is all twisted up and I can feel his stuff leaking out into my panties.

Blah blah blah, right?

Except I don't say all of that to Gort, of course. It's not like he needs the play-by-play. Nope. I wind it up at the part where we're sitting on the tailgate sipping whiskey, and I put the bit in about looking up at the stars early. What I do is put a cheery smile on my face and finish my five-dollar coffee and say, "I know, right? Even then I was thinking about aliens. And I'm glad, because you're a good friend, Gort. You really are."

He is, too. That's what I'm thinking as I dump my trash and rack the tray. So I reach up and take his elbow and we stroll out of Mickey Dee's together. Maybe people stare—it's not every day you see an alien like that—but I don't care. It feels so good walking arm in arm with Gort. It's like we own the place.

A few days pass this way, and then one morning I say to Donny, "It's my night off. Why don't we go up to Hooters for some wings?"—

because the truth is, I miss him. We've been married five years at this point. He's the only man I've ever had sex with, and even if you don't really like someone, if they're that big a part of your life, not seeing them anymore is a little bit like having a limb amputated. Plus there's the baby, which was a funny thing, because it pushed us apart and held us together at the same time.

So it hurt my feelings when Donny hesitated. I can see right away how much he's torn between tinkering with that ship and going out to Hooters—and I can see too that I don't have much to do with the dilemma. In Donny's mind, it's spaceship versus Star, and it's only when I say, "C'mon, Donny, please," that Star finally wins out.

"Alright," he says, and he shoots straight home after work to clean up. Me, I've got my best jeans on, plus a filmy white blouse Donny was always fond of. Gort's wearing his jumpsuit, the same as always. It didn't seem to need washing, and he didn't either. He'd been with us a couple of weeks at this point, and he didn't have any odor to him at all except that dry alien smell, plus a tinge of mulch and Milwaukee's Best. It wasn't a bad odor, and neither was Donny's once he scrubbed all the grease off, only he put too much aftershave on, the way he always does, and it reminded me of that night in the bed of the pickup. The way it always does.

We took my car. We always do when we go to Hooters, because Donny drinks too much. Pulling into the lot takes me back to the morning this whole thing began, with those Bible rays shooting down so that everything looked beautiful for a minute or two, and then the truth revealed itself, and the truth was a dumped ashtray and a dirty diaper and a bunch of people who can't be bothered to walk their buggies over to the cart corral.

In the misty October dark, though, you can pretend that everything really isn't so ugly, after all. You can ignore the abandoned carts, and the lights shine through these soft, yellow halos, like angels. Even the traffic whooshing by on Hasting's highway sounds soothing, like one of those oscillating fans on a summer evening.

It's a weeknight, so the Hooters isn't crowded, but we still have to

I Married a Monster from Outer Space

wait because Donny insists on a table in Star's section. Star acts like she hasn't seen us in a thousand years. "Where have you guys been? I've missed you!" she exclaims. She's this tallish blonde, only the blonde is mostly bleach, and the guys she's talking to is mainly Donny, not me. She's something to look at, all right. Her orange booty shorts are crawling up the crack of her rear end, and she's about to pop right out of her little Hooters tee-shirt as she takes our drink order—a pitcher of Coors Light—and sashays off to get it. Donny's eyes nearly bug out of his head when she comes back with a free appetizer of fried pickles, seeing as it's been so long since she's seen us. You can almost see him swell up, and by the time she brings out our wings and brushes her boob against his shoulder when she sets them down, steam is practically shooting out his ears.

Which is pretty much how it goes. Gort just sits there drinking beer and Donny focuses on the wings, pausing between bites to eye up the nearest Hooter girl. Me, I've lost my appetite. I don't have but one or two wings, but I hit the Coors Light pretty hard—we end up downing four pitchers of the stuff—because I know what's on Donny's agenda for the night and I have to kind of loosen myself up for it.

By the time we stagger out of Hooters, I've had too much to drink to drive us home. Donny's in no shape either, which is how I wind up in the back seat while Gort takes the wheel. He has to scrunch down with his brain between his shoulders to do it, but at least he's sober. As far as I can tell, he's always sober, no matter how much beer he pours down that lipless little mouth of his. He's not much of a driver, though—he's too heavy on the gas and too hard on the brake. He about jerks me out of my skin, driving like that.

Then we're home, and it's the usual stuff: Scrap screaming out from under the trailer, and Thing 1 and Thing 2 twining through our legs as we push our way inside. Some pretty hilarious moments follow. I remember them in flashes, the way you do when you've had too much to drink. Donny starts up with the drinking games and we all sit around the kitchen table bouncing a quarter at a juice glass.

This Island Earth

Me, I've never been any good at quarters, but Donny's a master at banging the coin into the glass. It's always me he chooses to drink. Gort isn't much good at it, and doesn't seem to get the game, anyway. He just takes a drink no matter what happens. Me, I miss the glass first time every turn, and around and around it goes, until I'm half-sick with beer.

And then we're dancing to some stupid death-metal band that Donny likes, and Donny and I are laughing so hard because Gort's getting his groove on, too. He's on his feet, anyway, bobbing his giant brain and moving his arms stiffly, pincers clicking, in that old robot dance, you known the one I mean.

After that, who knows how long, we're all crowded in front of the TV, stuffing our faces. I've splurged on a pint of Boom Chocolatta and Donny has his favorite, too, which is Salted Caramel. Even Gort's mulch is fresh. I'd walked over to the garden shop, which is pretty much dead this time of year, and snagged the last two bags. They looked kind of forlorn, and I thought maybe they had dried up, too, but I bought them anyway.

"It's a little late in the season for landscaping," Margo said when she rang me up. "What do you want those things for?"

"I just do," I said, and now I'm glad I picked them up, because the mulch is nice and moist right out of the bag like that and Gort is really chowing down. The only thing wrong with the moment is that I'm a little queasy, and Donny's put on one of those late-night Skinemax movies. You know the ones. This one's called *Stacked Racks from Mars*, which I figure might embarrass Gort, because it's another movie about space invaders. It embarrasses me, anyway, but Donny's Donny and there's not much you can do about that.

And then—I don't remember saying goodnight to Gort—Donny and I are in bed. I'm so drunk I can let go enough to enjoy it. But the truth of the thing is in the back of my mind even then, and the truth is that I'm just a picture on the wall to Donny, too, and it's usually a picture of Star—Star in her little booty shorts (or out of them) and her little Hooters tee-shirt with the stupid owl on it.

I Married a Monster from Outer Space

When we're done, I lie awake in the dark for a long time. After a while, I get to thinking about Gort, and what kind of losses he might be coping with. Finally, I can't help myself. There are things you have to know even if you don't want to know them. I say, "Donny."

He grunts and rolls over. I poke him. "Donny."

"Leave me alone, Ruth. I'm trying to sleep."

"It's Gort's ship," I say.

"What about it?"

"Did you find any"—I hesitate, and then, I can't help myself, I say—"Did you find any dead Gorts inside?"

Donny's quiet so long that I think maybe he's drifted off again. Part of me feels relieved, like it's better not to know. But it turns out he's only thinking, because finally he says, in this voice that's all of a sudden wide awake and sober, he says, "No. There's nothing in there at all, Ruth," and I know from the way he's said it that he's lying.

I choose to let it rest, though. Some things you just don't want to think about.

"I'm close to fixing it," Donny says. "I'm a day or two away. Maybe a week. I just want you to be ready."

"Well, sure," I say. "It's not like he's a pet, Donny. We're just putting him up for a while."

"Okay. I just want you to be ready."

"I'm ready," I say, but the truth is, I wasn't. The prospect made me really sad, and it sobered me up some, too. I didn't realize how attached I'd become to Gort, or how sorry I'd be to see him go. I thought on it a long time, and I was still thinking on it when I fell asleep.

I had this weird dream about his flying saucer. In the dream, it was all fixed up just like Donny said, only I was inside it. From the inside it was like looking through a glass dome, with only the blackness of space around us, and we sat without speaking in the dark, Gort and me, while stars slipped past on either side of us. I was thinking how quiet and peaceful it was when I woke up headachy from all the beer.

This Island Earth

It's after four by then, and I heave myself out of bed to get some Tylenol and a glass of water, only when I go out into the living room, Gort's not there. And Gort's *always* there. He doesn't sleep—he doesn't do much but watch TV and drink beer—but here he is, flat gone, the TV flickering silently in the dark. There's an infomercial for the Brazilian Butt Lift on. It promised you a supermodel's butt. Maybe Star used it.

That's what I'm thinking when I notice that the bedroom door in the hall is open, the one I told him not to go inside of. Something clenches inside me, and suddenly I'm not even thinking about how thirsty I am or how much my head hurts. Suddenly I'm standing at the door, and I don't even know how it is that I've gotten there. I mean, I know that I walked, but I don't have any memory of doing it. I'm just there. The room is lit up with this eerie light from the TV, but I force myself not to see anything but Gort. He's standing in the middle of the room, staring out toward the little window.

"Gort?"

He buzzes at me, but he doesn't turn or look. He just stands there.

That's when I step into the room, still not looking at anything.

"Come on," I say, tugging at the sleeve of his jumpsuit. "I don't want you in here. I don't like anyone to come in here."

Taking hold of one of his pincers—it's hard to the touch, it doesn't give at all—I coax him into the hall. I lead him to the sofa and we sit there together in the light from the TV, and suddenly I'm crying. It seems like all I do anymore is cry. Gort buzzes at me. What's wrong, he says, and I say, "I'm all right. Don't worry about me." Gort buzzes back, and then he's silent while I cry myself out. We just sit there staring at the TV after that, until the Brazilian Butt Lift infomercial gives way to one called *Hot Tub Fun*. The first hint of dawn is showing around the curtains by the time I steal back into the bedroom and slip under the covers beside Donny.

He's flat on his back, snoring to shake the house down. Me, I'm a long time going back to sleep and when I finally did doze off I fell right back into those crazy dreams. In one of them Gort was stroking my face—his pincer was warm and soft and it felt like old leather, I remember that like it was yesterday—and in another one he was sitting at the foot of the bed, buzzing away, only when I woke up it turned out to be Thing 2, purring at my feet. Donny had already left for work—he was good about not waking me up after a long night like that—and what I thought about was Gort leaving soon, and I felt so sad that I started to cry all over again.

First thing I see when I pull myself together and leave the bedroom is Gort, kicked back on the sofa, sipping a can of beer and watching Dr. Phil. Second thing I see is that door down the hall. It's still open, and what I think of is this old story I learned about in school—the one about the forbidden room and the secret behind the door. All the dead wives.

Some doors ought to stay closed, that's all I'm saying. This is one of them, too, only it's standing wide open, and I can't cope with it— not with the hangover that's just starting to set in, not with Gort buzzing at me.

"Good morning," I say, and if I'm a little short with him it's because I'm trying not to be mad about him going in there when I told him not to. He's a guest, after all. But now I'm going to have to walk down there and close that door myself. I feel like that kid in *The Shining*, tempted down the hallway to room 217, or whatever—that same feeling of dread that draws you forward, that you can't resist, no matter how hard you try. That kid, he had to open the door, he didn't have any choice. Me, I have to close this one, because Gort opened it, and in cajoling him out into the hall last night, I stupidly left it open behind me. I don't want to see what's inside it, but here I am.

Here I am, and when I reach in to pull the door closed, the room is filled with this golden late-morning light, shining through the blind covering the little window. I can't help but see it. Every day and every night I see it in my mind. But you can keep yourself busy, you can watch reality TV or eat ice cream or read those celebrity magazines

THIS ISLAND EARTH

they have on the last-chance rack at the Walmart—who has the best beach bod and who doesn't and who's together and who's not and who's in rehab and who's sobered up. The point is, it goes on and on, that kind of stuff. So when you're not really looking at what's in a room, when it's just inside your head, you can shunt it away to the back of your mind and pretend it's not there. You can drown it out with noise. I knew because I've been doing that for years. But standing there in the doorway, I can't shunt it away, I can't drown it out with noise, I can't do anything but see it. And what I see is— what I see is—

A pink room. The walls are this really light pink, and everything inside those walls is pink and baby blue. The crib and the dresser and the changing table that Donny picked up at a yard sale and refinished, they have these perfect pink and baby blue accents. Not to mention the little sheet and comforter set with the penguins on them that I just had to have when I saw it at Babies R Us. The matching penguin mobile—the penguins are wearing these powder blue tuxedos with pink bowties, and around the top of the room there's this border with more penguins marching along in more powder blue tuxedos and little pink bowties, and the thing about it is, it's a room with real stuff in it. It's like it's not even part of a rotting old trailer that you can't get the landlord to fix up and you've furnished it with a rental TV and a bunch of stuff your husband has plucked off the curb in some swank neighborhood. No. It's this perfect room, and there's a perfect dream house around it, and a perfect dream life where Donny has his mechanic's certificate and I'm a dental hygienist or whatever, and most of all we have this perfect little baby, and every night I sit down in the rocking chair in the corner and rock her to sleep in this perfect pink nursery.

I guess you knew all that already. It's not like you have to be Sigmund Freud to figure it out. But that dream life isn't mine. Which is why I just slide to the floor right there on the spot. I would cry but I've cried myself out. I've cried this whole story and I can't cry anymore. I'm just empty. Gort buzzes. I look up and there he is in the hallway, towering over me, staring down at me with those big bug-eyes of his.

"I'm fine," I say. "Don't worry about me."

The baby's name was Alice.

Gort buzzes, and I realize that I must have said it aloud, so I say, We'd have been better off not to name her at all. I think I knew from the start that she wasn't going to come home with us. She was such a tiny thing and she'd arrived so far ahead of schedule they wouldn't even let me hold her. I guess that's what I remember most, that and standing outside the nursery and looking through the window at her, all wired up to about a thousand machines and a tube down her tiny throat and the line on the heart monitor just flattening out. I was right there when it happened, standing at the window. I started screaming and pounding on the glass until somebody yanked a curtain over it, but by then there were so many doctors and nurses crowded around her that I couldn't see anything anyway.

Gort buzzes, and I say, I don't remember much after that. Donny says that somebody gave me a shot. All I know is that when I wake up, I'm in my room. Donny's sitting in the chair beside the bed, all hunched over like someone's just punched him in the stomach and I know it from the set of his shoulders, I don't have to ask. I can't help myself, though. There are things you have to know even if you don't want to know them, or even if you already do.

What I say is, "Donny," and he looks up at me. His face is gray and he just shakes his head. After that, I cried a little. He did, too, but he'll say he didn't if you ask him, and two days after that, when we had a little service for the baby, he didn't seem to have any tears left in him. Something had closed up inside him like a flower closes up at night, only it never opened up again and daylight never really came, just an endless flat dawn the color of sour milk. You keep hoping that something will happen on a morning like that, that the sun will break through or that maybe it'll just go ahead and pour, but it never does. It just goes on and on.

This Island Earth

Gort buzzs, and I say, If I'd known everything would turn out this way, I never would have gotten pregnant in the first place.

Gort buzzes, and I say, I wanted to hang on to him, I guess. I thought he really saw me, if you know what I mean. Mom was dead, and Dad, he'd hung up a picture on my face that wasn't really me, and my teachers had hung one, too, but Donny, he really saw me—only later I realized that he had pictures of his own, that I was a wall not a wallflower, and always would be.

Gort buzzes, but I don't have anything else to say. I just sit there with my back against the wall in the baby's bedroom. It smells of dust and disuse. And what I do is, I start to cry. Turns out I'm not out of tears, after all.

Which is more or less how this story comes to an end, except for one last part. We all hung on like that for a few days more. It was the usual thing: beer and mulch and TV dinners, and *The Price is Right* in the mornings and *Law and Order* after dark. Gort and me, we talked. It was buzz and blah, buzz and blah, all day long.

Then Donny comes home one night, we're passing on the lawn, and he says, "I think I've got it, Ruthie."

Which is how it ended up that I called in sick, and we all trooped out to Jim Hastings' old tree farm in the middle of the night. We saw the ship before we ever got there, lights twinkling through little gaps in the pine trees. And then we stepped into the clearing, and it like to took my breath away. It looked just like every flying saucer you ever saw, all lit up like that, but it was bigger than you ever thought one really could be, and you could tell it was practically aching to break free of the earth and shoot off toward the stars. Colors streaked around its rim: blue, then green, then red, and then the whole sequence started all over again. It hung about four feet off the ground, hovering on this column of white light, and there was a ramp sticking out you could walk up to get inside. It hummed, too, only you couldn't really hear it. You felt that hum in your bones. We stood there for a long time, staring at it, with the black pine trees pressing close around us and the night sky looming huge overhead and the full moon shedding down its light. All I could think was that soon Gort would be zooming through all that darkness up there. And I thought of my dream. Maybe on the inside the ship really *would* be see-through as glass, and you could sit there in peace and quiet, watching the stars slip past.

Then Donny kind of laughs. "It sure is something, ain't it?"

It sure was. It was something to look at.

Donny had that spaceship running like a tick.

Then it's like he's all business. He turns to Gort and he says, "It may not handle just right. I had to jury-rig a lot of it. I had some trouble getting parts, so you'll want to take it easy to start."

Gort buzzes. Donny reaches out to shake, but Gort just stands there, his pincers hanging at his side, and when I go in for a hug, it's the same thing all over again. I press my face up against his jump suit and I breath in that strange, dry odor of his. "I'm gonna miss you, Gort," I say, and all the time he just stands there. When I finally step away, he looks at us for a minute, the moonlight shining in his big googly eyes. He buzzes one last time and then he turns away and starts up the ramp. Something breaks inside me it's so sad, and before I know it, I'm halfway up the ramp myself, I'm shouting, "Gort, Gort—"

He turns to face me, and there I am with Gort above me and Donny below, staring up from the bottom of the ramp. I don't know what I'm going to say until I say it. But what I say is this: "I'm going with him."

"But Ruth," he says, "he's an alien."

I'm used to it, I want to say, but I hold it inside of me. I don't want to hurt his feelings any more than I have to. Then the strangest thing happens. Donny Sheldon starts to cry. It's like a dam breaking, those tears, the way they come. It's like catching a glimpse of a whole other man. I realized then how many Donnys I'd known since the day he showed up beside my locker in Crittenden Senior High. Some of them were pretty ugly, like the one who'd deflowered me in the back of his old F-150, and some of them were talented, like the Donny who'd fixed up Gort's flying saucer, and some of them were giving, like the Donny who'd quit school to go to work full time and take care of Alice and me. Some of them were loving, and me, I hadn't bothered to see any of them. I'd hung a picture up over his face instead and I'd never bothered to take it down and look at the grieving man underneath, who didn't want to open the door to Alice's room any more than I did. Gort had torn it open for the both of us.

I turned to look up the ramp at him. The bright door of the spaceship was empty. He was gone. *It* was gone, because the truth was, I never really knew whether Gort was a he or a she or something else altogether. But the doorway to its ship stood open all the same, and there was nothing to stop me from walking right up the ramp and stepping inside and flying off to the stars.

What I did instead was, I walked back down and took Donny in my arms. Some things would have to change, sure. Nights out we were going to the Applebee's, first of all, and Donny was going to learn to look at me in the light. And me, I was going to have to change some things, too.

That's what I was thinking when the ramp of Gort's flying saucer drew up inside it and the door slid closed. The ship just sat there for a minute, and then it rose straight up on that column of light until it was hovering above the trees. The colors around its rim picked up speed, blurring into a streak of light, and it shot off over the woods, and then it was gone. It was just me and Donny.

After a little while Donny got ahold of himself. "Cold out here," he says.

"Sure is," I say.

And so we struck off into the trees. We held hands for a little while, but it was hard going, and soon enough we were on our own again. But things have gotten better since then. These days we leave the lights on as often as not, and when we steal a night off we usually go to Applebee's. Donny's got his GED and started taking classes for his certificate at the community college. Me, it's my turn next. I think dental hygienist may be the way to go, at least to start.

I Married a Monster from Outer Space

I still think of Gort, though. I miss him, though I know now that he was always just an alien, no matter how much I wanted to believe otherwise. Sometimes I wonder if we aren't all aliens, hanging pictures on empty walls to show us what we want to see. And other times, I know, the pictures come down, if only for a minute or an hour, and on that fleeting edge of time, I love Donny for himself, a little or a lot, and sometimes he loves me, too. Maybe that's all any of us can ever know or hope for. Maybe it's enough.

Principal Ferguson's Testimony

BEFORE MISS FERGUSON FOUND Maude Lewis's body in the school gym, none of us believed in the teenage werewolf. There had been rumors, of course. There always are. But many of us viewed Miss Ferguson's discovery as confirmation of our worst fears.

Not everyone shared our certainty. There had been only a fingernail paring of moon that late February night, and a small but vocal minority of us argued that this precluded the possibility that Maude's killer had been a lycanthrope. It was common knowledge, they contended, that werewolves only struck during full moons, often adding that one only became a werewolf by surviving the bite of another werewolf. No such attack had been reported.

The rest of us refrained from pointing out the errors in this fount of superstition. Instead, we asked the skeptics to consider the facts of the case as Principal Ferguson reported them to the *Rockdale Gazette*. She had been working late as she did most nights, partly, we believed, because she was lonely, having no family to go home to,

This Island Earth

and partly to accommodate Maude's practice schedule. Maude was a talented gymnast who harbored hopes of a college scholarship and often stayed well into the evening to practice her tumbling runs and stunts.

Around eight o'clock on the night in question, Principal Ferguson had heard a brief shriek of terror. What she found when she investigated sent her flying back to her office in a seizure of panic and horror. She would not soon forget what she'd discovered in the gym. Some creature with superhuman strength—surely, it could not have been a man—had snapped Maude's back like a twig and draped her supine body over the balance beam. It dangled there like it had no bones at all. Her abdomen had been torn open, spilling out glistening loops of yellow entrails. The stench was terrible. You wouldn't think a pretty girl like Maude would have had such smells within her, Miss Ferguson said.

The Arrest of Tony Rivers

In a press conference the following afternoon, Police Chief Baker dismissed the rumors of a teenage werewolf, and announced that Detective "Don" Donovan, the lead investigator on the case, had already made an arrest.

Tony Rivers, a junior, had also been in the school that night. Tony had been working after hours as the custodian for almost a year by then, ever since his father had succumbed to brain cancer, leaving Tony and his mother to make their way as best they could. Tony had told some of us about his father's transformation as the tumor ate into his brain. A gentle man, Ted Rivers had, by the end, become foul mouthed, and prone to fits of rage. To those closest to him, Tony had confided that though he tried not to think about his father's death, it weighed constantly upon him: when he was doing his homework or watching TV, when he was pushing a broom down the halls of Rockdale High. It was the first thing he thought about when he woke up. It was the last thing he thought about when he went to sleep.

I Was a Teenage Werewolf

This was the grief-stricken young man the police had found standing over Maude Lewis's body. Tony's explanation for his presence was perfectly reasonable: he too had come running in response to Maude's scream, arriving scant seconds after Miss Ferguson had locked herself in her office to call for help. Detective Donovan had taken him in for questioning anyway. Under interrogation, Tony said that he always escorted Maude home after Miss Ferguson locked up the school. It seemed unwise to let her walk alone, given the rumors that a teenage werewolf stalked the streets of Rockdale. Tony also admitted to an unrequited crush on Maude. And yes, she had recently—the night before her murder, in fact—rebuffed an invitation to join him at the Junior-Senior Prom. Had her snub angered him? Detective Donovan wanted to know. Did he approach her again the night of the murder? Did he lose his temper when she rejected him? Where was he when Maude died?

Tony barely had time to respond to one query—often incoherently—before the next arrived. His panic mounted, and when Detective Donovan confronted him with the final and most damning question of all—why had his hands been so bloody?—Tony's answer made no sense. *I couldn't stand to see her all torn up like that*, he said. *I was trying to put everything back inside her.*

Detective Donovan consulted the police chief. Tony Rivers was in a cell soon afterward.

The streets of Rockdale were safe, Chief Baker told us at his press conference. We had nothing to fear.

Other Cases of Teenage Lycanthropy

Our situation was not unprecedented. Other towns had been plagued by rumors of teenage werewolves: strange tracks in the snow, lupine howls in the lonesome morning hours.

Usually the rumors came to nothing. But in some few cases, what began as uneasy whispers escalated into outright horror. Missing pets, mutilated livestock, and worse. Much worse. The captain of

This Island Earth

the football team had been arrested for decapitating the head cheerleader in Bailey Downs, Indiana; the star mathlete detained for disemboweling his algebra instructor in Beacon Hills, New Hampshire; the Homecoming Queen taken into custody for slaughtering her entire court in Baker's Park, California. These had all been crimes of unparalleled savagery and mysterious circumstance. No convincing motives could be discovered, no weapons capable of inflicting such appalling wounds.

Anonymous sources reported that the cheerleader and the teacher had been partially devoured. The Homecoming Queen had hunted down her friends on the court with uncanny speed, butchering six girls and their escorts in the space of two hours. In all three cases, the perpetrators had been tracked down in wooded areas hours after dawn. They had been uniformly drenched in gore.

The Rumors in Rockdale

None of us could have foreseen Maude Lewis's death when Jim Whitt, a fiftysomething graduate of Rockdale High, first set local tongues wagging. In the year since his wife had skipped town with a Bible salesman, Jim had taken to drink, often closing down the Four Roses Tavern. By the time he hauled himself off his barstool on the night of January 11th, he was more than a little unsteady on his feet. Halfway to his dilapidated farm—three miles out of town on Rural Route 41—he began to nod. He pulled over to rest his eyes in a wooded turnout just outside the city limits.

The howling startled him awake an hour later.

Just a dog, he assured himself as he pulled back onto the pavement. But he hadn't gone more than a quarter mile before something big sprang onto the narrow road in front of him. For a heart-pounding instant, the creature—he did not know what else to call it—froze there, pinned in the splash of his old pickup's one working headlight, its knees coiled, its arms flung up before it. Jim stood on the brakes, wrenching the wheel hard left. When the truck skidded to a stop, he reached for the rifle mounted behind him, but the thing was already gone, leaving him little more than a confused impression of slavering fangs, wiry fur, and hateful yellow eyes. It looked unnervingly human, he told Frank Lilly over bottles of Pabst Blue Ribbon the next day.

"Could have been a bear," Frank said.

But no bears had been seen around Rockdale for years. The whole thing was far more likely to be a figment of Jim's whiskey-saturated brain, we concluded—and that might have been the end of it but for the incident at Mike Talbot's farm. One early February night, the hunting dogs Mike kept kenneled near his barn woke him. When he walked out to check on them, shotgun in hand, he found them in a frenzy. They snapped and bayed at the surrounding woods. They gnawed at the chain-link mesh of their run. Then an answering howl clove the night—close, much closer than Mike would have liked. A wild, rank musk filled the air. Mike's dogs whimpered and shrank away, their lips skinning back in terror. Something thrashed in the undergrowth at the tree line. Mike didn't hesitate. He lifted his shotgun and discharged both barrels into the darkness. He was still fumbling with the breech—his hands were shaking, he would later report without shame—when the creature, whatever it was, crashed off into the woods. The animal stench faded. He'd driven the thing off, at least for now. He had no intention of waiting to see if it came back. He reloaded, retreated to the house, and put coffee on the burner. He didn't sleep till dawn.

This was a more difficult story to dismiss. Mike was an unimpeachable witness. A Deacon at the First Baptist Church, he'd never been known to take a drink in his life, so his testimony added considerable force to Jim's account of the creature on Route 41. Miss Drummond's poodle, Yankee, disappeared from his fenced-in yard a few days later. When his half-eaten remains turned up on the high school steps the following morning, rumors of the teenage werewolf began to circulate in earnest, and though none of us really believed them, we liked to pretend that we did.

This Island Earth

It was a pleasure to be afraid. We shivered with excitement when Andy Wilson swore that he'd seen an inhuman figure lurking in the gloom behind his father's toolshed. We swooned with delight when Debra Anderson reported hearing something snuffling at her bedroom window. We jumped at shadows and hid under covers. We roved the streets in packs for safety, immersed ourselves in werewolf lore, and debated the teenage lycanthrope's identity over chocolate malts at Mooney's drive-in. Fear united us, and granted some few of us social opportunities we'd never had before. Tony Rivers wasn't the only one who seized the chance to walk home with a girl who might not have given him a second glance beforehand.

Then Maude Lewis died.

Rockdale High Reacts

A feverish elation seized us at school the next day. The glamour of tragedy is contagious. Its aftermath permits no strangers. Maude's close friends sobbed, and even girls who'd barely known her—even girls who had never spoken to her at all—wept. The boys—not without self-interest—tendered solace when permitted, and swelled with false bravado. And had we wanted to forget, to declare ourselves free of any obligation to grieve Maude or honor or avenge her, we could not have done so. The teachers were long faced and solicitous, engorged with empty platitudes. Yellow crime scene tape adorned the locked gym doors, and uniformed policemen patrolled the halls. Speculation rang upon every lip. Who could have done such a thing, we wondered? Did a teenage werewolf truly walk among us?

The news of Tony Rivers' arrest, when it came that afternoon, settled the question for most of us. The crime did not conform to what we many of us believed about lycanthropy. A human suspect had been taken into custody, the investigation successfully closed.

But those of us who knew Tony could not countenance his guilt. He was, like his father before him, an essentially gentle person, soft spoken, shy. Surely he could not have committed such a crime—a conclusion confirmed in our minds by the publication of Miss Ferguson's account of the brutal attack in the next day's *Rockdale Gazette*. It had to have been the teenage werewolf, we concluded. Nothing else made sense.

Detective Donovan's Doubts

Though we did not know it at the time, we were not alone in our misgivings.

What seemed like efficiency to Police Chief Baker felt like political expedience to his lead investigator. What seemed like homicidal madness to his boss—the boy had been trying to stuff Maude's viscera back inside her abdominal cavity, after all—made a kind of bizarre sense to Donovan. In a similar situation—had someone gutted, say, his own beloved daughter, Sharon, a freshman at Rockdale High, and strewn her intestines around the room like garlands—Donovan could very well imagine doing the same thing. He could even imagine that it might seem reasonable.

In short, Donovan was skeptical. If Chief Baker hadn't ordered him to make the arrest, Tony Rivers would still be free. The narrative didn't hold up to scrutiny.

No one denied that Tony had had the opportunity—but he was hardly alone. The school had been unlocked, open to any passerby.

Motive, Donovan believed, was equally problematic. Chief Baker ascribed the crime to Tony's humiliation and anger at Maude's rejection. This made sense at first blush, but Donovan couldn't reconcile it with what he'd learned from Tony's interview. Maude had been kind to the boy. She'd brought a casserole to Tony's house after his father died. She'd attended the funeral. And she'd been gentle in telling the boy she didn't want to go out with him. She valued him as a friend. They would continue to spend time together. She hoped he would still walk her home after she worked out at night.

This Island Earth

More problematic still, Tony was a good kid himself—hardworking, kind. Donovan knew this from his daughter, and he'd sensed it in the interview. Tony seemed to have taken no offense at Maude's rejection. He seemed, sadly, to have accepted rejection as his lot in life. And he'd been genuinely distraught at her death—hysterical, even. Grief-stricken and destroyed. No doubt, a good prosecutor could make the motive stick at trial, but Donovan believed that it collapsed in light of any honest analysis.

As for means? Impossible. Tony had been a scrawny, ungainly young man before his father's illness. After Ted Rivers died, Tony had grown haggard and pale, attenuated, weak. Even in the grip of unmitigated fury, of a hatred that burned hot and clean, Tony Rivers simply wasn't physically capable of such a crime. Few men were. He could not have broken Maude's spine. Could not have disemboweled her with his bare hands. And could not have—

Donovan shuddered.

Tony Rivers could not have chewed off her face.

Detective Donovan had heard the same rumors as everyone else, of course, but he'd never believed in the teenage werewolf. Now he wondered. How else could he explain the tuft of coarse brown hair they'd discovered in Maude Lewis's death-clenched fist?

The Death of Helen Bissell

A week passed without incident, then another. Gradually, Rockdale returned to normal. We no longer roamed the streets in packs for safety. We dismissed as superstition the werewolf lore we had studied so intently mere weeks before. Talk at Mooney's turned from the teenage werewolf to the Junior-Senior Prom. Our younger siblings once again skipped rope and played pick-up basketball as the March dusk enveloped our sidewalks and driveways. After Maude's funeral, the crime tape came down from the gym doors, the police no longer patrolled our hallways, and the teachers turned their attention back to English and equations. At night, we slept with our windows open, and in the morning we walked to school without fear. Even those of us with doubts let down our guard as the days slipped by.

Then the teenage werewolf struck again.

Afterward, we would question our lack of vigilance. Many of us would blame Police Chief Baker for lulling us into complacency with his blind assurances that our streets were safe. Detective Donovan would blame himself. Others would blame the victims, Helen Bissell and Arlene Marshall, both seniors at Rockdale High. How could they have been so careless, we would ask ourselves.

But at the time, with Tony Rivers safely behind bars, the decisions Helen and Arlene made that evening must have seemed perfectly reasonable. They'd met at the public library to study for a geometry exam, and time had gotten away from them. One minute they were trying to figure out how to calculate the surface area of an irregular prism, the next Mrs. Landon, the Head Librarian, was ushering them into the night.

The *Rockdale Gazette* later reported that she'd closed the library five minutes early, a matter of some controversy, though most of us could not see how five minutes would have changed anything. There were no other patrons that night, and she'd hoped to make it home for *Alfred Hitchcock Presents*. How could she have known that a teenage werewolf lurked in the darkness outside?

How could any of us have known?

If we had, Helen and Arlene might never have been at the library in the first place. Failing that, they might have called a parent to pick them up. And in the unlikely event that they *had* decided to walk, they would certainly have taken a different route home. Their houses—they were neighbors, friends since childhood—lay on the other side of McComb Park. But going around the park added fifteen minutes to their walk. They decided to cut through instead.

By daylight, our park is warm and inviting. Sunlight slants down through ancient oaks, and old men gather on the benches to gossip and feed the ducks that cruise the lake. Lovers picnic on the lawn by the bandshell. Children climb on the monkey bars and chase each other through the woods bordering the asphalt path that bisects the grounds. At night, however, the park is an entirely different place, isolated and abandoned. The oaks loom like giants against the black sky. The monkey bars have a skeletal aspect. Inky pools of shadow gather between widely spaced lampposts (too widely, we would later contend) and the woods seem to press closer to the path.

Helen and Arlene were more than halfway through the park when a lupine howl shattered the pristine silence. Just a dog, that's all, they reassured each other, as Jim Whitt had before them. But rumors of the teenage werewolf asserted themselves with fresh urgency. Another howl split the night as they passed into the bright pool beneath a lamppost. They exchanged glances, their faces white with dread, and hesitated, unwilling to brave the darkness, terrified not to. The next light gleamed like a beacon through the trees, just beyond a long curve in the path, and beyond that, one more faintly visible, a hundred yards before the stone-columned exit of the park and the safety of the streets beyond. Another howl sundered the air. Reluctantly, they slipped into the gloom.

Maybe a third of the way to the curve, Arlene would later report, they realized that something was pacing them in the darkness under the trees. They began to walk faster. Their unseen shadow stayed with them. They got the first hints of a rank, animal stench, and when the next howl rent the air—the thing couldn't have been more than twenty or thirty feet deep in the trees—the girls panicked. Dropping their books, they broke into a run. The next instant, the monster came crashing out of the trees upon them.

As it carried Helen screaming to the pavement, the creature raked Arlene's face with razor-edged claws. She caught what followed in glimpses, through the blood sheeting into her eyes: caught a flash of the thing, wiry and agile, as it crouched over Helen on legs of tensile muscle, a flash of its outstretched arms and curving talons, a flash of its face, its snout lifted to the sky as it howled in triumph. When the monster looked at her, its yellow eyes blazing in the gloom, its fangs glistening, Arlene whimpered. It leered at her. It grinned in mockery—if such a thing could grin—and then it turned away, sweeping one massive hand down and across Helen's throat, silencing her in an arterial spray.

And then, God help her, it started to feed.

Arlene found her voice and ran screaming through the park into the streets beyond. She collapsed, still screaming, on the front porch of the first house she came to. It belonged to Larry Phillips and his wife, Esther, a childless couple with a penchant for jigsaw puzzles. When the door opened, Arlene lurched inside. Larry Phillips took one look at her, slammed the door behind her, and flipped the deadbolt. A moment later he was on the phone for help. His wife, meanwhile, was trying to stanch the bleeding from the gashes the monster had carved in the girl's face.

Arlene Marshall would never be beautiful again.

To his shame, that was Detective Donovan's first thought when he saw her in the hospital room where they had stitched her up. She was groggy with painkillers, and it took an hour or more—over the doctor's objections—to elicit even a fragmentary version of what had transpired. Despite the evidence before him, Donovan reeled with shock and disbelief. It could not be, he thought. None of it. It must have been the morphine that accounted for her story. Yet the final detail she'd confided before the drug carried her off to sleep would not leave his mind.

The monster had been wearing a Rockdale Rams letter jacket.

The Aftermath of Helen Bissell's Death

Most of what we knew of that night was the product of rumor and surmise, though we had some few facts at our disposal. The park was closed indefinitely, the *Rockdale Gazette* reported, and the contingent of policemen Detective Donovan had dispatched to search the grounds did not find Helen Bissell until well after dawn. Though the article was circumspect in its description, it was clear that Helen was no longer intact when they located her—that what was left of her had been discovered scattered throughout the woods, torn apart and half-eaten. We knew as well—or thought we did—that the teenage werewolf had been wearing a letter jacket, though Donovan had sworn the attending physician to silence.

Tony Rivers was released, but Vic Miller, star forward of the high school basketball team, a jealous ex-boyfriend of Helen Bissell, and proud owner of a Rockdale Rams letter jacket, was taken into custody. Released for lack of evidence soon afterward—his father was an attorney, a Rotarian, and a fast friend of the sitting judge—he returned to school, as did Tony Rivers, nursing a grievance. Tony's shyness had been replaced with sullen resentment and hostility. Vic's natural belligerence had been exacerbated.

Few of us—even the most skeptical—still doubted the existence of the teenage werewolf. Once again we grieved, ostentatiously, and with a kind of manic joy. It was exciting to be afraid, more exciting still to be feared—for now that the rumors had been confirmed beyond all doubt, we *were* feared. Tension gripped the halls of Rockdale High. Our teachers looked askance at us in their classrooms. Our parents sent our younger siblings to visit relatives in other towns. But why, we asked, smiling sly, secret smiles, because of course we knew. A teenage werewolf walked among us. Who could say who it might be? Who could say when—or whom—it would attack next?

Yet we were each of us confident in our invulnerability. Maude Lewis and Helen Bissell had met terrible fates, but no matter how well we had known them—and some of us had known them quite well—they were strangers to us in the end. To the young, the dead are always strangers, in transit of some inconceivable horizon, both proximate and impossibly remote. We understood that we could die, that we someday would, but we did not *know* it, and though we took precautions—once again we roved the street in packs and locked our windows at night—we felt at heart that they were not necessary. The teenage werewolf would strike again, but it would not strike us. We took comfort in our immortality, pleasure in our fear.

I Was a Teenage Werewolf

And we secretly thrilled in the power that the teenage werewolf had bestowed upon us.

For if we were both sovereign and slave to our terror, our teachers and our parents were slaves alone. As long as no one knew who the teenage werewolf was, it could be any one of us.

The Town Meeting

Two days after Helen Bissell's death—after the children had been dispatched into the safe keeping of faraway grandparents, uncles, aunts, and cousins, and after we ourselves had grown giddy with power and despair—placards went up announcing a town meeting. Such affairs were usually ill-attended, the speakers' voices booming in the half-empty hall. My neighbor's lawn is an eyesore, weedy and ungroomed. A red light should be installed at Third and Vine—traffic has picked up since the new A&P opened its doors. The proposed trailer park on State Route 321 must be opposed, lest visitors to Rockdale be given the wrong impression.

Such mundane matters interested few of us.

The teenage werewolf, however, engaged us all. Anticipating the turnout, the town fathers moved the meeting to the high school gym. We gathered in Section A, at center court, and watched our parents and our teachers, our coaches, our scout masters, and our pastors file grimly in. They did not acknowledge us. They did not speak among themselves. And when Mayor Flanigan called the meeting to order, there was barely a rustle as they settled their attention upon the makeshift stage. We wondered if they thought, as we did, of the bloodstains that had been scrubbed from the hardwood underneath.

Mayor Flanigan told us that we faced a crisis unlike any other that Rockdale had ever endured. He voiced our grief for Maude Lewis and Helen Bissell. He adjured us to cooperate with Police Chief Baker and Detective Donovan in the ongoing investigation. He quoted scripture and bowed his head in prayer. And then he summoned the witnesses. Jim Whitt was too drunk to testify (Mayor Flanigan summarized his account), but the rest of them took the stage one by one—Mike Talbot and Miss Drummond and Miss Ferguson, each of them building the case that something terrible haunted the streets of Rockdale.

Then Arlene Marshall mounted the stage, stitched up like a teenage Frankenstein. A whisper of shock ran through the gym. In the silence that followed, Arlene took the microphone with trembling hands and surveyed the crowd, letting her gaze come to rest at last upon us, her peers. We could not read her expression. We could not see beyond her ravaged face. The sutures—there must have been a hundred or more, black and knotty, the puckered wounds slathered with some glistening antiseptic balm—pulled her skin taut, her mouth into a snarl. Her voice was unsteady when she began, barely audible and difficult to understand, but as she shared her experience in the park she gained confidence. She held the audience rapt as she described the howling in the night, the stalker in the woods. Gasps erupted when the monster came crashing through the trees, and when she spoke the fatal words at last, when she said that the thing had been a teenage werewolf, clad in a Rockdale High letter jacket, a single cry of sorrow and horror—it was a woman's voice—scaled the walls and echoed in the raftered vault above.

Arlene left the stage, and—though the teenage werewolf sat somewhere in our section, hidden in a human skin—she took her place among us.

Detective Donovan was the next to take the stage. He begged of us our forgiveness. He had failed the town. He had assumed, even in the face of his own doubts, that Maude's murder had been the work of a merely human killer—despite the impossible violence of the attack and the tuft of coarse brown hair he'd found in one clenched fist. He'd ignored the evidence. His imagination had failed him. He would refine the focus of his investigation.

Mayor Flanigan and Police Chief Baker were not so humble. They did not acknowledge their own failures, and did not examine past error. For them, the only question was the course forward. New policies were to be implemented. A strict curfew would be established and enforced. All high school extracurricular activities—including sports—would be put on indefinite hold. And it went without saying (they said), that the Junior-Senior Prom—a mere week away—would be canceled. We stirred in discontent at the first of these pronouncements. A chorus of whispers sprang up in response to the second. An active outcry broke out at the third. Did Mayor Flanigan really think a curfew would contain a teenage werewolf? Had he forgotten that the basketball team was in contention for the state championship? And what about the prom? We'd purchased our dresses and sent our suits to the dry cleaners, made dinner reservations, ordered flowers. Did the Mayor intend to reimburse us for these expenditures—for a year's worth of yards mown and snow shoveled, drive-in food delivered, babies sat?

He hesitated. He didn't answer.

Police Chief Baker cleared his throat. He gave us a stern look, but we'd seen that look before. Our teachers used it when they caught us smoking behind the fieldhouse, and our parents used it when we came home late on Saturday nights. Our coaches used it when we took a bad shot or forgot the play, our pastors when we missed services. It no longer frightened us, that look. We knew it for an empty threat. We'd seen what a teenage werewolf could do, and we knew that Chief Baker too was afraid. What would we have him do? he wanted to know. Would we surrender the once-peaceful streets of Rockdale to a reign of blood?

We didn't answer him.

Then someone—none of us saw who it was—yelled that half-measures wouldn't do. By all means impose the curfew and cancel the prom. But something more had to be done! Our townsfolk roared their approval. Put extra policemen on the street! someone cried. And someone else: Issue the officers silver bullets! And then a clamor of competing shouts—wolf's bane and monkshood and lock them all away!—this last plunging the crowd into a deep silence as our parents contemplated the lengths that they would go to, to tame or contain us—

This Island Earth

A silence into which Arlene Marshall once again stood and approached the stage.

She leaned into the microphone.

"I always dreamed of going to prom," she said, and after what she'd been through, who could deny her?

Thus it was decided.

Our Thoughts about the Teenage Werewolf

Who would take Arlene to prom? we wondered.

Following her mutilation, Jonathan Bowling—her boyfriend—had rescinded his invitation (inexcusably, we agreed) on the pretext that she had not sufficiently recovered to attend. When we told him that his place then was at her side—and not at the prom—he had no counterargument. His face burned with chagrin, his eyes with fury. He clenched his fists and set his teeth. Many of us feared him. He was big, a tackle on the football team, and short tempered. Yet even he had no strength to oppose the force of our unified opinion.

He reinstated his invitation.

Arlene, to her credit, refused him. Even if she had no other options, she told him, she would not deign to accompany him. As it happened, however, she did have other options—a plethora of them. The attack and its aftermath, most notably her solidarity with us at the town meeting, had conferred a kind of celebrity upon her. But she turned her suitors down, and asked Tony Rivers to be her date. They were kindred spirits, she said. They'd both been scarred by the teenage werewolf.

But hadn't we all?

Hadn't the teenage werewolf come to shape and define us? Wasn't its existence, its endless capacity for violence, the single most important fact about us? Hadn't our townsmen, our parents, made that clear? They wished to curtail our freedoms, cancel our sports, deny, most of all, the zenith of our year—the axis about which our entire social calendar revolved. As far as they were concerned, until someone identified the teenage werewolf, we were *all* the teenage werewolf—and if at one level we resented this, at another it empowered us. In trying to save us, they had sought to imprison us. In seeking to imprison us, they had set us free.

The Friday before the prom, we cast our votes for queen. That night, we gathered to decorate the gym. We erected a band stand, unfolded card tables and disguised them with white linen cloths. We inflated balloons and draped ribbons. We hung a glitter ball from the rafters, like a shining silver moon, and felt wild currents flowing in our veins.

The Massacre at the Rockdale Prom

We woke to rain the next morning, but the weather cleared by ten. We heaved a collective sigh of relief. Cars needed washing, shoes polishing. We arrived early at the florist to collect our flowers—and sighed when we had to wait because everyone else had had the same idea.

Cliques clicked and gangs gathered.

We gossiped as we dressed. Our mothers clamped bobby pins between their teeth, plucking them out one by one as they constructed elaborate coiffures. Our fathers helped us knot ties purchased to coordinate with the dresses of our dates. Our stomachs churned with the magnitude of the occasion. We giggled in excitement. We put on stoic faces.

The prom officially commenced at 8:00, but most of us drifted in half an hour later. It wouldn't do to arrive too early, and besides, we had other things to attend to. Dates had to be picked up, corsages affixed. Pictures had to be taken. Our dinner plans ran long. We ate with mannered precision, conducting stilted conversations over our food. We pretended at adulthood and found it all a bore.

This was not what we had expected at all.

We longed for freedom, not a preview of the pinched years to come.

This Island Earth

Upon our arrival, we were alarmed to see that chaperones had attended in unusual numbers. Miss Ferguson was there, of course, as were our teachers. But Mayor Flanigan and Police Chief Baker had also shown up. Our pastors and our parents, too. Detective Donovan kept to the shadows, watching with a weather eye.

Even the gym's transformation disappointed us. The card tables were rickety. The folding chairs betrayed the illusion of elegance. The balloons drooped. The hors d'oeuvres left much to be desired. The cheese tasted ashy. The cookies were dry, the punch thin. And while we told ourselves that the band was fantastic, we knew that it was second rate. Their covers were pale shadows of the rock 'n' roll we'd grown to love, their harmonies off-key.

Yet we danced as if our lives depended on it. We danced like the twelve princesses in the tale. When the band played a slow song, we clutched each other close—too close, our chaperones would have said. In the shadowy reaches of the room they stirred as if to intercede, but then fell still. And when the band swung into a fast song, we whirled around the floor, waved our arms, drew each other close, and whirled away again. Our parents looked on in disapproval, but they did not speak.

The dancing became wild, frenetic, Dionysian. The staid adult masks we'd donned over dinner slipped and fell away entirely. And then the music stopped. We all froze, panting, on the dance floor as a spotlight illuminated Miss Ferguson, thin and pale upon the stage. It was almost eleven by then, the climax of the night, time to announce the prom queen. One by one, to squeals of triumph and delight, her court was appointed: four handmaidens and their escorts, arrayed in a crescent moon around the stage. And then, with a drum roll, Principal Ferguson opened the envelope containing the Prom Queen's identity. She unfolded the page within, she scanned it silently. She leaned into the microphone and read it aloud.

"This year's prom queen is Arlene Marshall," she said.

The room burst into riotous applause.

As Tony Rivers squired her to the bandstand, we stomped our feet for Arlene. We cheered, we roared as one, and when she dipped her head to accept the crown, we howled. We howled and howled, like wild things, like monsters and like wolves. Her tiara on her head, Arlene turned to the microphone. Before she could speak—had she even intended to speak?—her visage bulged grotesquely, stitches popping, and cracked along the fault lines of her wounds. We gasped when she reached up with her fingers and tore back her human face to reveal the muzzle underneath, slavering and snapping at the air. Her yellow eyes glowed with untamed freedom and with joy. She lifted her head, baying into the dark vault of the gym with its glitter-ball moon. And even as a tide of lupine transformation swept the crowded dance floor, as we too clawed apart our faces to free at last the ravening beasts that lay underneath, teenage werewolves each and every one—even as we assumed our true and long-hidden forms, unknown even to ourselves, our werewolf queen claimed her first victim, decapitating Principal Ferguson with a single swipe of her hand.

Our muscles tightened and grew tenfold strong, agile, quick. Our fingers sprang razor-edged claws, our pores coarse hair. And our senses sharpened. The gloom of the gym was blasted clean with white, hot light, and we could hear the pulse of blood in every human vein. We could smell it, too, metallic and hot. We could smell everything—the sweet tang of the punch and the terror of our chaperones in their sweat upon the air, even our own rank and randy musk—and we wanted to wallow in it all, to fight and fuck and eat, eat, eat. We were famished and insatiate, bottomless pits of raw appetite. Nothing had ever been so awful. Nothing had ever felt so good.

We reveled in it. Leapt on tables and smashed chairs. Snarled and howled and took our chaperones down. They stood in shock before our fury. Police Chief Baker died with his revolver still holstered. Detective Donovan got off a single shot before a teenage werewolf bit off his hand and took him to the floor. Someone kicked open a door and we eviscerated them as they fled into the night—pastors and

This Island Earth

parents, coaches, teachers, the mayor and the city council, too. We ripped out their throats and tore off their arms. We ate of their flesh. We drank of their blood. We killed them all and we devoured them, and then we stood on the roofs of their cars and howled our triumph at the moon. We were teenage werewolves and we owned the night.

We would never let them tame us.

> Times have changed here. We're not a bunch of kids anymore.
>
> — Hank Green

ALL THIS HAPPENED A LONG TIME AGO, in the summer when *Blackboard Jungle* ruled the screen, "Rock Around the Clock" shot up the charts, and Hal March asked the first *$64,000 Question*. That was the year our friend the atom lit up the streetlights of Arco, Idaho, the world's first atomic city. Reddy Kilowatt had slain Bert the Turtle, who'd been telling us to duck and cover for years, and for a moment we let ourselves forget that Uncle Sam had spent the better part of the last decade irradiating the Nevada desert. What did we care about the contradictions of America's Atomic Age? We were seventeen, and we'd thrown off the shackles of the classroom for another year. We slept late, and breakfasted on ice cream sodas at the New Graham Pharmacy. We played lazy games of pick-up baseball on the grass-worn municipal fields off Shippan Street. Most days, we went down to Party Beach.

This Island Earth

That wasn't its real name, of course. Maps had it down as Dane's Cove, after the ill-fated captain of a 19th-century clipper that had gone down in the waters churning just off-shore, and our parents, when they called it anything at all, mostly called it the sand beach, for it was the only stretch of anything remotely beach-like in a fifteen- or twenty-mile expanse of steep, rocky shoreline that left Maricove unspoiled long after the neighboring towns of Battleboro and Nash had bloomed into gaudy summer destinations. Even this unimaginative descriptor was not entirely accurate, for the sand beach was really too small and rocky—not nearly sandy enough—to appeal to acolytes of surf and sun, and the currents there were too dangerous for swimming. But it was the perfect spot if you wanted to put "Maybellene" on the radio and dance beneath the stars; so in the summer before my senior year, the summer when rock 'n' roll was born and for one golden moment everything was possible, it came to be called Party Beach. And though the name would fall out of use after the horror that unfolded there, it has always remained Party Beach to me.

I'm an old man now, and most of my memories have faded like old photographs left too long in the sun, but my recollections of that summer—my recollections of Party Beach—stand apart. They are crisp and well-preserved, and if they are not wholly free from nostalgia, that nostalgia is tempered with the hard lessons that came at the end. That was the first summer that I had a car—a battered '49 Mercury that I'd purchased with a loan against my earnings from bagging groceries down at the A&P. That was the summer I lost my virginity. Most of all that was the summer of Elaine Gavin.

These were not unrelated phenomena, as you have no doubt surmised. But I don't want you to misunderstand me. Elaine wasn't fast. There was nothing lurid or cheap, nothing shameful, about the moments we shared in the backseat of that old Merc, however fumbling and inexpert our amours might have been. Sometimes when I close my eyes, I can still smell the faint lavender scent of Elaine's shampoo, and I can feel, for a fleeting heartbeat, the warmth of her

THE HORROR OF PARTY BEACH

embrace. But then the final horror sweeps over me once again, and I shudder and I jerk myself awake to stare out into the darkness, and listen. And though my house is almost a mile away from the sea, on those nights I can still hear the surf pounding upon the rocky shingle we called Party Beach.

We met in Mr. Taylor's chemistry class in the spring semester of our junior year, Elaine and I—really met, I mean. We'd known each other for years in the casual way you know kids that move in other circles—the ones you nod at as you pass in the hall, but never really pause to exchange a word with. And why would we talk? She was a loner, aloof and isolated—stuck up and wicked smart. Me? I was quiet, but well-liked. I knew the most popular kids, and even if I wasn't quite one of them, I was always welcome in their company.

Not that it mattered to Elaine.

"I'll take care of the thinking," she told me when Mr. Taylor paired us up in lab. "You follow orders."

It turned out to be a good arrangement. When it came to chemistry, I was fumbling and dim at best. Elaine, on the other hand, was brilliant. She regarded Mr. Taylor's labs as dumbed-down lessons for kids with the intellects of capuchin monkeys.

She had, in short, inherited her father's aptitude for science. Dr. Gavin—the Mad Scientist of Maricove—was widely regarded as a savant of the first order. A widower, he'd fled to Maricove from some southern university, for ill-defined but possibly scandalous reasons. He'd gone through two teaching jobs since then—first at Maricove College, then at the high school downtown—departing each attended by a fresh round of whispers: midnight power surges in the physics building, clandestine experiments in the chemistry lab. By the time Elaine matriculated as a Maricove Red Raider, he'd become a recluse in the sprawling Victorian house they shared out on Fingel's Point. He hadn't been seen in town for years, though passersby on Route 13 occasionally observed odd blue light flickering around the edges of his heavily curtained windows, and his mailman complained of the place's persistent fishy miasma.

But there was no fishy stench to Elaine. She smelled—indefinably—wonderful, and she looked wonderful, too. She was lean and dark-eyed and quick to smile, with a pixie haircut that flattered her almost as much as Audrey Hepburn's had flattered her in *Roman Holiday*, and maybe more. I soon came to look forward to our twice-weekly labs more than anything else in school, or out of it. I was halfway in love with her by mid-February, and more than halfway by the beginning of April. She said things like "Don't drop that beaker, Mike" (I was always dropping beakers) and "Be careful with the Bunsen burner" (this, after an unfortunate accident involving a lab report and the sleeve of my second-best shirt). I was always saying things like—

Well, I was rarely saying things at all—and certainly not the things I wanted to say—though I didn't do a very good job of hiding them, I guess, since I was always getting harassed about them in the locker room before gym. "When you gonna ask Brainiac from Planet X out, Mikey?" Scott Becker would ask, and John Moore would say, "Maybe she's as mad as her mad scientist daddy," and Floyd McKay would snap me with a towel and raise his eyebrows like Groucho Marx and add, "Mad in the sack, maybe," and it would go on like that until finally Brad Clarke, quarterback of the Red Raiders, Big Man On Campus, and stand-up guy, would weigh in and put a stop to it, saying, "Lay off, fellas. Mikey here can ask out whoever he wants to." But Mikey did nothing of the sort until one day—it was late in May, by then—Brad pulled me aside before English and batted me lightly on the back of the head. "You should go for it, Mike," he said. "Can't you see she's wild about you?" In fact, I couldn't see it, but I trusted Brad's instincts. Wasn't he dating Tina Laurel, the head cheerleader, homecoming queen, and all-around prettiest and most popular girl in school?

He was.

Which is how I wound up in chem lab the next day, stuttering,

"Hey, Elaine, you think we should go see a movie this weekend or something?" And then, when she didn't answer right away, "We don't have to. It was just an—"

"Shut up, Mike," she said. "I think that would be grand."

She touched my hand, and I dropped my beaker in surprise. I stepped back and caught my sleeve on fire. "Gosh," I said, as she shoved my arm under the spigot, twisted the handle, and doused the flames.

She laughed and gave me a quick peck on the cheek.

I felt like I'd caught fire all over again.

I didn't know anyone who'd ever been to Elaine's house—had never heard of anyone even getting near the place aside from the aforementioned mailman. So it was with some apprehension that I turned my rusty beater of a Merc down Route 13 toward Fingel's Point, and with greater apprehension still that I climbed the steps of the old house itself. The porch sagged, the wooden cladding had long since weathered gray, and if I detected a faint piscine tang in the air—nothing like the stench the mailman had described—I attributed it to the salty wind whipping up over the point.

I had just lifted my hand to knock—tentatively—when the door swung open before me.

Elaine stood on the other side, looking glamorous in a skirt and cardigan. She gave me another chaste peck on the cheek—more flames—and pulled me inside. "You have to meet Daddy," she said, leading me through the dim foyer and into the room beyond, which swam with a strange, blue undersea light—a light reflected and refracted through dozens of huge aquariums, each schooling with fish. Some of them were the exotic beauties you saw in every hobbyist's saltwater tank—clownfish and angel fish, dartfish and dottybacks. But some of them were exotic in other ways, in their sheer ugliness and unfamiliarity. I saw fish that seemed to be little more than mouths and curving, razor-edged teeth, bioluminescent fish and bewhiskered fish and heavy-lidded, drowsy-looking fish the size of my forearm. And in the largest tank a bizarre-looking fish that must have been four feet long.

"What is that thing?" I asked Elaine.

"That thing," said a disembodied voice, "is a living fossil, young man." And then the mysterious Dr. Gavin himself materialized out of the shadows, a tall man, well over six feet and gaunt to the point of emaciation, with a shock of dark hair that made him seem two or three inches taller still. His lab coat was filthy and he smelled of cigarette smoke and algae—though maybe that was only the odor of the room, which had through his long occupancy permeated his clothes and skin. Elaine would later tell me that he often fell asleep at his work. "He's very devoted to his research," she would say, though his devotion sounded more like obsession to me, a point that I remained silent on, as I would remain silent on other points as the summer went by. When I reached out to shake his hand, he didn't seem to notice. He had the distracted air of a man who lived deep in his own thoughts. He had eyes only for the hideous fish.

"That thing," he said, gesturing, "is a coelacanth, thought extinct for sixty-six million years until some lucky fisherman pulled one out of the waters off South Africa not two decades since. His kind—the fish, not the fisherman—swam the ocean waters in the last days of the dinosaurs, young man. Impressive, isn't it?"

"I...guess so."

He nodded. "It's a handsome creature," he said. "Do you know the Cretaceous, then?"

I sputtered.

"My peers," he went on, "such as they are, contend that volcanic activity caused the demise of the dinosaurs. They are wrong. I believe that the impact of an enormous meteor wiped them out in the blink of an eye." He drew his gaze back from the deeps of time and focused his considerable powers of concentration upon me. "Well, what do you have to say for yourself?"

"Um, I—a meteor? Sir?"

He clapped me on the back. "Good. Elaine has told me of your aptitude for chemistry."

"My aptitude for—"

"Ah. Well. You kids have fun tonight."

With that, he turned away. I knew a dismissal when I heard one.

Outside, as we pulled out onto Route 13, I glanced at Elaine. "You told him I had an aptitude—"

She leaned over to kiss me on the cheek once again. When I felt her hand fall upon my thigh, I thought I might spontaneously combust.

"Didn't you say something about a movie?" she asked.

Which is how we wound up seeing *Revenge of the Creature* at the Granada Theater downtown. We shared popcorn and a Coke, we ate a box of Junior Mints—and just as the Gill-man made his escape from captivity, I yawned and stretched, draping my arm as if by chance across the back of Elaine's seat. She leaned into me, resting her head against my shoulder. We watched the rest of the film that way. When the credits rolled and the lights came up—altogether too soon—she reached for my hand and we strolled out together into the night.

In the car, she said, "Do you know a place where we can talk awhile?"

"Won't your dad be worried?"

She laughed quietly. Maybe there was a tinge of sorrow in the laugh. I couldn't say for sure. "My dad doesn't worry about things like that," she said.

So we went to Party Beach.

It didn't occur to me to ask what kinds of things her dad did worry about—not then, anyway. And by the time the question did come to mind, it was too late: events had ground to their inexorable conclusion.

But that night I could not imagine the horror yet to come. That night, the unpaved turnout overlooking Party Beach was empty. We had only a glittering multitude of stars for company. "Earth Angel" played softly on the radio as we gazed out across the black water. I wanted desperately to kiss Elaine, but I didn't know how to go about it. I launched into some tedious observations about the movie instead.

Elaine pressed a finger to my lips. "Hush, Mike" she said, and I hushed—enthusiastically, if it's possible to hush enthusiastically. I was certainly enthusiastic about what followed. Elaine's next kiss was neither shy nor chaste. We must have made out for an hour or more, as only seventeen-year-old virgins can make out. We made out until our lips were bruised, we made out until I could barely breathe. And by the time Elaine put an end to the proceedings—just as my hand was about to close over her breast—I was, literally, aching with desire.

"We'll have another chance, Mike," she said, and it was on that promise that I left her at her door.

Elaine was true to her word. There *were* other chances—plenty of them, though never quite enough. Neither of us ever formalized the matter, but after that first session at Party Beach, we didn't really need to: we both understood that we were going steady, in the parlance of the day, which translated to spending virtually every waking moment together—or every waking moment that I didn't spend bagging groceries at the A&P, anyway. We shared chocolate shakes at Frankie's Diner and movies at the Granada. We went parking out at Party Beach. My grades, never very good to start with, plunged. I might have failed my junior year altogether if I hadn't managed to run out the clock on the semester.

But summer came, and I escaped unscathed. On my days off Elaine and I went down to Party Beach with Brad and Tina Laurel and the rest of the gang—with Scott and his girlfriend Annette, with Floyd McKay and Susan Carver, with John Moore and half a dozen others. The radio was always on. The beat of the music—"Ain't That a Shame" and "Good Rockin' Tonight" and "Skinny Jim"—was like the beat of our hearts and we danced to that beat like no one had ever danced before. When we couldn't dance anymore, we cooled our feet in the surf or sunned ourselves like cats and talked of dreams and love and rock 'n' roll. At night, when the breeze off the water turned cool, we built a fire and sat in a circle around it and talked some more, until we finally ran out of things to say and drifted away in pairs, up to the turnout where we'd parked our cars or off into the deeper shadows of the rocks, where we would spread blankets and make out until our lips were sore and chafed.

And Elaine would swim, of course. Nobody else ever went more than knee-deep into the water off Party Beach. No one else wanted to chance the vicious riptide. But Elaine was fearless. She would swim at any time of day or night. "I think I'll take a quick dip," she'd announce, and the next minute she'd be gone. It scared the hell out of me every time she did it.

I wasn't the only one who thought it was a bad idea.

I remember the first time we joined the gang down at Party Beach, two or three days after school got out. Everyone made Elaine feel welcome that day, even though she'd never moved in my circle and had always been held in disdain by those who did—mostly, I think, because she was the only kid at Maricove High who didn't care about their opinion. With her dark good looks, her Audrey Hepburn hair, and her father's brains, Elaine was above all that. She was a nation of one, and when that nation wanted to go swimming, it went swimming.

And on that first day, when the strains of "Baby, Let's Play House" died in the afternoon air and we all collapsed in exhaustion, Elaine, flushed and beautiful from dancing, announced that she thought she'd take a swim.

"Maybe that's not such a good idea," Brad said.

"Why not?" she wanted to know, and as Brad answered, I saw a change come across Tina Laurel's face. Sometimes I tell myself that everything that happened afterwards hinged upon that moment. But who can say? Maybe it was all foredoomed, from the minute I worked up the courage to ask Elaine Gavin out in the first place. Sometimes, I think it was. Sometimes—when I let myself—I know it.

This Island Earth

But all I knew at the time was that Brad was being his usual fundamentally decent self.

Why not swim? Elaine wanted to know. "The rip is really dangerous here," he said.

"The rip doesn't scare me," Elaine said.

And when Brad started to speak again, Tina interrupted him. "Let her swim if she wants to, Brad."

"But—"

"What's it to you?" Tina said. "Mikey's the one that brought her here, isn't he? Let him worry about it."

And the thing is, I *did* worry about it. Worried as I turned to register my own anxieties on the point (too late, Elaine was already waist-deep in the cold Atlantic) and worried as I watched her dive into an incoming wave and worried most of all when she didn't surface on the other side.

Silence, then. The sigh of the ocean, the cry of a gull.

"Now she's stepped in it," Floyd said.

And John Moore, "Where'd she go?"

I glanced down at the second hand of my watch. A full minute slipped by, and then another one. By then I was *really* worried.

I started toward the water. I don't know what I was planning, exactly. I guess I was going in after her—there didn't seem to be any other choice—though I was a lousy swimmer even in calm water. Heck, I was a lousy swimmer in the shallow end of a bath tub. The riptide at Party Beach would have chewed me up and spat me out to sea in no time. I could already feel the relentless pull of the current when Brad dropped a hand on my shoulder. "Hang on, Mikey, I'm coming, too."

"No, Brad, stop," Tina harangued him from behind. "Come back here! I *said* come back here!"

But Brad ignored her. He followed me into the water not because he wanted to show me up or claim Elaine's affections for himself. No, Brad did it, as he did most things, out of a kind of selfless good will. He was everything any of us wanted to be. A natural on the gridiron and in the classroom, he had the handsome, blond charisma and self-deprecating wit of an A-list movie star. We should have hated him, but we could not. He was too open-hearted for that. He could no more have left Elaine at the mercy of the rip than he could have passed an accident on the highway without stopping to make sure everyone was okay. But we were both saved from heroics that day. We were still thigh-deep in the water when Elaine surfaced maybe fifty yards out.

"Come in!" I called.

And Brad: "It's dangerous out there, Elaine!"

Her voice boomed across the water. "I'm fine!" she shouted. "I'll be in soon!"

She was as good as her word. Five minutes later, ten at the most, she came wading out of the surf like a Nereid. Tina was waiting behind us, and as the three of us turned back to the beach, I saw in her cold, adamantine glare that she now hated Elaine, and thus we all came to ruin.

By the middle of June, Elaine was eating dinner with my family two or three times a week. My mother smiled and said that she had beautiful eyes. My father clapped me on the back and said that I was playing out of my league. My little sister asked if she could get a pixie haircut, too. In short, my family adored her.

I was less sure that Dr. Gavin approved of me.

I had not seen him since that first night. I had not even been admitted into the house again. When I picked her up, Elaine was always waiting outside for me. When I dropped her off, she left me with a kiss at the bottom of the stairs.

The first time I asked her if her father minded us spending so much time together, she told me not to worry about it. The second time I asked, she said that he was very busy with his research. The third time I asked, she invited me to dinner.

"Dinner?" I said.

"Dinner," she said.

This Island Earth

"At your house?"

"Yes."

"But who's going to cook?"

Elaine rolled her eyes. "Who do you think cooks, Mike?"

She cooked—and she did a darn fine job of it, too. She served a far more exotic meal than my mother's customary fare of roast beef or fried chicken: firm white swordfish steaks (I had to ask what kind of fish it was), potatoes au gratin, and pan-roasted asparagus and mushrooms. We ate in a room off the lab. Fresh flowers and a white linen tablecloth, candles and wine. Nothing like I'd ever seen before.

Dr. Gavin sat at the head of the table, picking at his food. Elaine and I sat to either side.

There was little conversation until I asked Dr. Gavin what he was working on. He dropped his napkin beside his plate. "Evolution," he said.

"Evolution?"

"Evolution." He finished his wine and sat back in his chair, steepling his long fingers before him. "At some point in the Devonian, a primitive fish crawled out of the sea and took its first breath of air. Four hundred million years later, here we are. Surely, you've wondered how that happened."

I hadn't. My curiosity at that time pretty much came to an end with my own evolutionary urges—most of which I hoped to someday visit upon this man's daughter—but now that I'd gotten him talking—

"Sure," I said. "But I thought we had fossils—"

"The fossil record is laughably incomplete," he said, waving a hand dismissively. He leaned toward me. "And I'm not interested in old bones. I want to *see* how it happened. I want to see it for myself."

"But that's impossible."

"A generation ago perhaps, but now, well—what's the secret of evolution, young man?"

I had no idea—did anyone?—but I cast around for some phrase or other to toss into the conversational mix. I came up with "survival of the fittest."

Dr. Gavin looked pained. "It's a poor synonym for natural selection. How does one become more fit than one's fellows?"

"I— I don't know."

"Mutation," Elaine said.

I looked at her. "What?"

"Mutation, Mike," she said, speaking as you might speak to an especially dense child. "Some kind of random error in the organism's DNA."

"Exactly," Dr. Gavin said. "Nine times out of ten, ninety-nine times out of a hundred, it's not particularly useful—you have blue eyes and I have brown, but we both see just fine. But sometimes, over thousands of generations, a gill becomes a lung, a fish comes crawling up the beach to colonize a new environmental niche, and from that—"

"Everything," Elaine said, "elephants to insects," and the way she said it, it sounded like she was repeating something she'd heard a thousand times over.

Dr. Gavin patted his daughter's arm. "Elephants to insects—well, not insects, exactly, but it's a handy mnemonic isn't it, dear?"

Elaine smiled, and I saw in the radiance of that smile how devoted she was to her father and her father's work. "But you just said mutation takes thousands of generations. How—"

"Ah. Good question, young man. Come with me."

He stood, and led us into the lab. It was like being in a bathysphere made of glass, with oceanic blue light all around us. I stared at the fish in their abundance, the enormous coelacanth among them. The thing hung motionless at the bottom of its cramped tank, large-eyed and armored, with fins that looked almost like—

"Legs," I said.

"And a vestigial lung in its abdomen," Dr. Gavin said. "Fascinating creature. A window upon the past. Evolution in action."

THIS ISLAND EARTH

He gazed at it fondly.

Elaine said, "Fish reproduce in far greater numbers than we do—"

"They spawn," Dr. Gavin said. "Fish spawn," and out of the entire conversation it is that phrase that most haunts me—that and what he said next. "The common carp can spawn multiple times in a single season, producing as many as 300,000 eggs each time. The odds of mutation expand exponentially with each clutch of eggs, young man. And if you goose the process along..."

"How would you do that?" I asked.

"Radiation," Elaine said. "How else?"

Mushroom clouds bloomed in my mind on the drive home. I could almost see them in the windshield before me, hanging over the atom-blasted cinders of Hiroshima and Nagasaki. I'd spent my youth playing in backyard bomb shelters and hiding under my desk when the air-raid sirens went off. From the time I was a kid, bizarre rumors had abounded: giant ants in the sewers of L.A., monsters in the Sea of Japan.

Talk of the atom was always in the air.

The atom was going to destroy us. The atom was going to set us free.

One way or the other, the atom was going to remake our world.

I hadn't expected it to remake *my* world, though—not so soon, anyway.

Yet the minute Elaine had said the word—

—*radiation*—

—I felt the geography of our relationship shift. I saw her for the first time not as a mere observer to her father's experiments but as an active collaborator. Elephants and insects, that radiant and adoring smile.

I imagined a leaking metal barrel overturned in a patch of dead weeds out on the windswept precipice of Fingel's Point. Dr. Gavin hunched over it, drawing up into a syringe a glowing green fluid that he would soon inject into the waters of an experimental aquarium. Fish spawn, he said, and 300,000 irradiated eggs drifted to the mossy bottom to rest.

What if the mad scientist of Maricove really *was* mad?

What if his daughter was as mad as he was?

I managed to shunt these questions aside until a Saturday night toward the middle of July. I still remember the sky-blue pedal pushers and black ballet flats Elaine wore that night. I had planned to take her out for a burger at Frankie's, followed by the creepshow down at the Granada. But we wound up in a booth near the door of the diner, shooting the breeze with Floyd and Susan instead. Scott and Annette joined us after a while, and then Brad and Tina stopped by, and before you knew it we'd missed the start of the movie.

Outside, rain lashed the windows.

Somebody suggested we stop down at Tom's Billiards Parlor to shoot a couple games of pool. "Sounds good to me," Brad said, tossing a handful of silver on the table. "Let's blow this popsicle stand"—which clinched the matter. But as we stood to go, Elaine said, "I think I'm going to have to pass tonight."

"What's wrong?" Brad said, and Tina shot him a murderous glare.

"I'm feeling a little queasy."

"Maybe something disagreed with you," Tina said.

Elaine ignored her. "Do you mind driving me home, Mike?"

I tried to hide my disappointment. "Sure," I said.

But five minutes later, as I pulled out of Frankie's lot and spun the wheel toward Fingel's Point, my windshield wipers slapping the rain away, Elaine said, "Let's go out to Party Beach instead."

"I thought you were sick."

"I'm feeling better now," she said.

But if she was, it was hard to tell. She spent most of the drive in a brown study, gazing out at the rain. When "Shake, Rattle, and Roll" came on the radio, I turned it up loud. I always did go for the fast ones. Elaine didn't say a word. She just reached out and dialed it

This Island Earth

back to a whisper. Without the backbeat to pound out the rhythm of my heart, I felt more lonesome than I'd ever felt before—and this though she was right there on the bench beside me, everything I'd ever dreamed of and then some.

I wheeled the Merc into the turnout and killed the engine, nose out to the ocean. Rain hammered the roof. On the radio, just barely audible, the Platters swung into "Only You." Inspired by the sentiment, I slid my arm around Elaine and leaned in to kiss her. She pressed her palm against my chest. I turned away and looked out into the night. I took the steering wheel in both hands. Outside the rain came down and down. A sense of foreboding possessed me.

"Did you bring me here to break up with me, Elaine?"

She didn't answer for a long time. Then, quietly: "No, though maybe I should."

A tide shifted within me, dark water drawing back to reveal the jagged stones beneath. "Elaine—"

"I'm afraid, Mike."

"Of what?"

"I've never felt anything like this. It scares me. It's like a current way out in the deep water, pulling at me. Pulling and pulling. And I'm afraid I'll drown." She hesitated. "Do you ever think about our first date?"

And what came back to me was the way she had pillowed her head against my shoulder as the movie flickered on the screen before us. That, and the way her hand had slipped so naturally into mine as we exited the theater. She'd brought me out to Party Beach that night, as well. I remembered the taste of her lips against my own. Did I think about our first date? "All the time," I said, turning to look at her.

"Me, too." She laughed. "Sometimes I think about that silly movie. How sad it made me."

"Sad?"

"Well, the creature was lonely, wasn't it? It wanted to be loved. And who doesn't want that?"

Who indeed?

"Do you love me, Mike?"

Something quickened inside me.

"Yes," I said. "I love you, Elaine."

Elaine didn't say anything, but she came into my arms and this time when my hand crept up to her breast, she leaned into me and kissed me hard and I took that as answer enough. Her pedal pushers ended up on the floor that night, her blouse beside them. As she rose up over me, headlights illuminated the interior of the car. In a panic, I pulled her down out of the line of sight, but it was too late. I'd seen her frozen above me. Whoever was in the other car must have seen her, too. And then the lights swept past. The other car accelerated back onto the highway, engine roaring.

"Shit," I said. "They must have—"

"It's okay. They're gone now," she said, and she began to rock against me once again, and then there was only the heat of her body in the car, and outside the rain and the dark ocean muscling up the beach.

The Moonglows lit up the radio dial, crooning I'll do anything for you.

"Promise me you'll forgive me, Mike," she whispered at my ear. "Whatever happens, promise me you'll forgive me."

I promised.

Outwardly, things were better than ever after that. Elaine and I scarfed down burgers at Frankie's. We took in the latest creature features at the Granada. And we made love with increasing frequency, parking out at Party Beach when no was around, and scouting out other locations—an abandoned quarry, a forsaken mill—when someone was.

In many ways, it was the happiest time of my life.

But disquieting questions—questions I could not bring myself to ask—shadowed my thoughts. When we saw *Creature with the Atom Brain* (radioactive zombies) and *It Came from Beneath the Sea*

This Island Earth

(radioactive octopus), I couldn't help recalling her father's unorthodox obsessions. And sometimes, as I drifted off to sleep, I heard her urgent plea for forgiveness and I wondered what it was she had to fear.

There were portents of the horror to come, as well, though I did not recognize them at the time. When we'd started dating, Elaine had barely picked at her food. Now she routinely put away her burger—she liked them rare—and a double order of fries. She drank chocolate shakes like water. When my mother served apple pie for dessert, she always took the largest slice. And she spent more time than ever in the treacherous waters off Party Beach, often disappearing for an hour or more.

"Maybe she's a mermaid," John Moore remarked one night as we sat talking around the fire.

"Maybe she has a boyfriend with a boat," Tina said.

"Tina!" Brad said.

But Tina shrugged and flipped her hair. "I'm just looking out for Mikey."

"Mike can look out for himself."

"I'm not so sure of that," Tina said, and the truth was I wasn't so sure of it myself.

I tried not to listen to Tina, but I had my own worries about Elaine.

After the party broke up, we lingered on the beach alone, watching the fire burn down. "Tina says you have a boyfriend with a boat," I told her.

"And what do you say, Mike?"

"Well, I don't think you have another boyfriend," I said, "but I do worry about you out there. Every time you disappear like that, I wonder if you're going to wash up downshore somewhere."

"Well, you needn't worry about that."

"But what if you get a cramp or something?"

"I don't get cramps."

"Elaine—"

"Hush, Mike," she said, pulling me down to the sand beside her, and when I protested again, she put her lips to mine and one thing led to another and we ended up making love right there on the beach, with the surf crashing at our feet and a million stars looking down. It wasn't everything it's cracked up to be—sand gets in the damnedest places—but it was pretty fine, and by the time we finished, my questions were—for the moment, anyway—forgotten.

But "Hush, Mike" could only work for so long, even when paired with her considerable physical charms. The bathysphere glow of her father's lab irradiated my dreams, and as the summer crested and began its long decline toward my senior year at Maricove High, strange fish schooled in my thoughts. Where did Elaine go during her long sojourns at sea? What promise had she exacted from me?

I got my answers—and terrible answers they were—one night toward the end of August, with school looming just over the horizon. The whole thing began down at Frankie's.

We'd just finished eating—Elaine had put away two burgers, to my amazement—and she had excused herself to the restroom to powder her face. She'd taken her compact and a lipstick, leaving her purse open on the table, another chance decision that changed everything—for the ladies' room door had no sooner swung closed behind her than Jeff Callahan and Chris Smith walked by. It was innocent horseplay, nothing more, but Jeff happened to give Chris a playful body check as they passed. Chris staggered against our booth—

"Watch out!" I said.

—nearly upsetting the table.

A half-empty milkshake went over, spilling cold, soupy chocolate into my lap.

Cursing, I yanked a handful of napkins from the table-top dispenser in a futile effort to contain the damage. Chris and Jeff just stood there, mouths agape.

This Island Earth

"Wow," Chris said, "that doesn't look good."

"Why don't you watch what you're doing?"

"Hey," Chris said. He held up his hands, palms out, an innocent man. "Blame Jeff, he's the one that pushed me."

"Here," Jeff said, reaching for a napkin, "let me help you."

"It's all over my pants. What do you think you're gonna do? Just get out of here!"

"Fine," Jeff said, and as they beat feet out of the place, he gave Chris another playful shove. "He didn't have to get bent about it," he said, pushing out into the night.

I reached for another wad of napkins, did a little more damage control, and tossed the whole soggy mess onto the table. That's when I saw that my pants weren't the only casualty of the impact. Elaine's purse had gone overboard, spraying half its contents across the bench opposite. The other half—and the purse itself—had wound up under the table.

Cursing again, I leaned down to retrieve it, shoving the debris piece by piece back inside its gaping mouth—a rubber change purse that you squeezed open to get at the silver inside, a wallet, a little package of Kleenex, a—

"What happened?" Elaine said.

I straightened up, startled, clutching her purse in one hand and some random bit of flotsam in the other one. I caught my head on the lip of the table. Another milkshake—this one empty—came crashing down beside me. I sighed.

"Here," Elaine said, reaching out to haul me up. "Watch your head!"

I watched my head.

Back on the daylit side of the table, I handed her the purse.

"What happ—" she started to ask again—and broke off, abruptly silent. She swallowed.

"What?" I said, and then I realized that she was staring at my hand.

I looked down—and that's when I saw what I had plucked up

from the shadows: the narrow glass barrel of a syringe. When I held it out toward her, a little ripple ran through the glowing green fluid inside.

"What is this, Elaine?"

"Come on, Mike," she said. "Let's go for a drive."

Neither one of us said anything for the longest time. I drove without destination, I drove by reflex, I drove to Party Beach, and at last, as the night rushed past the windows, Elaine said, "I never told you about my mother."

"You did. You told me she died from complications when you were born."

"I never told you the truth."

I drove.

I said, "Is that all you've lied to me about?"

Her silence was all the answer I needed. I felt that tide receding, the jagged rocks beneath.

"I'm not sure this is going to work out, Elaine."

"You promised me, Mike. You promised me that you'd forgive me. No matter what happened, you said that you'd forgive me."

I drove.

"So tell me what happened to your mother."

"I was just a kid."

"What happened to her, Elaine?"

"They blamed my father, but it was the cancer that got her. It was in her bones. The last time I saw her, she looked like a skeleton, she'd lost so much weight. I could see the skull inside her face. It was so painful at the end. I can still hear her screaming."

"Elaine—"

"It's okay," she said. "Just drive."

I drove.

"Why'd they blame your dad?" I asked.

"He was so close to saving her, Mike. If she'd lasted another six months..."

This Island Earth

I looked over at her. In the backwash from the dash lights, I could see tears on her face. "But why would you lie?" I asked.

"I was afraid."

"Of what?"

I turned on my signal. We pulled into the turnout by Party Beach. I inventoried the cars. The whole gang was there. Floyd and Susan were there. Scott and Annette. And Brad and Tina, of course. I sometimes tell myself that things might have turned out differently if they'd chosen to see a movie that night instead.

I parked the car and killed the engine. We sat there and listened to it tick. Outside the sea heaved, gnawing down the edge of the continent. A fire burned on the beach. Figures stood in silhouette against the flames.

"I didn't want you to leave me, Mike."

"But that doesn't make any sense. Why would I leave you over that?"

"Not that," she said.

"Then what?"

"What if my mother's disease was inherited?"

"What are you talking about? Are you sick?"

She sighed. "My father made the diagnosis at Christmas."

"Cancer?"

"He thought he'd perfected the treatment. We thought I'd be okay."

"Are you going to—"

I couldn't bring myself to say the word.

"No. But—" She took a long breath. "I'm changing, Mike. I can't control it anymore."

I thought of the syringe—I thought of that glowing green fluid—and those bizarre rumors came back to me: giant ants in the sewers of Los Angeles, monsters in the Sea of Japan.

"What's in the syringe, Elaine?"

"Radiation to kill the cancer cells," she said. "And—"

She broke off. She turned away.

"And what?"

She hesitated. "Blood. Blood to bolster my immune system."

"What are you talking about? What blood?"

"The blood of the coelacanth," she said.

Much of what she said afterward is a blur—unexpected side effects, rapid cellular mutation, re-emergent DNA. None of it meant anything to me, and I couldn't focus, anyway. I kept seeing that massive armored fish floating serenely at the bottom of its aquarium: evolution's abortion, a Darwinian dead end that had never quite managed to crawl out of the sea. The thought of that monster's irradiated blood flowing in Elaine's veins nauseated me. Recoiling in horror, I clawed at the door and flung it open. I stumbled outside, into the cool air sweeping in off the ocean, and collapsed against Scott's car, too dizzy to stand on my own. When the vertigo passed, I stood unsteady on my feet, and surveyed the night. A full moon hung overhead and a breeze swept in off the ocean. A fire burned down by the water. Brad's voice came to me—

"Hey, Mike, why don't you guys get yourselves down here!"

—and I lurched off toward the beach. I didn't feel any better by the time I got there, but I must have looked okay. No one seemed to notice anything other than the lingering stain of the milkshake, anyway—and even that elicited only a few jokey asides ("You might want to see a doctor about that," John Moore said) before the gang lost interest and Brad asked me what I'd done with Elaine.

"She'll...be down in a few minutes," I said.

But she was already there, coming along behind me. I hadn't heard her, she moved so lightly on her feet, and when she said, "I'm here," it startled me.

I turned, but she lingered in the shadows.

"Well, aren't you going to join us?" Scott asked.

"I think I'll take a swim first," she said, moving on down toward the water.

"Weirdo," Tina said and Brad sighed and said, "Why can't you be nice to her?"

This Island Earth

"Maybe because you're too nice," Tina retorted, and after a brief, awkward silence, talk turned to the upcoming school year. I think we all felt it slipping away, that one golden summer, and there was a funereal solemnity to the conversation. In nine months we'd graduate to adult life: jobs, college, marriage: everything we'd longed for and dreaded for so long. But for one shining moment we were still teenagers.

Or they were.

I felt like I'd already slipped across the line, into the fuzzy gray territory beyond. Promises you couldn't keep, losses you had not anticipated—such was the price of love. I'd been a fool to think that I could bear it.

I didn't want to grow up. In some sense I already had.

So I sat on a rock at the periphery of the circle and gazed into the fire and when Brad hunkered down beside me and asked me if I was okay, I didn't know how to answer. I wasn't, of course. I didn't know if I'd ever be okay again.

"You and Elaine have a fight?"

"No, we're fine."

"Are you? Because you don't seem fine."

"I'll be okay."

"If you need to talk—"

"Sure."

"Okay, then." He clapped me on the shoulder and moved back toward the fire.

"What's wrong with him?" I heard Susan ask. Brad said something I couldn't make out and the conversation resumed, leaving me to my funk.

I was still sitting there when Elaine came back and everything went to hell.

There was something wrong with her gait. There was something wrong with her face.

These were subtle changes, invisible, in that light, to anyone who didn't know her as intimately as I had come to know her in the last few months. No one else seemed to notice, anyway. But they did notice the sallow cast to her face.

"Hey, Elaine. Are you okay?" Brad said. "You look a little green."

I stood. "Elaine?" I said.

"I think I'm going to be sick," she said.

"You know what causes that, don't you?" Tina said.

Elaine turned to look at her—we all turned to look at her. Tina raised her eyebrows. "Maybe you've been spending too much time in the backseat of Mikey's car."

"Tina!" Brad said sharply.

But it did no good. Now that she had the stage, Tina was determined to give us a show. "We saw you that night in the rain, Brad and I," she said. "I hope it was good for you. When's little Mikey due?"

Elaine was too sick to answer.

She clutched at her midsection and retched and retched again, spewing the contents of her stomach into Tina's face. Tina reeled away, shrieking and swiping at her eyes. The stench was atrocious—a noxious piscine reek—and as I stood by, stunned, I saw, in the stew of fish guts steaming in the sand at Tina's feet, a single severed tentacle, still twitching.

Elaine cried in horror, lifting her hands to her face.

Only they weren't hands—not human hands, anyway. They were the hands of some monstrous thalassic super-predator: enormous hands with long webbed fingers and hooked, black talons. When she saw them, Elaine moaned. She met my gaze across the fire. I felt some obscure communication—sorrow or regret—pass between us. And then she melted back into the gloom.

"Elaine!" Brad shouted. "Come back!"

He looked at me. I was still standing there stupefied, wondering—I am ashamed to say—how many times Elaine had returned from such a filthy repast to press her lips to mine. Brad must have seen the shock in my eyes. "I'll get her," he said. "You take care of Tina."

THIS ISLAND EARTH

Before I could speak, he was gone, sprinting off into the shadows. I stood there, staring after him, listening to Tina rant. "Look what that bitch did to me," she screamed. "Look at me!"

So I looked at her—she was a mess, all right—and then, when she called Elaine a bitch for the second time, I did the only thing I could think to do. I slapped her across the face. Her head snapped back, and she stared at me with the huge, bewildered eyes of a spoiled child who has run hard up against reality for the first time in her life. She reached up to touch the corner of her mouth, where a thread of blood had started down her chin, and I felt an influx of shame stronger than any shame I'd ever felt before.

"You hit me," she said.

I said nothing in reply. What was there to say?

I turned away instead.

They were all standing there, dumbfounded, mouths agape. Annette was sobbing quietly. Floyd was the only one who tried to stop me.

"Wait, Mike," he said as I pushed past him. "I don't think I would go out there if I were you. There was something wrong with her hands. Did you see that, guys? There was something wrong with Elaine's hands." He reached for me. "Mike, buddy, please—"

"Get off me, Floyd."

"Mike—"

He fell back at the edge of the light. After a minute, the surf drowned out his voice.

I kept walking, following Brad's footprints out across the damp rocky sand.

I needed to find Elaine. I had a promise to keep.

Floyd was right about one thing: Brad should never have followed Elaine out into the darkness. If he hadn't, I think she might have retreated to the sea. As it was—well, her appetite had been increasing for weeks. I'd seen that for myself. She must have been burning all kinds of energy managing the transformations, with her long swims alone providing some relief. When she finally lost control, the thing she'd become had glutted itself, choking down a surfeit that she couldn't stomach when she regained her human form. So now the atavism that lurked within her was ravenous.

Brad was dead, of course.

She'd taken him down in a maze of rocks, where the fingernail paring of beach gave way to the great seaside cliffs that ran all the way north to Battleboro. The crash of the incoming tide was so loud down there that if he had cried out I wouldn't have heard him. But it must have been quick. His head was rolling around at the edge of the surf when I found them, and Elaine—the thing that had been Elaine—had already begun to feed. She'd torn his guts open with those hooked talons, and she was scraping out the cavity within. When I said her name, she looked up, loops of viscera dangling from her teeth.

Those teeth. My God, the thing was all teeth. They must have been three or four inches long: curving, razor-edged needles, blood slick and dripping with the tissue of Brad's intestines. Its yellow eyes were set far back beneath a bony shelf, its face framed in folds of tissue that must have been gills—all of it, everything, swept back, streamlined as a bullet, perfectly evolved for hunting the warm Devonian seas.

When it saw me, the thing sprang over Brad's body on legs sheathed in muscle. Its momentum carried me backward to the beach. For a moment, supine upon the rocky sand, I struggled to free myself, clawing in vain at its slick, armored carapace. And then I was still. The monster hissed, its jaws unhinging not two inches from my face. Its gullet stank of blood and shit and rotting fish.

I said, "Elaine—"

And the creature paused.

"I forgive you," I said.

In the end, the story we settled on was that Brad and Elaine had decided—against our advice—to go for a swim. We told the police that they'd never returned. The vicious riptide must have dragged them out to sea. An early-morning search of the beach turned up Brad's remains. In the end, the investigation concluded—officially, anyway—that he'd been attacked by a shark out there in the midnight waters. Even the most cursory examination of his body would surely have shown otherwise. No shark would have inflicted that type of damage. But if the authorities had some other theory, they weren't talking.

As for Elaine? Presumed drowned.

I knew better, of course—I'd watched her disappear into the dark water—but I wasn't talking. And that might have been the end of it. But I kept thinking about that night I'd eaten dinner with Elaine and her father. Elephants and insects, Dr. Gavin had said. I want to see evolution in action. It was those words more than anything else that led me to turn my old Merc out toward Fingel's Point a month or two later.

The whole world had changed by then. School had started back, but it seemed like a formality. Those of us who'd been on Party Beach that night had already graduated into adulthood, with its attendant griefs and ambiguities. We didn't spend much time together after that—I think the truth was too unbearable—and none of the other kids wanted much to do with us either. Without Brad, we each of us drifted into our solitary orbits. Floyd and Susan broke up almost immediately. Scott and Annette hung on a little longer, but by Homecoming they too had gone their separate ways.

The house on Fingel's Point, however, remained unchanged. Its porch still sagged. Its cladding was still gray. Stepping out of my car was like stepping into the past. When I rang the bell, I half-expected Elaine to open the door, gorgeous in her skirt and cardigan. Dr. Gavin opened it instead. His shock of hair stood up uncombed. His lab coat was filthy.

"I suppose you want to come in," he said.

"No, I just came to ask you a question."

"Hurry up, then. I have things to do."

I took a deep breath. "Elaine was never sick, was she? Or her mother either?"

Dr. Gavin stared at me for a long time. He laughed. "You're brighter than I thought you were," he said, and then he shut the door in my face. I heard the deadbolt turn, and I turned away and drove back to Maricove, where seven months later I graduated high school at last and became a manager down at the A&P and went on to lead a long and ordinary life. I'm an old man now and that really is the end of it.

Except—

Except I happened to turn on the TV the other morning to learn that the savaged bodies of swimmers have started showing up on beaches all up and down the coast. Twenty-four of them so far, and it's not yet June. Shark Summer they're calling it, the deadliest year on record. The best guess is that fished-out hunting grounds and polluted ocean waters are altering predation patterns. But the marine biologist on TV had his doubts. The force quotient of the bite is all wrong, he said, the wound structure atypical.

"What could it be then?" the anchor wanted to know.

"You tell me," he said.

You tell me. I wondered if he really wanted to know.

When's little Mikey due? Tina Laurel asked inside my head, and what I thought of was Dr. Gavin schooling me on the mating habits of the common carp. Fish spawn, he'd said, and as I sat there in front of the TV, I imagined 300,000 eggs drifting to the ocean floor, and I thought about those polluted ocean waters and those fished-out hunting grounds, driving my children into the shallows to feed.

AFTERWARD—AFTER THE INCIDENT and the investigation following; after the shock, but not the guilt and sorrow; after he'd grown accustomed to the dreams, their portents and intimations; after he had embarked upon the strange half-life that he would live hereafter—after all that and more, Ezra drove down to the station, chasing his headlights into the night as it billowed down like a shroud over the narrow roads and fields patchy with snow and winter rye.

He hadn't been there in months, and he came late today, uncertain why he'd come at all or what he hoped to accomplish, looking for a sign. If John had left for the night, he would pass on, burrowing deeper into the warren of dark roads, putting miles between his old life and the one that lay ahead.

But John's ramshackle old pickup was there when he steered the Chevy into the lot, gravel crunching under his tires. He killed the engine, listening to it tick as he pulled himself together. When he finally forced himself out of the car, a '57 Bel Air—you could still smell the new—he stood hesitant in the January cold, fixed in the

This Island Earth

red neon haze of the call letters bolted to the sign high above him: KNWC. The windows of the station glowed yellow. Behind it, the shadowy tower of the transmitter array printed itself against the sky.

Against these frail assertions of human dominion, a wall of night and the sigh of wind combing the rye; above them, the black arc of heaven: a thousand stars like still points moving and billions more unseen beyond them. Nothing else: only the vacuum of space running on to the edge of all things, expanding.

Into what, though? It was inconceivable.

He looked at his watch. 9:37.

He was going to do it now. He was going to go inside.

But he was still standing there when the station's door swung open. John appeared, pausing in the light to dig out his keys. The dim, ceaseless murmur of the studio—piped low into the station's every room, the bullpen, the offices beyond—spilled out around him: the comforting timbre of the DJ's voice and the platter spinning, the needle crackling as it dropped into the groove and music poured out from the transmitter, flowing invisibly across the fields to the small towns and the lone farmhouses between them.

"Ez?" John said, compact and gray, edging into his sixties. "Is that you? I haven't seen you in a month of Sundays!"

"You're on your way home," Ezra said. "I'll come back later"—knowing that he would not.

"Like hell you will. I can call Mildred if I need to. She won't mind. She's been worried about you. We both have."

He didn't say why he'd been worried, just waved Ezra across the lot.

"You're a sight for sore eyes, anyway," he said in the bullpen: checkerboard tile and a rump-cratered lime sofa with a coffee stain on the right arm where Ezra had once dozed off, too tired to drive home after an overnight. Tattered back issues of *Radio News* and *Confidential*—"uncensored and off the record since 1952"—lay on the table in front of it, along with a spine-broken western, *Sixgun Fury*, that Ezra had dropped there months ago. A clock hung on the

Night Caller from Outer Space

wall opposite, a deranged cat that rolled its eyes and switched its tail on the beat of every second. The air smelled of damp coffee grounds from the stainless-steel percolator by the sink, where Darla had abandoned a lipstick-smudged mug.

Carl was in the box, the *On Air* sign aglow. Ezra nodded at him through the glass. Carl offered a tight smile in return, his face settling into a mask of wary reserve.

Ezra had become accustomed to it. For three months he'd ventured out only when he had to: to buy coffee and bread, peanut butter when he'd scraped the jar clean; to draw down his paltry savings until he had none left to draw. These few errands had been enough, though. The grocery store, the bank, the courthouse when they had some questions: everywhere he went people wore that wary mask—people he'd known his whole life. A strained smile, a brief word if they couldn't avoid it. What could they say to him? A wall stood between them: questions that could not be asked or answered; condolences that they could not offer.

They watched him when he turned away.

"Here we are," John said, settling behind his desk.

Ezra shut the office door. He flipped a ladderback chair around and straddled it. Eyed John over crossed arms.

Carl set a new platter spinning. The Everly Brothers felt so lonely they could cry.

"How are you?" John asked. "You okay?"

"I don't even know what okay means anymore, John."

"Well, hell. Who does?" Opening a drawer, John produced a pint of Ten High and two dusty glasses. He shook out a handkerchief, smeared the dust around in one of them, and poured a finger of whiskey. He nodded at the other glass. "You want a drink?"

"Dreams are bad enough when I'm sober."

"You wanna talk about it?"

"No."

What could he say?

It was too big, too strange, to talk about; you had to talk around it somehow. It was all madness: lights in the sky, that pervasive hum, so deep you could feel it in your molars, so deep you could feel it in your bones. And Abby.

Tell us about Abby, the lean men in dark suits said.

What could he possibly say about Abby?

They sat in silence, John sipping at his whiskey. "What can I do for you, then?"

"I need money."

"You looking for a loan or a job?"

"You still have a job for me?"

John leaned back and drew a long breath. A tension passed out of him. Ezra saw it only when it was gone.

"You're family, Ez. You'll always have a job here, long as I own the place. Bill's got to stay on mornings, him and Helen having the baby now. I can put you back on overnights."

"That's fine."

"You can start Monday, then. I can advance you a few bucks if you need it. Darla might fuss, but that's Darla."

"Let Darla be. I can get along till payday."

"Alright." John finished his whiskey. "Well. Mildred's waiting."

Ezra knew a dismissal when he heard one. He stood and put the chair back. "Tell her I appreciate everything she's done for me. Dropping off the food. I should've called. You and Mildred—you're family to me, too. Everybody down here is."

Ezra pushed the words out fast and went off down the hall before John had a chance to reply. In the bullpen, he stopped to glance at his watch. It was 9:37. He went on outside, into the cold. He didn't look up as he walked to his car. He was afraid of what he'd see there.

Ezra took a deep breath. He drew down the mike, leaned in close, and came in low over the fade with the handoff, saying, "That's Carl Stewart's been spinning the records for you this evening and no man does it better. I'm gonna pick up where he left off and carry you through till morning. I'm Ezra Hill. That's Easy Ez to my friends, and if you're out there in radio land tonight, you can count yourself among them. It's been a while since I joined you on the airwaves, and it's a real honor to be back behind the mike at KNWC, cranking out country music new and old on 1000 watts of late-night AM power. It's a quarter past as the hour moves toward eleven, so we're gonna throttle back on the honky-tonk dance tunes and lend an ear to the low and lonesome ones, a little night music for this long, cold Iowa night. Let's get started by reaching back almost a decade to hear old Hank tell us what it's like when your sweet love ain't around."

He set the record spinning and slotted the needle in the groove.

Hank Williams' plaintive tenor filled the studio and rolled out across the swells of rye grass. Ezra imagined someone, some man or woman in some dark house, tuning the volume low and taking comfort that in their loneliness they were not alone.

He never had been one for church. But at night, with the radio playing, he sensed something moving in the airwaves. He always had. Comfort, God, whatever you called it, he'd been made to summon it down, to give it shape and voice. The words that everywhere else eluded him came easy in the studio. He could untie the knot of his thoughts there, unbind some other self—not his truest self, maybe, but a self comfortable behind the mike, easy in his own skin. He brought the second turntable up to speed and rolled straight into the next cut, Webb Pierce, "It's Been So Long," and then the next one after that, Kitty Wells and Red Foley, "As Long as I Live." He doubled back to I.D. the songs, laid a music bed on the turntable, and read off a block of ads against it before moving into the next set.

"We're a quarter and change short of the hour here at KNWC," he said when he was done. "We've got Patsy Cline's new one, 'Walkin' After Midnight,' coming down the line. You'll wanna stick around for that one. Meantime, why don't you pick up your phone and dial in a dedication at KN-5692? That's KN-5692. Could be someone out there might like to know you've got 'em on your mind. As a certain young man from Tupelo, Mississippi, reminds us, it can get mighty lonesome when you take up residence in that old 'Heartbreak Hotel.'"

That's how it went. Though he pushed the request line, there wasn't any action on the phone. Overnights were quiet. It didn't matter. Fifteen minutes and it had all come back to him. The records unracked themselves, they came so readily to hand. All he had to do was run the patter in between, lay down the ads, and keep an eye on the VU meters, adjusting the pots now and then to keep the needles out of the red. Riding the gain felt the same as it ever had. It felt like breathing—as natural and as necessary, as empty of volition.

He'd been holding his breath for months. He hadn't even known it.

It was half an hour short of 6:00 before the request line lit up. He snugged the receiver into the nook between his ear and shoulder as he pulled the next set. "This is Easy Ez at KNWC. What's your pleasure at this early, early hour?"

Nothing. Only the hiss of an open circuit.

"Hello, you've got Easy Ez here, down the line at KNWC. You there?"

A burst of static, then, and through it dimly, like a transatlantic call—like a call from the moon or from a distant star—a voice came whispering, thin and faraway. He caught a single phrase: "...they're coming..."

A buzzsaw of interference drowned out everything that followed.

"Let me have that one more time," he said.

No reply. The crackle of static. Nothing more.

He was just ready to rack the phone when the line cleared again. At the far end of it silence, vast and empty as the midnight sky, and in the silence the sound of something waiting. And then an echo—or the ghost of one—rang hollow in his ear, interspersed with sharp bursts of static:

"...watch keep..." And then, urgent and sharp: "Ezra!"

The line went dead.

Night Caller from Outer Space

Ezra rocked back in his chair, cloven by loss and longing, riven by shame.

Only one person in the world had ever called him Ezra. Only one. That's all it took: a single word, a name—his own name—and he was shorn from the world of men. He skipped a block of ROS ads. He didn't trust his voice to lay down the copy steady. He didn't front the next cut for the same reason: just queued it up, his hands trembling as he slotted the 45 on the spindle: Johnny Cash and the Tennessee Two, "So Doggone Lonesome."

On the other side of the window, Bill Archer—Big Bill to the faithful listeners of KNWC, and at six-four he lived up to every inch of the name—swung into the bullpen. He threw Ezra a wave and busied himself with the percolator. Ezra still didn't trust his voice—

—*one person only one*—

—so he rolled straight on into "Cry, Cry, Darling" and "Just Call Me Lonesome" after that. He had "There Stands the Glass" spinning up on the second turntable when Bill leaned in and handed him a mug of coffee. "You're supposed to say something now and again, Ez," he said. "You okay?"

"Yeah. Sure. Worn out is all." Ezra forced a laugh. "Been a while since I pulled an overnight."

"You wanna head out, I'll take it from here."

"You're not on for another ten minutes."

"You don't look like you got another ten minutes in you. And what am I gonna do? Sit out there flipping through Darla's gossip rags? Might as well get to it."

"Yeah, okay then," Ezra said. "Thanks." He stood, shaky on his feet, cradling his coffee with both hands. It was all he could do not to spill it as Bill shouldered by him to the soundboard. The rip-and-read came chattering in over the line: news and weather from the AP.

Bill adjusted the mike.

On the speakers, Webb Pierce was yearning for the glass that would ease all his pain. Ezra—forcing the words out, as if by will alone he could weave himself back into the fabric of the world—Ezra said, "Hey, you and Helen, about the baby. I'm sorry I— I should have—"

"You've had a hard time. We know that."

"How's fatherhood treating you?"

"A lot of dirty diapers."

"I can imagine."

"You *cannot* imagine. You cannot *begin* to imagine. Now get outta here. Get some rest, okay?"

Ezra was at the door when Bill called him back, his face curious and open and empty of judgment. "Hey, Ez," he said. "Whatever happened out there—"

"Thanks for the coffee, Bill," Ezra said. He shut the door behind him.

Ezra stood in the bullpen, stricken. He was halfway aware of Bill doubling back to clean up the mess he'd made with the song titles and then sliding on into the early news. But most of his mind was far away—fixed on that light in the sky, that hum throbbing in his bones; on that name—*his* name—coming urgent down the line; on Abby. Abby—the only person in his entire life who had called him Ezra.

He'd always been Ez. Ez to the father who'd abandoned him and the mother who hadn't, Ez to his teachers and his friends, Ez to John and Mildred and everyone at the station, who'd taken him in when he'd lost his mother. Seventeen years old. He had the house she'd left him, a '46 Plymouth De Luxe that was more rust than Plymouth, and three months of drudgery remaining to earn a piece of paper she'd cared more about than he ever had. And a radio.

A radio.

Tune in, turn the volume low, and bask in the comfort coming down the airwaves. In the honky-tonk heartbreak Ezra heard the echo of his own sorrow; in the dance numbers a glimmer of future contentment. Every day the songs came sweeping out across the fields. One day he hopped into the Plymouth and followed them back to the wellspring where they spilled out into the world.

Night Caller from Outer Space

John looked at him skeptically across his desk. "What do you even know about radio?"

"I know the way it makes me feel."

Something flickered in John's eyes. "You know how to clean a toilet and take out the garbage?"

"Sure."

Which is how he came to work at KNWC; came to know John and Mildred, Carl, Darla, Bill, and the rest; and came, three or four years down the road, to take his seat at the soundboard and send the voice of Easy Ez, the self he aspired to be, rolling out across the farmland.

It was also how he came to know Abby.

His twenty-third birthday Bill and Carl treated him to beers at a juke joint outside of Udell. Their waitress—a slim redhead with a crooked smile and a spray of freckles on her cheeks—caught Ezra's eye as soon as they sat down. He wanted to ask her name. He didn't know how to. Outside the studio, words had never come easy to him. How could he even begin? But for three sweating, longneck bottles of Pabst Blue Ribbon, icy to the touch, he might not have. Instead, beer-emboldened, he said, "I'm Ez," when she came by with another round. "You might of heard me on the radio. Easy Ez."

"Not unless you're on that swing station over in Mystic," the redhead told him. "Which you aren't. And your name isn't Ez either, is it? And it certainly isn't Easy. If I wanted to call you anything, I'd have to call you by your true name. I'm betting it's Ezra."

Ezra, he thought. Here then was a third self. Not the self who could find no words to unbind his thoughts, and not the self he aspired to become—not Easy Ez—but the self he'd been all his life without ever even knowing it. His true self. His true name. Hadn't he always been Ezra in his thoughts? He wondered that it hadn't occurred to him before.

"I guess you like this hillbilly music here, Ezra," the waitress said.

It was a test.

"I guess I do," he said.

THIS ISLAND EARTH

The redhead blessed him with that crooked smile. "Well, nobody's perfect, are they?"

"I suppose some folks go for Duke Ellington. There's no accounting for taste, is there—" He tilted his head.

"Abby," she said.

"Not Abigail?"

"That's my legal name. Abby is my true name." She put his beer on the table and walked away. Not so much as a glance back.

Just then somebody dropped a nickel in the jukebox, and Hank Penny launched into a tune praising the merits of red-headed women. Call it coincidence. Call it fate. But Ezra vowed on the spot that he was going to marry a red-headed woman—and not just any red-headed woman. *This* red-headed woman. Abby.

Six months later he did.

A justice of the peace presided. John and Mildred stood witness. Afterward, alone in Ezra's little house, Ezra and Abby danced: Tony Bennett, "Because of You"—Abby's choice.

Ezra didn't care much for the fancy stuff, but no song had ever sounded finer.

Somewhere between the bullpen and Darla's office Ezra lost track of his coffee.

It didn't matter. The words coming down the request line had stunned him into a stupor. The memories they triggered had jarred him wide awake.

He closed a mental door on the memories—or tried to—and opened the physical door before him. The office inside took him by surprise. It always did—the discrepancy between the person who worked there and the space she worked in.

There was Darla, and then there was Darla's office. Darla was, as Ezra's mother might have put it, as neat as a pin. Ezra figured she had five years on him, which put her in her early thirties; he knew better than to ask. But she looked at least half a decade younger, fresh out of school, dark and petite, with bobbed hair, bright lipstick, lacquered nails. Her office, on the other hand, looked like a tornado had just torn through it, depositing on her desk every scrap of paper in a ten-mile radius. Maybe it was a comfort to her. Some people found drink, others God. Maybe Darla had found a way to project all the human turmoil roiling within her upon the world around her: maybe outward chaos was the price she paid for inward tranquility.

If it *was* chaos: to Ezra's perpetual amazement, she could pluck any document from the midden on her desk with unerring speed and accuracy. He had no such luck. He had to excavate her telephone. He had to steel himself to make the call.

A relay clicked. A circuit closed. "Operator."

"Hi, Ruth. This is Ez, down at the station. That call you put through around five-thirty—any chance you can trace that back for me?"

"I didn't put a call through around five-thirty, Ez. It's been dead quiet here all night."

"It was five maybe. On the request line. It was a real bad connection. It might have been long distance."

"Well, I don't know what to tell you. It's been dead quiet here all night."

"Could it have come through another exchange?"

"There aren't any other exchanges out this way. You know that." She hesitated. "Are you alright?"

"Yeah. Yeah, I'm fine."

"Well, after—after what happened, I guess—"

She broke off abruptly. He wondered what she'd been about to say. Did it matter?

You're saying a flying saucer took her?

He heard the skepticism in every voice. He saw it in every eye.

He'd lived in the rolling hills of southern Iowa his whole life. Farm country: soybeans and corn, milk cows, pigs. A handful of small towns and a few wide spots in the road that had ambitions. Bloomfield and Moulton, Bladensburg, Udell. Two or three others.

THIS ISLAND EARTH

Growing up, Ezra had known most everybody. Who didn't? Six weeks behind the mike at KNWC, he knew the rest of them—or they knew him. Set aside a handful who were mindful that the world was a mysterious place, strange beyond reckoning. The rest of them viewed the whole matter with stoic midwestern skepticism—or worse.

He wondered which group Ruth fell into, and if it mattered.

"I'm fine," he said. "You have a good morning, hear."

He cradled the receiver before she had a chance to respond. On his way out, he picked up *Sixgun Fury*. The story had washed clean out of his head. Maybe he'd give it another go.

Outside, a few snowflakes eddied in the still air. He glanced at his watch—it was 9:37—and then he walked to the car.

Nothing happened.

Three overnights following and Ezra had taken only ten or twelve requests, standard stuff. The schedule wasn't an adjustment. He'd been sleeping day for night since mid-October. Nothing much changed now. He was home from the station before dawn stitched color to the sky. Outside, farmers were an hour into the day's chores, milking cows, slopping pigs. Inside, he stood with a peanut butter sandwich in the flicker and buzz of the fluorescent bar over the sink, listening to Big Bill low on the radio, easing a little Johnny Horton and Carl Perkins—music to get the blood moving—into the morning mix of weather and news, the daily livestock reports. By 10:00, Ezra would be pulling the curtains in his bedroom. He slept restlessly, plagued by nightmares that felt too much like memories, and in his wakeful moments by memories that felt a lot like nightmares.

He was awake again by 4:00–4:30 if he could shake the nightmares. An hour later, he was bundled up against the cold, sitting in a rocking chair under the porch light, *Sixgun Fury* on his lap, though he didn't read much. He looked out across the yard instead, gaze fixed on the frigid dark settling over the land. His neighbors would have thought he was crazy, sitting out in the cold, but the house nestled in a shallow swale. He was invisible down there unless you took the trouble to look for him.

Friday night somebody did.

Ezra watched the car wind down through a screen of trees, the flash of headlights blinding him as it crested the low rise in front of the house, gravel crunching. He winced, touched by the fleeting edge of dream or memory. The engine died and the lights went off. A shadow came up out of the dark, the old stairs creaking: Darla, clutching in one hand a grease-stained brown bag. After 5:00, and she looked like she'd just finished dressing for the morning: immaculate, unsullied by the vexations of the day.

"You're back working for almost a week, you haven't dropped by, Ez," she said. "Thought I'd come down and say hi, since you weren't taking the initiative."

"I meant to," he said. Lying maybe. He didn't know.

"Well, you made it to my office anyway."

"I needed to use the phone. I didn't look at anything private."

"Nothing private to look at," she said, easing herself into the neighboring rocker.

"State of that desk, I'm surprised you could even tell I was there."

"Desk only looks messy. Somebody moved stuff around. Bill was in the box. No one else around that time of morning. That leaves you." She held up the bag. "I picked up a couple burgers at the drive-in over to Bloomfield. You want one?"

"Sure."

"Maybe we could eat inside, seeing as it's twenty degrees out here."

"It's a mess inside."

This *was* a lie. Abby had always kept a neat house. It had been neat when they'd walked out the front door three months ago, on an overcast October afternoon, to drive up to Ottumwa, an hour or so away. They'd decided to trade Ezra's rust-eaten De Luxe on a new car—Abby was insistent. The old Plymouth wouldn't be coming back.

This Island Earth

Neither of them had foreseen that Abby wouldn't be coming back either.

In her absence, the house had remained unchanged. Her glasses were still on her nightstand, folded on a copy of *Peyton Place*, dog-eared at page 143. Her shoes still lay under the coffee table, one heel to the floor, the other sidewise against it. The cookbook she'd left on the counter lay open to a recipe for beef stew. Everything—the whole house—looked like she might any moment return. But she wouldn't. Not ever. This realization, daily renewed, was revelatory to Ezra. The malice of the world was unspeakable.

The house wasn't a shrine. It was a tomb. He'd been living inside it for weeks, a dead man caught between the life he'd lost and the life to come—if any such life existed.

Darla snorted. "Must be one hell of a mess if we're eating out here." She handed him a burger wrapped in white paper. "I didn't know what you liked on your burger, so you'll have to make do with everything. Eat."

He ate. The first bite flooded his mouth with flavor. Like his return to the airwaves, it woke something up inside him. It was like taking a deep breath after gasping for months in air too thin to nourish or sustain him. But the next instant, the memory of that phone call—his name sharp and desperate down the line—left him breathless once again. He might as well have been chewing sodden cardboard.

"Awful early to be making phone calls," Darla said.

"Yeah."

They ate in silence. Darla's observation—the unspoken question behind it—hung in the air between them. Ezra wadded the last chunk of his burger into the paper and dropped it into the bag. Darla finished hers in three precise bites, folded the wrapper in half, in half again, and twice after that, producing a square the size of a matchbook. She ran pinched fingers along the edges and tucked it into the bag, which she rolled carefully, frowning at the unsightly bulge of Ezra's discarded burger.

"You wanna talk about it?" she asked.

"The phone call?"

"Anything. The whole thing."

"I don't know. I don't know how to talk about it. Who would believe it? I can hardly believe it myself."

"I don't think anyone believes you're lying, Ez."

"But do they believe I'm telling the truth?" he asked. He shook his head. Exhaled. Said, "What I want to know is why."

He didn't finish the question: *Why did they take Abby?*

Abby.

Tell us what happened to Abby, the lean men in dark suits had said. And so he'd told them. He'd told them, and he was ashamed of what he told them. And then they'd made him tell it again. And again after that. *Let's just go back over it one more time, if you don't mind,* they'd said. Ezra *did* mind, but they were not the kind of men you said no to. They were unfailingly courteous, but the courtesy masked a certain ruthless expedience. They had the eyes of surgeons or assassins. They bore him no animosity, but they weren't averse to the knife.

When they finished with him, they made it clear that he wasn't to talk about what had happened. *It's a matter of national security, Mr. Hill,* they'd said.

Now, on the porch, Ezra recalled coming to himself in the brand-new Bel Air he and Abby had closed on only three hours previously. He recalled coming to himself *alone*—alone in that brand-new Bel Air, clenching the steering wheel white-knuckled. The interior was full of whirling red light, and it was only through a strident blast of terror—

—what is it Ezra what's that in the sky—

—that he recognized it as something altogether more mundane than the blinding kaleidoscope of godlight that had descended upon them out of the storm-riven night. A police car had pulled up behind him, its cherry dome spinning. Rain hammered down. Beyond the windshield, the road lay narrow in the night, a slick, merciless ribbon running on before him. Trees pressed close against the shoulders. He looked at the dashboard clock.

This Island Earth

A familiar face leaned in at the window. A familiar voice in his ear.

Clyde. Clyde Wilson, soaked to the skin despite his yellow deputy sheriff's slicker. Ezra couldn't remember a time he didn't know Clyde Wilson.

Are you alright, Ez? Clyde asked, and Ezra had begun to weep.

The lean men with assassins' eyes had shown up two days later. When they told him he wasn't to speak of it, Ezra had laughed bitterly. *It's a little too late to lock the barn door,* he'd said. *Those horses got loose long before you got here.*

Clyde would have told his wife, Almada. Almada would have called Marge Simmons. Marge would have told her husband Bob, who would have told the loafers over at the feed store in Bladensburg. Trying to contain it would have been like trying to contain a gallon of water in a bucket full of holes.

All this passed through Ezra's mind as he sat there under the porch light. "I wish I knew why," he said. "It came down out of the sky and took her. That's all I know. How do you even start to talk about a thing like that?"

"I don't know," she said.

So they didn't talk, just sat rocking. Their every breath fogged the air before them. Ice-barbed air tore at their lungs. Ezra didn't know why she stayed there with him in that lacerating cold. He was glad for the company.

She said, "You've been reading?"

"Trying. I can't concentrate."

"Maybe you could read aloud or something, you don't feel like talking."

"Alright." He cracked the book to the first page. Cleared his throat. Began:

After ten days on the trail, Lance Brogan was itching for gunplay. He had a line on the desperado who had robbed the Waco bank a year ago. Wanted: Dead or Alive, the bounty papers said. Dead was fine with Brogan. It was less trouble, and it paid the same. But it was more than that. He hungered for the stink of gun smoke and the hiss of lead punching tunnels through the air. He loved the feeling of hot iron blazing in his hands. But Lance Brogan's heart was cold.

Ezra paused for breath.

"On the other hand," Darla observed, "we could just sit quiet for a spell." She gave him a wry smile, and Ezra felt a spark of familiar energy leap between them. From his first day at the station, all those years ago, he'd sensed in her a core loneliness not unlike his own. Darla kept her business to herself. If there were men in her life, she didn't share it. Heartbreak in her past was generally suspected, never confirmed. Either way, that current had always flowed between them; but for three Pabst Blue Ribbons and a slim redhead with a crooked smile it might someday have drawn them together.

"After ten days on the trail, Lance Brogan was itching for gunplay," Ezra said, dead sober.

"Who isn't, really?" Darla asked, and after that they sat alone with their thoughts, looking out from the porch into the vast sky, empty of any light but that of the stars, unmoving as they hurtled blindly into the dark.

Darla was gone by 8:00.

By 10:15, Ezra was settling behind the soundboard.

The night's first two requests were standard overnight fare: bleak, lonely voices sending out bleak, lonely songs that expressed feelings they maybe couldn't voice themselves: Hank Williams and "Lovesick Blues," Jean Shepard and "Beautiful Lies." Ezra spun both cuts and moved on, pulling the records for each set and laying down the patter in between them, deep into the rhythm of the work. Five-thirty and he was bringing turntable two up to speed when the phone lit up again. He was already dropping a platter on number one when he flipped the receiver off the hook, pinning it between his ear and shoulder. "You've got Easy Ez down at—"

THIS ISLAND EARTH

A blast of static, deafening. Ezra jerked the phone away, wincing. He was not going to do this. He was not going down this path to madness. He was going to hang up and go on. He was going to—

"Who's there?" he said.

The static died abruptly. Silence, then: an absence seething with presence and the sound of words impending. A voice—

—*her voice*—

—came down the line, thin and impossibly remote. ...Ezra..."

"Who is this? Is this some kind of joke?"

"...me, Ezra..."

"I don't beli—"

"...play...Bennett, Ezra...play...'Because of...'"

Interference burned through the word that followed. But Ezra didn't need to hear it. He knew what it was: *you.*

Play me Tony Bennett, Ezra. Play me "Because of You."

Time slipped: Abby lifted her face to his as they turned and turned again to the rich timbre of that voice and the sweep of the orchestra in the air around them. Ezra's small living room had never been so large before; in the light of candles flickering, it had never been so bright.

Abby. Abby Hill, he'd whispered, marveling at the sound of it.

Now, he said her name again, dredging it up from a pit of longing and despair. "Abby?"

The waste places between the stars shrieked in the receiver. Then words broke through the static, phrases taut with rising panic. Ezra scrabbled for a pad to jot them down: ...listen...you've got to listen...they're coming...spread the...God, they're here, they're—"

An electronic squeal erupted down the line.

Afterward, nothing. Nothing there. Nothing to come.

Ezra sat utterly still, numb with horror. Had she screamed? Had there been a scream buried in that final shriek of interference? No, he told himself. No, there had been no scream.

But there had been. He was almost sure of it.

NIGHT CALLER FROM OUTER SPACE

What happened to Abby? the lean men in their dark suits had wanted to know. They might have been cast from the same mold: Agent This and Agent That. Dark hair cut close around sharply angular faces. Dark eyes, flecked with points of light, intent and courteous. Cold.

What happened to Abby?

I could have saved her, Ezra had said. *I could have.*

In retrospect, he could see the whole day unfolding—how it might have been different, how half a dozen decisions and indecisions had doomed them to arrive at that moment in that place, on that desolate stretch of road between Ottumwa and Bloomfield, cresting a long hill in a hard rain. Alter any one of those decisions and Abby would be at home waiting for him now.

If, he thought, running his finger across the words he'd incised on the tablet.

If they had gotten away earlier, the way they had planned. If they hadn't gotten turned around looking for the Chevrolet dealership in Ottumwa. If they'd been able to agree on the car.

That most of all maybe.

Abby had insisted on a four-door Bel Air Sport Sedan, painted a lustrous pale blue that the salesman, to Ezra's amusement, insisted on calling Larkspur. To Ezra, it looked like a sky-blue Saturday morning with the whole weekend still ahead of you. It also looked like more than they could afford. Top of the line, with all the options: the Powerglide automatic transmission with power steering and power braking. Power windows and a Wonder Bar auto-seek radio. Air conditioning. Seat belts. *Seat belts?* Ezra had said, incredulous. He thought the base model One-Fifty would do just fine.

Abby had won of course. By some mysterious alchemy she'd acquired two votes to Ezra's one in their conjugal democracy. But he never questioned the wisdom of Hank Penny's encomium to redheads.

Abby could be volatile, and she was not opposed to casting her second ballot; but she was also independent, fair, fiercely intelligent, and deeply committed to him. Passionate, even. Most of all, her wry irreverence countered his tendency to brood. Before Abby, Ezra could seize little more than a few moments of fugitive contentment behind the mike. With Abby, he'd been—not content. No.

Happy. He'd been happy.

Abby calmed the gale of anxiety constantly roaring inside him. She brought him into balance with the world: not Ez and not Easy Ez.

Ezra.

Nonetheless, he didn't concede without a fight.

They'd quarreled about the car for an hour or more, trying to conceal their discord from the salesman hovering just out of earshot. *You folks take your time,* he'd said, clearly curbing his own impatience. *It's a big decision, a new car. You don't want to rush it.*

They should have rushed it. Ezra had known from the start that they would drive off the lot in that Saturday-morning-blue-sky Bel Air. But it had been full dark before he'd surrendered—grudgingly—and there had been all the red tape to get through after that. If he'd just given in at the start. If they'd gotten on the road an hour earlier. If they hadn't—

"Ez, man, you okay?"

Ezra looked up, startled. Cut loose of memory, he plummeted back into the here and now. Big Bill stood in the doorway, bearish and tall, his brow furrowed.

"What?" Ezra said.

"Dead air," Bill said, and suddenly Ezra heard—*really* heard—what he'd been hearing since that raw electronic squeal had chopped off—

—*Abby it was Abby*—

—the caller: the crackle of the stylus trapped in the run-out groove.

"Hell," Ezra said, snatching blindly for a record with one hand and swinging down the microphone with the other. He held up a finger to silence Bill, leaned into the mike, and flipped the switch,

Night Caller from Outer Space

saying, "This is Easy Ez at KNWC. Apologies to you folks in radio land for going quiet on you. Gremlins got loose in the works down here and it took us a minute to round the little fellas up. We're sure glad you stuck with us. I'm gonna step away for the day now. Big Bill Archer's here to see you through the morning. He'll have all the news you want, all the weather you need, and the livestock reports you depend on." Ezra read off the title of the 45 as he spun it up to speed. He laid his voice over the opening riffs. "Now here's Carl Smith with 'Go Boy Go' to start you off on an extra-long set of the country music that sees you through the day *every day*, right here on KNWC."

He dropped Tommy Collins, "What'cha Gonna Do Now," on turntable two and rolled away from the board to let Bill squeeze in. Bill squared up to the mike and put his coffee down.

"What's this?" he said, holding up the pad.

"It's nothing," Ezra said, grabbing at it. He tore off the top sheet and crumpled it into his pocket.

"Sure doesn't seem like nothing."

"Don't worry about it, Bill."

Bill shook his head. "Whatever you say." He flapped his hand. "Go get some rest."

But Ezra didn't go. He turned at the door, struck by a question: "Who was doing overnights when I was out?"

"You didn't listen?"

"No. I thought I was done with radio."

"You're never going to be done with radio. You're radio to the bone."

"Who was it?"

"Carl, mostly. John and I spelled him. It wasn't easy, but John wasn't going to hire someone new. None of us wanted him to. We're all of us on your side, you need to know that."

"I didn't know there were sides."

"Come on, Ez. You know that's not what I meant."

"You get any strange calls?"

"Calls?" Bill asked, fading out the Carl Smith cut and bringing Tommy Collins in over top of it.

This Island Earth

"When you did overnights."

Bill snorted. "They're all of them kind of strange, aren't they, overnight requests? Always something sad and lonely. What I like about mornings, at least you can put something on with a little kick to it."

"No, I mean... weird calls. Interference on the line, like a call from overseas or..."

Space, he didn't say. *Like a call from outer space.*

"Huh. Now you mention it, I guess I did get one or two. One that I remember, anyway. Static mostly. But this voice, too. A woman, I'm pretty sure. I couldn't make out anything she was saying." Bill bit his lip, thinking. Sighed, as if coming to a decision he didn't much like the taste of. Said, "Funny thing, though. One thing I might've caught, it sounded a little like your name. Not Ez, though. *Ezra*, like Abby used to—" He broke off, flushing. "It was nothing. Really." He laughed, a forced jovial chuff. "It sure is weird, isn't it, the way your ear can make something sensible out of the noise on an open line. Like the snow when a TV channel signs off for the night. Stare at that stuff long enough, you'll start to see things. It's weird."

"It's weird, alright," Ezra said.

In the silence that followed, they realized simultaneously that "What'cha Gonna Do Now" was tracking dead wax. Neither one of them had thought to fit another 45 over the second turntable's spindle when Bill had flipped over from "Go Boy Go." In houses and towns for miles around them, people spun tuning knobs and adjusted antennas, trying to coax down the chords of a song that wasn't there.

"I hope John's not listening," Bill said, though this time of morning he would be. Bill plucked down a record. "He's not going to like it," he added, pointing Ezra out the door.

Ezra collapsed on the sofa in the bullpen and propped his feet up on the table, pushing two or three copies of *Radio News* overboard.

The cat on the wall opposite switched its tail to the tune of six and a quarter.

He closed his eyes—just for a minute, he told himself.

It was after eight when he woke up, blasted out of an anxious dream by a burst of arctic air. The gust carried John in from the foyer, shrugging off his coat. "Christ, it's cold out there," he muttered. He glanced at Ezra. "You still here?"

"I fell asleep."

"Well, pour yourself some coffee and come down to my office. Bring me a cup, too. Heavy on the sugar."

"I know how you like your coffee. I poured you plenty when I started here."

"Another episode like this morning, you'll be pouring me plenty more."

John disappeared into the hallway.

Ezra scrubbed his eyes with his knuckles. He heaved himself to his feet, trying to recall his dream: he was on an island, calling out futile warnings to ships foundering in heavy seas.

His whole life, he'd never remembered his dreams—only the last three months. The details always differed; the sense of foreboding did not. Isolation. Grief and impotence. A certainty of doom impending.

In the bathroom, he splashed cold water on his face. He studied himself in the rusty mirror and shook his head. Went out to the bullpen to fetch the coffee.

"You busting me back to gofer?" he asked, shutting John's door.

"You know better."

"I suppose." Ezra flipped the chair around, back to the desk.

"What happened?"

"It was my fault. I distracted Bill during the handoff."

"Before that."

"I don't want to talk about it."

John leaned back in his chair and blew across the surface of his coffee. Took a sip. Waited.

"You doing ads today?" Ezra asked.

"That's not what we're talking about here."

"What we're talking about, it's not an easy thing for me."

"As long it doesn't affect you on the air, I can respect that."

"It won't happen again."

"Just ignore the request line for a while. Make them up. It's an overnight. Nobody cares."

"What about the request line?" Ezra asked.

"Just ignore it, okay?"

"John, level with me."

"I have."

"Bill told me you took some overnights while I was out."

"Fifteen, twenty times, maybe. I could look back. Carl and Bill carried the load. I brought in ringers from Mystic to fill the gaps. You know."

"When you were on nights, you get some odd calls? Is that why you're talking about the request line?"

John put his coffee down. He leaned forward. "Look, I'm not holding out on you. It's a radio station after midnight. You're gonna get strange calls. The ones I'm thinking of, I wouldn't even call them strange. Bad connections, that's all. Static."

"You hear my name?"

John held Ezra steady in his gaze. "No," he said. "No, I didn't. But if I were in your state of mind—if I'd spent the last three months pushing away everyone who cared about me, if I'd spent all that time alone, if Mildred had died, God forbid—well, sometimes I might hear what I wanted to hear."

"Abby didn't die. They came for her. They took her."

John cradled his forehead in one hand, massaging his temples, thumb and forefinger. "Christ," he said. "Flying saucers. Aliens." His voice was flat, empty of skepticism or conviction.

"You say it like that, it sounds like some kind of bad movie. It wasn't like that. I don't know how to tell you what it was like."

"Ez—"

"These calls—I've had two of them now. First one, I checked with Ruth down at the switchboard. She didn't put that call through."

"Ruth's seventy if she's a day. Seventy-five. She's lucky if she remembers what she had for lunch."

"It was Abby. She said my name."

"It was a bad connection. It was just noise. It could have been anything."

"Are you taking me off the air?"

John looked away, lips pursed, silent. "No," he said. "Not right now. Not if you keep it together. No more dead air, okay?"

"Yeah. Of course, no more dead air," Ezra said.

He stood, turned the chair rightside round, and picked up his coffee.

"Don't let this destroy you, Ez," John said.

Ezra stepped into the hall. Over the speakers, Bill was running through the rip-and-read. The news wasn't good. It never was. Darla stood at the sink in the bullpen, washing out her mug.

"Talking to John?" she asked.

"Yeah. I botched the handoff."

"I heard. I was tuned in." She shook out the mug. Reached for a towel. "He pull you off the rotation?"

"No."

"Anybody else, he would have. You're like a son to him."

"I know."

He set his cup on the counter and looked at his watch. On the wall opposite, the deranged cat flipped its eyes and tail.

Darla touched his arm. "You're going to get through this."

"Yeah." Ezra pulled on his coat. "Thanks, Darla."

He went out into the cold. He would never get through it.

Home, Ezra dug out the crumpled sheet he'd jotted Abby's panicky phrases on. He smoothed it flat on his kitchen table and stared down at it, walked away. Two shifts off, and he left it there without looking at it, trying not to think about it, to let the part of his mind attuned to dreams and mysteries sort it out.

He kept to his nocturnal rhythm over the weekend. Slept restlessly for a few hours in the middle of the day. Continued his nightly vigil, sitting under the porch light until the cold finally drove him inside. He turned on the radio low and tried to read *Sixgun Fury*. He must have read the first chapter half a dozen times. Lance Brogan was a cold man. Hot lead flew in the final paragraphs. Nothing else stuck.

He didn't leave the house; no one came to see him.

It wasn't a problem. He'd spent three months alone; he'd grown accustomed to his own company. When the phone rang, he hadn't picked up. When someone had stopped by to check on him, he hadn't answered the door. Everybody came for a while—Bill and John, Carl, too, though not as often. Darla had been steady the whole time, calling his name, knocking. Mildred had dropped off casseroles two and three times a week, leaving them on his porch with cards that he threw away unopened. He threw away the casseroles, too, though he was ravenous for them.

Penitence. Mortification of the flesh.

It was not enough. It never would be.

Monday afternoon Ezra sat down at the kitchen table. He smoothed out the crumpled sheet once again:

—listen...you've got to listen...they're coming...spread the... God, they're here, they're—

They had taken her. That much he knew. That she had somehow escaped them, that they were coming after her, that they had come—that much seemed clear. The thought of it was shattering. Horrific beyond words.

What else?

Ezra ran his fingers over the words. He'd carved them into the page he'd been pressing so hard.

Listen...spread the—what? The word? *Listen. Spread the word.*

What word? Who would he spread it to?

He rubbed his eyes.

In the windows, the light was failing. He pushed back from the table. He stood on the porch, low hills before him and above him the cosmos unveiling itself, vast beyond human comprehension.

Night Caller from Outer Space

Against that magnitude everything was meaningless: a million million galaxies and all their sheltering stars, and the creatures that swarmed like vermin on the skins of their captive planets. Human beings and every human passion. Fear and hatred. Love.

Done at the car lot—at last, and considerably poorer—Ezra had mentioned dinner.

"Let's get something out," Abby'd said. "It'll be too late to cook by the time we get home."

"Not sure we can afford it," Ezra said. "Maybe if we'd gone with the One-Fifty."

"We can afford it," she said. "If it wasn't for me, you'd never get anything nice."

"The One-Fifty was nice."

"Nice!" she exclaimed, punching him on the arm. "The One-Fifty was shitty!"

"Abby!"

"Well, it was!" she said, dissolving into laughter. Ezra tried to resist, but her hilarity was infectious. Among the many things he loved about Abby—maybe the thing he loved the most, though there were a lot of contenders—was her talent for cheerful blasphemy. He would never have thought of such a thing; having thought it, he could not have said it. The One-Fifty wasn't quite shitty—not compared to his old Plymouth De Luxe (the Plymouth De Yuck, Abby had christened it). But it wasn't much to get excited about.

The Bel Air, on the other hand, was a joy to drive.

The Powerglide transmission was not a gimmick with a fancy name, though Ezra would have said it was—in fact had said it, that very day. The car did indeed glide: a smooth glissade over pavement glistening in a rain that had held off all day and was only now beginning with heavy, slow drops to fall. Still—

"We could have compromised with the Two-Ten."

"Never compromise," Abby said, turning up the radio. First thing, she'd tuned in the swing station out of Mystic. The air sparkled with

THIS ISLAND EARTH

the jaunty brass flourish of Count Basie's orchestra, Joe Williams at the mike—"Alright, Okay, You Win."

Ezra laughed. "What can I do?"

"Anything I say. It's just got to be that way," she sang.

"Your voice is terrible," he cried, laughing, and she sang louder.

A drive-in appeared ahead, a neon shimmer in the rain. Ezra put on his flicker.

Abby's hand dropped over his forearm. "No compromises, Ezra Hill," she shouted. "Not tonight!"

Which is how they wound up cruising around Ottumwa until they found a place that measured up to her expectations: nothing fancy, but compared to the options around Moulton, positively cosmopolitan. Italian: white tablecloths and a smiling young woman to seat you.

"Seat belts?" Ezra grumbled, after they'd settled at their table.

"Safety first," Abby said over her menu.

"Did we really need the four-door?"

"You never know," she said. "Four doors might come in handy." She smiled at him across the table.

Despite John's directive, Ezra continued taking requests.

His first few shifts, every call honed the edge of his anxiety. When he lifted the receiver, he halfway expected—he more than hoped—to hear the hiss and crackle of the infinite dark. He longed for the sound of Abby's voice; he dreaded the panic he would hear there. He knew that he was powerless to help her. But knowing that she was still alive out there, that she still existed—that was something. That was better than the hole she'd left in his life. That was better than not knowing anything at all.

So he waited.

But no call came. Just the same old heartbreak and sorrow: Marty Robbins, "Singing the Blues"; Ray Price, "Crazy Arms."

A week passed, a week and a half. The days dulled that edge of tension. Maybe Bill and John had been right: listen long enough to static on the line, you might hear what you want to hear. Maybe. Maybe in the company of the people he loved, he could begin to heal.

Carl maintained his reserve. The others drew him back into the circle.

Mildred came by one morning as he dozed in the bullpen. John had forgotten his lunch, she said, brandishing a brown bag as Ezra shook himself awake.

"You look so thin," she said.

Ezra choked out an almost incoherent protest—he was fine, she'd kept him plenty well fed—and endured an embrace, rigid in her arms. Then something passed out of him. He sagged against her with a bottomless groan that they both pretended was not a sob.

John was as warm as he ever had been.

Bill griped without rancor about the sheer volume of shit a single baby could produce. "Loose yellow shit," he remarked one morning with a sigh. "Gallons of it. What I wouldn't do for a good old-fashioned turd!"

Darla came by twice to join him in his vigil on the porch.

She brought junky drive-in food—hot dogs and greasy fries, pizza. They devoured it with cold-stiffened fingers, anxious to pull on their gloves.

"You ever gonna let me in the house?" she asked.

"No," he said. But in his head he said, *Not yet.*

And then—halfway through the first week of an icy February—Ezra picked up a request at 5:30. For ten seconds, maybe fifteen, the line howled with interference. He had time to call Abby's name twice before the connection broke.

It was like taking a gut punch; it left him clawing for air, a white roar in his head. Big Bill trudged into the bullpen, waving his hand vaguely in Ezra's direction as he fumbled with the coffee. Ezra spun the turntables and skipped the final batch of ROS ads.

"You missed the last ad-block," Bill said during the handoff.

"Did I?" Ezra asked. He'd recovered enough to feign confusion.

This Island Earth

He kept his hands busy. He didn't want Bill to see them trembling. "Double back and pick it up for me?"

"Sure thing. You okay?"

"Yeah, I'm fine," Ezra said.

But he wasn't fine.

Not when he left the station. Not when he pulled into Carl's driveway twenty minutes later. He sat idling in the Bel Air, looking at the house, two stories of white clapboard, grayish in the gloom. Silent. Every window dark.

Carl was a crepuscular creature. He worked late. Stayed up late. Slept late. His day intersected with Ezra's for half an hour, usually less, when he handed off the mike at ten. That mask of reserve never slipped. He did not ask for intimacy; he offered none.

Coming here was a mistake: a violation of the boundaries Carl had drawn. But that call, that fifteen seconds of static, compelled Ezra. A tempest whipped through him, a wild panic, impervious to reason. John had denied him. Bill would give him nothing more. He had nowhere else to go.

So he pocketed his keys, and climbed the porch stairs. Rang the bell. A light came on, laying a bright trapezoid across the lawn. The porch light followed. The door. Carl's wife, Rose, stood in a threadbare robe on the other side.

"Do you know what time it is, Ez?"

"I'm sorry, Rose. I—"

"What do you want?"

"I need to talk to Carl."

"Carl's asleep. Go away." She closed the door. Switched off the porch light.

Ezra waited. Rose's inner weather was unpredictable. She was one moment gregarious and cheerful, the next solitary, despondent. She was quick to anger, slow to forgive. She was prone to grudges.

Carl, reticent and cool, steadied her. He might not welcome Ezra, but he wouldn't leave him standing on the porch. If Ezra didn't go,

Carl would come down. Two or three minutes later—five at the most—he did, scruffy in paint-stained jeans and a flannel shirt, his hair in disarray. "What do you want, Ez?" he asked.

"I need to talk."

"It's pretty early. Let's talk later."

"Just a few minutes, Carl. Please."

Carl grunted, resigned. "Well, I guess I'm up," he said, waving Ezra in.

They went back through the house to the large, shabby kitchen. Ezra had been to the house two dozen times over the years, but he'd known the kitchen only in its warmer register, when a mellow amber glow suffused the worn wallpaper and sun-bleached linoleum, and the wobbly Formica table had a kind of raffish charm. He'd crowded around that table for meals; he'd sat there long into the night, listening to honky tonk on Rose's transistor radio and drinking beer until he felt wobbly himself. Last time he'd been here, Abby had gotten tipsy on red wine, pushed him up against the counter, and kissed him with an enthusiasm that promised enthusiasm to come.

Now her absence was palpable.

A thin, wintry dawn limned the hills in the eastward-facing windows. The wallpaper had a jaundiced cast, and the linoleum was scuffed. The wobbly table where Carl seated him was merely wobbly. The radio was silent. Rose glowered at him from the counter where she was pouring coffee. The clanking radiators could not dispel the cold.

"What is it you want to talk about?" Carl asked.

"John said you did some overnights while I was out."

"I did a lot of overnights when you were out. We were stretched thin."

Rose sat down with the coffee—two cups, one for herself, one for Carl.

"Is this about the calls?" Carl said.

"What calls?" Rose asked.

"Ez has been getting some calls on the request line. A lot of static. Voices."

"One voice. Abby's voice."

"Oh, for Christ's sake," Rose said.

"You got them, too, didn't you?" Ezra asked Carl.

"I didn't get any calls. Nothing out of the ordinary. Only reason I know anything about this is John told me."

"Tell me the truth, Carl. You owe me that."

Carl's mask slipped. Ezra caught a faint flicker in his eyes before he cut his gaze away. He turned his coffee cup on the table. Cleared his throat. Looked up. Whatever Ezra had seen in his eyes, it was gone now. "Look, Ez, I know you're hurting. But this doesn't help, this fixation."

"Please. Just tell me what she said. I need to understand. I need to know why."

Rose laughed. "You think some staticky phone calls are gonna tell you why? You wanna know why, you should—"

Carl touched her hand.

"Listen to yourself, Ez. Listen to these things you're saying."

"Where's she calling from?" Rose asked. "Outer space?"

"Rose," Carl said.

"Don't 'Rose' me. I wanna know. Do flying saucers have phone booths, Ez? Refresh my memory. I don't recall."

"I don't know where she's calling from. I don't know how she's calling."

"You have to let this go," Carl said.

"I can't. I don't know where else to look."

"Look in the mirror," Rose said.

Carl laid his hand across her forearm.

"Don't touch me," she said, wrenching herself free.

Enough, Ezra thought. There were no answers to be had here. Carl had made his decision. Whatever he knew or didn't know, he wasn't going to waver.

Ezra stood. "I'm sorry I barged in like this," he said.

"You should know. This is some thin ice you're walking on. John's concerned."

Night Caller from Outer Space

"Maybe he won't hear about this, then."

"Maybe," Carl said.

Ezra nodded. He went out through the hallway and down the stairs into the bloodless dawn.

Rose caught up with him at the car. She grabbed him by the wrist, yanked him around. "You're the not the only one who loved Abby, you know. You think you're the only one hurting?"

"No, Rose—"

"You think you have everyone snowed. You don't have me snowed. What really happened out there? What really happened to Abby?"

"I don't know," he said. "I wish I knew."

He pulled away from her. Slid into the car. Rose stepped back when he started the engine. He turned the car around and went up the driveway toward the road.

A steady drizzle had settled in by the time they left the restaurant. They hesitated under the awning, curtained in by rain. The car glistened under a streetlight half a block away, bright as a scrap of Saturday morning sky on a rainy Sunday afternoon. "That is a fine-looking car," Ezra said.

"That fine-looking car is *our* car, Mr. Hill!" Abby announced, breaking into a lamentably tone-deaf version of "Singing in the Rain." She swept Ezra into an awkward dance that carried them out onto the sidewalk. He lumbered. She floated. Both of them got soaked. Neither of them cared. They rode out of town on a wave of exhilaration, with the heat blasting and Artie Shaw on the radio.

By the time they crossed the Skunk River on 63, they'd dried sticky damp. The storm had grown fierce, reducing their exhilaration to the simmering anxiety of a long night drive in dangerous conditions. They'd turned off the radio so that Ezra could concentrate. A vicious rain slammed down, sheeting across the windshield. Lightning slashed the sky, revealing the road in stark negative flashes. Ezra hunched over the wheel as they curved up out of the river valley and came into a long straightaway that climbed all the way to the crown of the timbered hill.

He rolled his shoulders, trying to unkink the tension in his spine, and leaned on the gas.

"What's that?" Abby asked.

There was something in her voice, a note of awe that Ezra had never heard before. He glanced over at her, puzzled. She was cinched in tight, one hand braced against the seat, the other one flat against her stomach. The lightning on the windshield washed her face in blue shadow. She was very still and pale.

"What?" he said.

"There's something in the sky. A light. Up over the hilltop."

"It's just—"

—*lightning,* he was going to say. But it was too steady, a constant ripple of light and shadow, scrubbing her cheeks clean of the freckles which on a lark he had once tried to count, and might have succeeded if all the kissing hadn't distracted him.

"What is it?" she asked.

They were moving at a steady speed, heavy-footed on the gas.

Ezra searched the sky. *There.* He saw it now, high above the hill in the rain-lashed dark: a lambent funnel, whirling dim and bright.

The radio came on: a dissonant screech of noise and voices and rags of melody peeled clean from songs.

He gritted his teeth. "What'd you do that for? I'm trying to concentrate."

"It wasn't me. I didn't touch it."

"I don't understand."

"It just came on. I didn't touch it."

Ezra glanced at the radio. The frequency needle was a white blur, zipping back and forth across the band. Right off the lot and the fancy radio's already on the fritz, he thought. Frowning, he ran his eye along the dash to the clock, a chrome-accented circle set in the smooth curve that enclosed the model name: *Bel Air*, styled with embossed letters, gold on black and raked forward with speed. But the clock—

Ezra shook his head, trying to rattle some sense out of what he was seeing.

The clock's hands were spinning wildly in both directions, untethered from time.

Abby's hand closed around his wrist. "Ezra!"

He wrenched his head around.

They crested the hill too fast. Ezra dropped his foot on the brake. The car slipped away from him, whipping around twice—maybe three times—before it lurched off the pavement. It skidded across the gravel shoulder. Ezra jammed the brake to the floor. The car rocked to a stop, snapping them forward with checked velocity.

Everything went dead at once. Radio. Headlights. Engine.

Light spilled through the car, half-blinding him. The air buzzed with a steady hum: almost sub-audible, but ramping rapidly into an air-choked drone. Raw panic cascaded through him. *Abby—*

—*"are you okay, Abby?"*

"Seat belts," she gasped with queasy bravado. "You didn't bust up our new car, did you, Mr. Hill?"

"No, I—"

"Then get us out of here. *Go!*"

"Did you see the clock did—"

"*Go! Goddamn it, g—*"

That vibrating drone swallowed up everything that followed—loud, so loud now that he could feel it throbbing in his bones. Ezra didn't need to hear her to know what she was screaming. It was screaming through him, as well, a blind imperative to—

Go! Go! Go!

He twisted the key. Nothing. Cursing, he yanked the shifter up into neutral and twisted the key again. Nothing. Nothing nothing nothing until the key snapped off in the ignition.

The cabin blazed with light, a whirling incandescent godlight

This Island Earth

sliding down the spectrum into lightning-gashed streaks of red blue green—

The hair on his arms crackled to attention.

Then, abruptly, silence.

It was there.

It hovered a hundred feet above the hilltop, on a radiant pedestal of flickering blue. Big. Too big to take in. It swallowed the sky and every star within it. It swallowed everything—not a spaceship or not only. It was more, infinitely more: a godmachine fashioned by inconceivably powerful beings to ride the black currents that flowed between the stars. Against it, the Bel Air was a toy. Against it, every human venture—from splitting the atom to probing at the edge of space—was little more than the paltry achievement of an infant.

It hung above them in utter silence.

It was there.

"We do thank the folks down at Singley's Farm Supply over in Bladensburg for throwing some support KNWC's way," Ezra said, lifting the needle on the music bed. He dropped his voice a register to drive the pitch. "We hope you'll throw a little their way, too. That's Singley's Farm Supply, serving your farm needs since 1941, with tractors, tool kits, and everything in between."

He glanced at the clock on the bullpen wall.

"We're at the bottom of the hour, climbing toward four o'clock," he said, his mouth close against the mike. "We're gonna kick off a long set right now by reaching all the way back to 1952. Here's Kitty Wells, the queen of country music, giving Hank Thompson a piece of her mind on 'It Wasn't God Who Made Honky Tonk Angels'—and if you want my two cents, gentlemen, she's got a point." He backed the turntable around and brought it up to speed, laying his voice over the fade-in. "Stay faithful to your ladies, hear?"

He was out. He had two minutes and change to splash some heat into his coffee and empty out the coffee he'd already taken on board.

Both needs were pressing, but he had the efficiency of long practice on his side. He slipped back behind the soundboard with more than half a minute to spare—long enough to take an actual sip of the coffee, snatch a glance at the VU meters to catch a needle drifting, and adjust the pot to bring it back to true. He piggybacked "I Walk the Line" on the final chords of "Honky Tonk Angels." Sleeved Kitty Wells and staged the on-deck turntable with "I've Got a New Heartache." He liked building a set, liked the way one song talked to another. But he didn't think about it. It was muscle memory. Flow. What he was made to do.

Contentment ghosted through him, gossamer thin, gone.

You're never going to be done with radio, Bill said. *You're radio to the bone.*

Maybe. But it wasn't hard to imagine a future in which radio was done with him. Thin ice. Thin: like a rime of February glass on a mid-March lake, so clear you could see the water lift and pull on the other side. So thin you could feel it.

He stood in Carl's kitchen, the ice cracking underneath his feet. Too proud to beg, begging all the same: *Maybe he won't hear about this, then.*

Maybe.

Two days off had followed that fiasco. Ezra had folded up the scrap of crumpled paper on his kitchen table and slipped it into his wallet. Slept his uneasy afternoon sleep. Stood at the kitchen sink to eat, working the bolus of peanut butter and Wonder Bread between his teeth until he could finally choke it down. It was all he could do to eat the stuff. He threw half of it away. He didn't know why he ate it. He could not imagine a future in which he ate anything else.

You ever gonna let me in the house? Darla asked.

Not yet, he thought, turning his face to the stars.

All weekend that way. Waiting for John to call. Wondering what would happen when he rotated back onto the schedule—whether he'd even *be* on the schedule.

He was.

Ten o'clock, the evening handoff, he said, "I take it you didn't tell John, then."

"I figure you can't afford to lose anything else. I don't wanna be the guy. Don't make it so I have to be."

"Carl—"

"We're not gonna talk about this anymore, okay? We work at the same place. That's as far as it goes."

"I just wanna—"

"Don't. You're fine. Make sure you keep it that way." Carl tipped his head at the mike. "You're on in thirty. Don't fuck it up."

That was it. After that, the nightly handoff was like an encounter between brothers after a decades-old rift: every word and every gesture measured lest the old strife reassert itself. It was okay. It wasn't the same.

He ran a series of ROS ads and moved into another set.

Five minutes short of four, the request line lit up.

He'd drawn a line at five o'clock.

It wasn't even four.

He picked up the phone.

"Ezra," Abby said.

Calm. So calm.

"Yeah?"

"It's a flying saucer, isn't it? Like in the movies."

"Yeah. Only it's real."

The thing squatted over the road on its pedestal of light. The timber on either side had been blown into twisted wreckage.

It was nothing. God had set his foot here. It was that and nothing more.

"I'm afraid," Abby said.

"Me, too." Ezra licked his lips. His throat was dry. His tongue. "I'm afraid, too."

But the fear was like no fear he had ever known. It was there. He knew it was there. But it lay under an integument of absolute calm. He could not touch it. He could not act upon it. He could do nothing with it at all. He could not even feel it. He'd been dispossessed of all that.

"I have to go now, Ezra."

"I know."

She opened the door.

"Here," he said. "I'll walk with you."

"I'd like that."

They got out of the car.

The saucer loomed above them, a shimmering, faintly iridescent disc marbled with dark currents that gathered and dispersed in a constant lazy flow. Massive beyond belief.

Hand in hand they walked slowly toward that flickering pedestal of light.

As they drew closer, Ezra could see them. Two of them. Aliens: dusky shadows adrift in the high blue light, like men stretched thin and tall, their limbs rippling with the languid grace of seagrass in slow ocean currents, their faces featureless as spades. But he knew—he was allowed to know—that this was only the form they chose to show him. Their true bodies extended through dimensions of space and time that he could not perceive or imagine: vast, cool intellects that existed apart from the merely human world. The word aliens was utterly inadequate. The word aliens could not encompass the mystery of these creatures that had come here, to this moment, this place, across black gulfs of space and time. The word aliens could not encompass their power.

He and Abby walked on.

Ezra could see the madness in this blind submission. Knew that Abby must see it as well. But he could not tear his way through the placental calm that enveloped him. Like a man buried in nightmare, he tried to scream himself awake. He slept on.

"I wish you didn't have to go," he said.

"I wish that I could stay."

THIS ISLAND EARTH

A kind of grace was granted them, a brief freedom from the ineluctable structure of the moment. Abby leaned into his arms.

"I love you," he said.

"Me, too, Ezra. I love you, too. Despite the damn hillbilly music." She tightened the circle of her embrace. "Don't wait, okay? Go on. You go on now. Promise. Promise me."

"Yeah."

He released her. She drew back.

And for a single heartbeat, Ezra clawed himself free of that dread capitulation. For a single heartbeat, he existed wholly in the ephemeral human world. It was hot and still under the saucer, silent as a breath suspended. It was like standing in the flat, even warmth of an oven. It was like standing in a noon-day desert, the air scorched of moisture.

He dragged a single word up the parched tunnel of his throat. "Don't," he rasped. And then that inhuman calm descended upon him once again, bathing him in cool serenity. Everything else was far away. The desperation remote. The terror inaccessible. Action impossible.

Abby turned away from him.

Abby turned away from him.

Abby turned away.

She stepped into the light or was drawn into it. The dusky shadows closed around her. They took her up through the blue light.

Finally, with an exertion of will he could not have imagined he possessed, with every muscle straining, Ezra once again tore himself free of that awful tranquility. He staggered toward the light. He collapsed on the pavement, one hand outstretched.

"Abby," he whispered. "Abby."

I'm here, Ezra, she said.

She said, *They're dying. They're all dying.*

She said, *Without us, they'll die. They'll all die.*

She said, *Listen now:*

Night Caller from Outer Space

She told him what he had to do. And then—there was so much more to say, a whole lifetime of words that would never be given voice—they came for her.

Abby, he cried into the void. *Abby!*

But she was gone. He would not hear from her again. She'd gotten a clear line at last. She had done what she had to do. She had not flinched. She had not turned away. He would have to do the rest. It did not matter the cost.

Ezra pushed back from the soundboard. Walked to the door. Turned the lock. An Ernest Tubb cut—"Keep My Mem'ry in Your Heart"—was spinning on turntable one, sending out across the night-plunged fields some comfort to all the sleepless people sitting out there in dim rooms, their ears turned close to quiet radios, their hearts knotted up with sorrows they could not themselves untangle into words.

Ezra lifted the stylus.

He pulled down the microphone, thumbing it to life. The words flowed through him as they always had when he took his place there. He said—

Listen.

I bring you the most important news you will ever hear. The most important news any human being in history has ever heard. For a long time we have believed ourselves safe here, alone on a warm, green island in a lifeless, black sea.

We are not alone. We are not safe.

Creatures immensely more powerful than we are have taken notice of us. They have come down from outer space. You hear rumors of them. Jokes. Flying saucers. Little green men.

I tell you they exist. I have seen them. I have witnessed their power.

They are dying. Their whole race is dying. They are already waging their war upon us, taking up those among us who can give them life. They are fighting for their survival. Now we must fight for our own.

This Island Earth

Spread the word. Spread it everywhere. Tell everyone. We are at war. The enemy will come from above. Watch the skies. Keep watching the skies!

By the face of the lunatic cat on the bullpen wall, Ezra began broadcasting this message at 4:11.

He was still broadcasting it when Bill broke down the door.

The men in the dark suits had shown him a photograph of the site where Abby had been taken up: the slick, narrow road running up to the crest of the hill; the woods pressing close against both shoulders.

There were two hills in Ezra's mind.

On one hill, the road ran through the wreckage of those trees.

On the other hill, they stood tall and unbroken, their rain-shiny boles flaring with the red shadows cast by Clyde Wilson's dome light.

Ezra laid these memories down on the photograph and asked himself which one was true.

Tell us what happened to Abby, Agent This or Agent That said.

I could have saved her, Ezra said. *I broke free twice. Twice. If I'd been stronger, I could have saved her.*

A dozen times he told them.

Finally, they were done with him. They packed up their briefcases at the courthouse conference table. They'd been sitting there for two days, going through it all. They thanked him for his time. That was it, then. They were just going to leave him there, with those two memories unreconciled, and only a photograph to test them against. The first agent was already out the door when the second one—Agent This maybe, or maybe Agent That—turned to look back at him, slumped at the table

There's nothing you could have done, the agent said. *Nothing.* And then, with a curt nod, *Thank you for your time, Mr. Hill.*

The door closed behind him.

Night Caller from Outer Space

Ezra crossed his arms on the table to pillow his head. He had been asleep for two hours when Clyde woke him. *It's over now, Ez,* he said. Ezra glanced at his watch before he stood. It was 9:37.

It was 9:37 when Clyde leaned in the Bel Air's window. It was 9:37 when Agent This or Agent That turned in the doorway.

It was 9:37 when John walked him out to his car.

"Now what?" Ezra said.

"We'll see," John said. "Let me think on it. Go home."

Ezra went home. He ate a sandwich at the kitchen sink. It was like chewing paste. He threw it away and went to bed. He slept seven hours straight. No dreams, or none that he remembered.

When he woke up, it was already dark out. He pulled on a teeshirt and walked through the dark house to the porch. He sat in the rocking chair, looking out into the night. He'd lost track of *Sixgun Fury*. It didn't matter. He was never going to read it.

A car came down the driveway, its headlights flashing as it came over the rise. Darla walked up on the porch.

"You cold, Ez?" she asked.

"I'm fine."

She sat down in the rocker beside him. "You oughta put something on."

"It's alright."

They sat for a few minutes.

"John send you?" he asked.

"I don't think you're gonna hear from John for a while."

"Yeah."

"You wanna go inside, Ez? Let's go inside. Get you warm. Get you something decent to eat. You look like a scarecrow."

"I could have saved her."

"I don't know about that. I don't know what happened out there. But I know you, Ez. I know you tried. I know you did everything you could. That's all anybody can ask. Some things you don't get to decide."

"She was pregnant."

THIS ISLAND EARTH

"Christ," Darla said. She sat for a long time and didn't say anything. "Christ," she said.

"Come on," he said. "Walk out here with me. I want to show you something."

"You don't have any shoes on, Ez."

"Come on."

"Let's go inside. You need to get warm. You're gonna freeze to death."

He stood and walked down the steps. She followed him out into the yard. The ground was rough underfoot, the dead grass crunchy with frost.

Ezra spread his arms wide to the clear winter sky, each bright star graven with a jeweler's precision in the black vault of heaven. All of them still. All of them moving. Hurtling away from one another. Every day more darkness between the lights.

"See?" he said.

"See what, Ez?"

"Everything. It's everything. And it's dark. So much darkness and every minute more of it. It just keeps piling up."

"Maybe it does, Ez. Probably. All the more reason to look for the light."

"I am. That's what I'm looking for."

"Well, maybe you're looking for the wrong light. The real light, the one that matters—maybe it's not up there. Maybe it's down here. Right here. All around you, Ez. What if it was?"

Ezra looked over at her. Everything was still and cold. Everything was silent. That ship and more than ship, that godmachine made to navigate the winds that howled between the stars, hovered in his mind, faintly luminescent, those dark currents flowing in their lazy gathering. He didn't know how to live outside its shadow.

"Even if it is, it doesn't matter. This is bigger than I am, Darla."

"Ezra—"

"You go on, now," he told her.

Suddenly she was furious. She drew close to him and pushed him.

"Do you think you're the only one ever lost somebody?" she cried, and she pushed him again. "Do you think you're special, Ezra? Do you? Do you?"

"You go on, now," he said.

She pushed him again, but he only stood there, immovable. She waited and she waited some more, her breathing disordered by tears. She wiped the back of her hand across her nose. "Do you?" she whispered, and a hard look came into her face.

Ezra looked away. He looked at the sky.

He heard her go, her shoes on the frost-rutted earth, the thunk of her car door and the engine starting up, gravel crunching under the tires as she moved off up the driveway.

He heard it clearly, but he didn't look around.

He kept his face turned to the stars, searching for a light in the vast tonnage of the black midwestern night.

for Wayne Singley

DURING BREAKS IN SHOOTING, the Creature from the Black Lagoon usually rests in a pond on the studio back lot and dreams of home. The pond isn't much even as ponds go. It's maybe four feet deep at its deepest point and a hundred yards or so around, an abandoned set carved out of the scorched southern California earth for some forgotten film or other: cattails and reeds and occasionally a little arrow of ripples when a dry breeze skates across the surface. Not even a fish if he's feeling peckish. Which he often is. The catering is suspect at the best of times, and it's even more so when you're accustomed to a diet of raw fish and turtle flesh prized living from the shell.

This is Hollywood.

"Don't expect too much," Karloff had advised him over sushi not long after he'd arrived, full of ambition and optimism, and Lugosi, strung out on morphine and methadone by the time the Creature made the scene, had been even more blunt. "They vill fuck you every time," he'd said in that thick Hungarian accent. Both of them

This Island Earth

typecast by their most famous roles. The Creature had assumed he could beat the odds, but on those blazing afternoons in the pond, now and again scooping up handfuls of water to moisten his gills, he'd begun to reconsider. The water was unkind, perpetually casting his reflection back at him: the bald, barnacle-encrusted skull, the eyes sunk beneath shelves of armored bone, the frills of tissue encasing the gills around his neck. Not what you would call leading-man material.

To think, he'd once been the king of his little world—the vast, dark Lagoon, overhung with the boughs of enormous trees, and the mighty Amazon itself, where anacondas slithered through the algae-clotted water, caiman slid into the flood without a splash, their tails lashing, and catfish the size of Chevrolets trolled the mossy bottom. Not to mention the jungle, humid, rank, and festering, clamorous with the chitinous roar of millions of insects. And here he was in southern California instead, spending his days in waist-deep water and sleeping his nights in an oversized bathtub in a crummy apartment.

Such are the Creature's thoughts when a member of the crew—it's Bill, a gopher who's trying to break into the biz as a lighting tech—walks down to the pond to tell him that Jack's finished setting up the next shot. It's time for the Creature to come back up to the set and stagger around the deck of the *Rita*—not even a real boat, just a cheap mock-up in one of the soundstages on the Universal lot—and menace Julie Adams for another hour or so. She's a real scream queen, Julie, the genuine article, but she's nice enough in real life; she even walks down to the pond to chat once in a while between set-ups. They're all nice enough. Even Jack's okay, though he's always badgering the Creature to focus on his motivation when the Creature has enough trouble just hitting his marks. To tell the truth, the Creature's heart isn't in it anymore, but he's signed a deal with Universal, and his agent—who rarely returns his calls anyway—tells him there's no way to break the contract.

So the Creature hauls himself out of the pond and tramps back

THE CREATURE FROM THE BLACK LAGOON

up to the soundstage, trying not to think about the fact that he could decapitate Bill with a single stroke of his taloned hand. Trying not to think that he wants to.

It wasn't supposed to turn out this way.
You never know happiness until it's gone, that's the way the Creature figures it. The present always seems like a mess. It was only once he left the Lagoon that he realized how good he'd had it there. In Hollywood, he recalls its dark waters with longing. Sometimes at night, his head pillowed on the bottom of his brimming bathtub and his webbed feet slung over either side to brush the peeling vinyl floor, he even dreams of it. How perfect it seems now, the murky bottom where he'd nestled for hours among the drifting fronds of plants he cannot name and the hidden channel that led to his rocky underground lair. Armored with scales and impervious to jaguar and piranha alike, the Creature had hunted both the overgrown shores and the black fathoms, snatching spider monkeys screaming from their roosts and feasting on the great fish that slipped through the Lagoon's sulfurous depths. He recalls even his isolation with melancholy regret. What had seemed like loneliness—he'd never known another of his kind—now seemed like freedom, and when the boat that spelled his expulsion from paradise had first steamed into the Lagoon, he had approached it with a curiosity that now seemed like folly.

He hadn't planned to leave the Black Lagoon, but life always takes the unexpected turn: caiman poachers in this case, though he hadn't known that then. It had been the boat, anchored in a sun-dappled inlet, that fascinated him. He'd taken it for some kind of novel creature, and because no denizen of the Amazon posed a threat to him—because he pined for novelty in those days—he hadn't given a second thought to approaching the thing. He'd been backstroking along, his face turned to the sun, when it came chugging into the Lagoon, stinking of gasoline. When he saw it, the Creature dove into the sun-spangled water, surfaced in the shadow of the boat, and dragged a talon along its rusting keel. He hadn't seen the net until it was too late. He found himself entangled. Panicked, he began to claw at it. He'd have freed himself had the poachers not reacted so quickly, winching him out of the water even as his talons tore long rents in the ropy mesh.

"My God," one of the poachers screamed, staggering back.

"Jesus, what the hell is that thing?" his companion cried, reaching for a spear gun. (The Creature reconstructed this dialogue only later.) The Creature was thinking the same thing. What could these soft, distorted reflections of his scaly self be, he wondered—

Then the harpoon punctured his shoulder, and he stumbled flailing into the water. He'd never felt such agony. By the time he bobbed to the surface, he was unconscious. When he woke, he found himself imprisoned behind steel bars.

The poachers weren't dumb—grimy, stubbled, and foul-mouthed, but not dumb. Three times a day, they tossed a fish, still flopping, between the bars of his cage. When they saw him pour his bucket of drinking water over his head, they realized that he needed to moisten his gills regularly. Using a spare gaff, they poked fresh buckets into his pen on the hour. The rest of the time he spent curled in a corner, whimpering. His terror of the boat at first overwhelmed him: the roar of the engine, the stench of his own waste, the curious faces (if you could call such doughy parodies of his own batrachian features faces) staring at him jaws agape from outside his cage. But you can get used to anything. By the time they anchored in the headwaters of Peru, his terror had dwindled to a dull simmer of anxiety.

What next?

He had no concept of the worst possibilities—not then, anyway. He could have been sold to a marine biology institute, where sooner or later scientists would have gotten around to dissecting him to see what made him tick (the Creature's rudimentary knowledge of scientists derives mostly from horror movies; scientists are all mad, as far as he is concerned). He could have been sold to a zoo, and spent the rest of his life paddling around in a wading pool, while small children gawped at him and tossed half-eaten ice cream cones through the bars. These would no doubt have been more profitable avenues. But the caiman poachers weren't anxious to disclose their reasons for cruising the Amazon. So he was sold instead to a carny scout combing the region for freak-show specimens, shipped north, and sold yet again, this time to Southeby & Sons Travelling Carnival, a fly-by-night operation that worked the south-western circuit through the spring and fall, wintering in Gibsonton, Florida, along with most of the other carnies in North America.

And here was happiness again—sort of, anyway—though he didn't recognize it at the time. By then, he'd pretty well been tamed. After he'd raked the shoulder of one of the poachers with his claws, a cattle prod had been brought into play, and three or four applications of *that* had been sufficient to cool his heels. So when he came to Southeby & Sons he'd been pliable enough. Besides, he fit right in with the freaks. They too were unique: the Living Skeleton; the Fat Lady (fat hardly did her justice); Daisy and Violet, the Siamese Twins; and half a dozen others, midgets and bearded ladies and the Monkey Boy: a community of sorts, a family that assuaged the loneliness that had been his lot back home in the Black Lagoon.

What's more, he had a vertical glass aquarium he could call his own, smaller than he might have wished, true, but brimful of water. Southeby billed him as the Gill Man and his sideshow performances were no hardship. He could bob in the green water, or kick to the surface for a breath of rank air (the Monkey Boy wasn't particular in matters of personal hygiene), or even doze if so inclined. Something of a romance—unconsummated, for the Creature's sexual organs, if he had any, were incompatible with those of human beings—blossomed between him and Daisy, much to Violet's dismay, who for unknown reasons took an immediate and abiding dislike of him. It was Daisy who taught him to talk, though his vocal cords, unfit for human speech, rendered his voice guttural and unintelligible to the untutored ear. And there was a kind of freedom during the winters in Gibsonton, this perhaps most precious of all. A simple

This Island Earth

walk of a mile or so brought him to the beach, and he sometimes lazed for hours in the warm, briny waters of the Gulf.

So he might have passed his life, or at least a longer portion of it, for who could say how long he might yet exist? The Creature had no memory of his birth and growth. He was then as he always had been and might always be. But restlessness possessed him. Violet's inescapable abhorrence was a constant blight on the affection he shared with Daisy, his tank grew cramped, and even his sojourns in the waters of the Gulf too brief, restricted by nine months on the road, burning the lot in one town to set up the next day in another. The midway—the flashing lights of the rides, the alluring chants of the barkers, the sugary reek of cotton candy and funnel cake—grew oppressive.

So when the chance to escape presented itself, in the person of a low-rent Hollywood agent who paused before his tank, the Creature was quick to take it. The agent took the time to decipher his rasping tones, sensed his discontent, and persuaded him to give the silver screen a try. L.A. was close to the beach year-round, after all, and the Creature was already in show biz. If stardom didn't suit him, he could always return to the carny circuit. So it was the Creature signed up to be a contract player for Universal. He didn't count on being typecast as, well, the Creature, forever flapping about on his great rubbery feet after one nubile beauty or another, his scaly green arms outstretched. Didn't count on being mistaken for a stunt man in a rubber suit. Didn't count on the bathtub or the crummy apartment.

Most of all he didn't count on Julie Adams.

This is Hollywood.

As Bela Lugosi put it, "They vill fuck you every time."

The Creature has begun to believe that he might be in love with Julie Adams.

"Are you lonely?" she asks him one day down by the pond.

He floats on his back in a stand of cattails, keeping an eye on her through a screen of gently bending stalks. He understands all too well what it's like to be stared at. Every time he strolls outside his apartment, people stare. He's learned to ignore the occasional cries of "Hey, Fish Man," and no longer stops to explain that he's not a fish, but an amphibian. Yet the mockery has had its effect. The Creature has begun to wonder if there's something cannibalistic about him every time he chomps into a fish taco or spears a sushi roll on a single curved claw—with his webbed fingers, chopsticks and silverware are out of the question. The truth is, that's another reason the Creature has given up on the set's catering: he senses that people would just as soon not see him eat. He's never quite overcome the gastronomic habits of the jungle. He wolfs down his meals, smacks his oversized red lips, chews with his mouth open, gets gobs of food caught in his fangs. The whole thing is unsightly. The studio has ignored his requests to stock the pond with bluegills and catfish so that he can eat in privacy, and rather than protest—the negligent agent again—the Creature elects to spend his days hungry. He figures it sharpens his hostile motivations in the film; he's become a student of Stanislavsky.

The Creature has, in short, begun to accept the norms of Hollywood. He no longer sees any beauty in his fellow denizens of the freak show (the mere thought of Daisy now repulses him)—but he has very much come to see the beauty in Julie Adams, a tall, busty brunette who spends most of her days in their scenes together wearing a white one-piece bathing suit that accentuates her considerable curves. He's not sure that what he feels is love—love is a relatively new concept to him—but he knows that he eagerly anticipates her occasional visits to the pond, that the sound of her voice sets his heart racing, that sometimes he has trouble sleeping nights, and not merely because the bathtub provides no comfortable accommodation for his dorsal ridge. No, he has trouble sleeping because he can't stop thinking of Julie Adams.

Is he lonely? In a word, yes.

But the question begs closer examination. He glides out of the bed of cattails and gives Julie his full attention. Perhaps she's come to suspect his amorous intentions, for she has taken to wrapping herself in a thick white bathrobe before she walks down to the pond. Perhaps she's merely cold. It's hard to know.

"Lonely?" he says, hating his inhuman rasp. He cannot help comparing it to the rich, clear timbre of Richard Carlson, the (let's face it) star of the movie, despite the Creature's eponymous billing. With a languid kick he turns to face Julie. She sits at the edge of the shore, with her knees drawn up and her hands clasped around her legs. The Creature can't help staring at her bare ankles. Lonely? He muses on the question.

"That's right."

"I suppose I haven't really thought about it."

"Well, there are no other Creatures, are there?"

"None that I know of," he says, recalling the splendid isolation of the Lagoon.

"It must be very lonely, then. I wouldn't like to be all alone."

"I'm not alone anymore."

Implying that he has become a companion to the human race in general, and perhaps, hopefully, to Julie in particular.

She doesn't take his meaning. "Sometimes I think we're all alone, every one of us. Do you ever think that?"

The Creature composes his largely immobile features into an expression of tragic acceptance. "I suppose we are," he says. "But if you can find someone to love—"

She interrupts him. "I guess that's true. But it must be especially difficult for you. You're not human, but you're not...not human, either, if you see what I mean." She sighs, resting her chin on her knees. "Dick says you're the Missing Link." She seems to be blind to the cruelty of this statement, but the Creature has become as accustomed to this appellation as he is to "Fish Man." If he really thinks about it, he supposes he does stand somewhere between the modern human and his piscine ancestry, but he doesn't much like what this implies about his place on the evolutionary spectrum.

Annoyed, he backstrokes off in a snit, arcs his body gracefully

The Creature from the Black Lagoon

backward, and dives, dragging his armored belly on the muddy bottom of the shallow pond (oh, how he longs for the fathomless depths of the Black Lagoon!) He surfaces to face Julie across the stretch of sun-shot water—only to find her striding back to the soundstage. Bill is waving him in from the water's edge. It must be time to resume shooting. Sighing, the Creature breaststrokes toward shore. Once the scourge of the Amazon, he has been reduced to a bit player in his own story.

For it *is* his story. Or was supposed to be.

History will record it differently—attributing the film's origins to Maurice Zimm, but Zimm did little more than transcribe the Creature's narrative during a series of interviews conducted while the Creature lounged in producer William Alland's swimming pool. That's how the Creature remembers it anyway. He would have pounded out the screenplay himself if he could have. That task fell instead to two inveterate Hollywood journeymen, Harry Essex and Arthur Ross. When he read the final draft, the Creature recoiled in disbelief. The caiman poachers had been transformed into intrepid paleontologists, the Black Lagoon into an arena of horrors, the Creature himself—an innocent victim!—into a vicious monster. About the only thing the trio of scribes had managed to do right was add a love interest—otherwise, the Creature thinks, he might never have met Julie Adams.

"I won't do it," the Creature protested. "I'll go back to the carnival. Hell, I'll go back to the Amazon!"

His agent—a balding, mousy little man named Henry Duvall—shook his head dolefully. "You've signed a contract."

"I didn't sign anything," the Creature growled. "I can't even hold a pen."

"I signed *for* you in the presence of two witnesses and a notary public," Duvall replied. "Same difference."

Cue Bela Lugosi.

So the Creature reported to the set as ordered, climbed aboard the

This Island Earth

Rita to terrorize Julie as required, shrank before the virile posturings of Richard Carlson (as required)—and fell in love.

"Love," he tells Karloff, pacing the actor's capacious study. By this time, Karloff has long since settled into stardom. He lives comfortably in L.A. and has steady work, though he's still typecast as a horror icon. Smaller than the Creature expected—the Creature towers a good two feet above him—Karloff in his late sixties remains handsome and slim, his dark hair silvering. Five times married, he is perhaps not the best person to approach for romantic advice, but the Creature's options are limited. His film, the first of a projected trilogy, is not yet completed, much less released, and he is beginning to see that he has been played for a fool. If Boris Karloff can't escape his defining role—if this charming, gentle man still clumps around in the American zeitgeist wearing elevator boots and bolts in his neck—then what hope has the Creature, who cannot even shuck his costume? There are no Oscars in his future, just endless sequels to this initial pack of lies. *Revenge of the Creature. The Creature Walks Among Us.* Even *Abbot and Costello Meet the Creature*, if things go badly enough (or well enough, from Universal's perspective).

"Love?" Karloff says. He leans back in his armchair and steeples his fingers. "Love is always a delicate matter."

"Tell me about it," says the Creature.

"If your love is unrequited"—Karloff retains a trace of his native British accent, a genteel formality—"then there is little you can do."

This is not the advice the Creature sought. This is not advice at all. This is a statement of fact. The Creature has come to suspect that Julie's visits to his pond are little more than kindnesses. After all, he sees the way she looks at Richard Carlson, the way she moistens her lips and gazes up at him in adoration. Carlson is nice enough to him, but nice won't do. While the Creature occasionally daydreams of raking Bill's head off in annoyance, his fantasies of violence toward Carlson burn icy and pure. He would like to kill him slowly, to spear each eyeball upon a talon and pop them into his mouth like jellybeans, to unseam his belly and feed upon the steaming offal, to wrench off his limbs one by one. For a start. The Creature does what he can to repress these unsavory flights of imagination, but they retain a vividness he cannot deny. He may work in a black-and-white 3D horror flick, but his fantasies are projected in widescreen Technicolor. Perhaps this is his true nature, savage and immutable, antediluvian and, yes, appropriate to the Missing Link. You can take the Creature out of the jungle, but you can't take the jungle out of the Creature.

He senses that this is not the way to Julie's heart.

Karloff clears his throat. "You face many obstacles, of course. You are not handsome. You are not human. You have, insofar as you have been able to detect, no potential for procreation. Yet there might be a way."

A way? The Creature pauses. He takes a seat across from Karloff. He'd like to lean back, but his goddamn dorsal ridge is, as always, in the way. Another reminder of his inhumanity. Yet there might be a way past even that.

He is all attention.

"Beauty comes in many forms," Karloff says. "It is, as the expression goes, in the eye of the beholder. But that eye is often best attuned when its object is set against its natural environment."

"What are you saying?"

Now Karloff leans forward. He smiles. "Underwater, my friend. Water is your natural milieu."

True enough. In his pond on the Universal lot, submerged to the waist and ladling up clear freshets with one spade-like hand, the Creature looks ridiculous. In the Black Lagoon, however, he glides through the water with a grace and beauty no man can hope to match. Human beings are no more suited to thrive underwater than he is suited to a purely land-bound existence. Clumsy and ill-equipped for a submarine life, they don wet suits that are but sad reflections of his own glistening hide. They have rubber flippers where he has feet, heavy oxygen tanks and re-breathers where he has gills. If he shambles gasping across the Universal lot, his adversary in love will shamble—or anyway flail—beneath the surface. In the water, Carlson's beauty will be but a paltry thing. And while a return to the Black Lagoon is cost-prohibitive, the underwater scenes are scheduled to be filmed in Wakulla Springs, Florida, a return to his beloved Gulf and (yes, he has researched the location shoots) the largest freshwater cave system in the world—if not his beloved Lagoon, the next best thing. Flush with renewed optimism, the Creature thanks Karloff and takes his leave.

The same optimism carries him across the continent, canted awkwardly in his seat—his dorsal ridge, again—and staring out at the blur of the propellers. Halfway through the flight, Julie walks down the aisle to take the seat beside him. She leans past him to look out the window, so close that he can smell the faint lavender scent of her perfume. "Isn't it beautiful?" she says, gazing down at the green hills unscrolling below the streaming scud. "It makes me think of the film."

"How?" says the Creature, who can see no clear connection.

"Well, it seems so deep, you know, so...dimensional...looking down from up here like this. I imagine the way the audience will experience it when they see us swimming out of the screen like that."

Ah. 3D. If he's been told once he's been told a thousand times. Alland's ambitions for the film hinge upon two factors: the realistic creature effects (which certainly *should* look realistic, the Creature ruminates) and the use of 3D, only the second Universal film to be released in the innovative format. But then he realizes that Julie has dozed off against his shoulder, and he wonders if he too can have a three-dimensioned life.

Wakulla Springs is everything the Creature had hoped it would be. There are shortcomings, to be sure. He could have wished for a more tropical setting—strangler figs, lianas, and buttress-rooted trees—but there is much to be thankful for as well. The alligators slipping into the murky water recall the caiman of the Black Lagoon; the bulky manatees, the nine-foot piracuru and catfish that call his

The Creature from the Black Lagoon

native waters home; the boom of insects, the constant roar of the jungle. And the springs themselves are fathoms deep and riddled with caverns. Against his better judgment—Julie will think him hardly human at all, he fears—the Creature dispenses with the pretense of his trailer and abandons the on-set catering altogether. Halfway abandons the film, in fact. More often than not, when Jack dispatches Bill to summon the Creature to the set, he's off touring the depths. He explores the cave system in search of a rocky grotto like the one he'd had in the Amazon. He dozes in deep, cold currents where no human being can follow. He gluts himself on the abundance of prey, devouring fish raw in clouds of ichthyic blood. Life is good, or better anyway, but he is not happy (or if he is, he does not recognize it). Thoughts of Julie torture him like an inflamed scale under a ridge of his armored breast.

Finally, Jack calls him in for a meeting. Like Karloff, Jack is a kind man. Anger is not his natural métier, yet the Creature is forced to stand dripping on the carpet in the director's trailer, listening to his gentle rebuke. Somehow that makes it worse, Jack's generosity of spirit. "I have no choice, you see," the director admonishes him. "We're on a tight schedule. We're not making *Gone With the Wind*, you know."

"It's going to be a good picture," the Creature says.

"I didn't say it wasn't going to be a good picture. I said that we have to make our release date or both our careers are on the line."

"Your career," the Creature rasps. "What kind of career am I likely to have, Jack?"

"You're unique. After people see this picture, offers are going to come rolling in."

"Don't patronize me, Jack. We both know there's only one role I can play."

Jack sighs. "I guess you're right. But still, this is going to be a good film. You'll get to play *this* role again."

The Creature laughs humorlessly, snared in a dilemma even his human colleagues must share, forever trapped in the prisonhouse of self. That's the appeal of acting, he supposes: the chance to be someone else, if only for a little while. And isn't that what he's doing here, playing at being something he's not? He's not a monster. He never has been. If his range of roles is limited—if he is doomed to be the Creature from the Black Lagoon—well that's Hollywood. He thinks of Karloff and Lugosi. Who does he want to become? Does he wish to accept his fate with grace or does he wish to rail perpetually against it, strung out on drugs and bitterness? Is being the Creature any different than being a carnival freak? Yet still he longs for his lost home. How he hates the poachers who have done this to him. He'd like to poke *their* eyeballs out, too. And eat them.

So maybe he's a monster, after all.

"I need you on the set on time," Jack is saying while these thoughts run through the Creature's head. "It's expensive to shoot underwater, especially with the 3D rig. Every time you don't show up when you're supposed to, you cost us money."

"I'm sorry, Jack," the Creature says.

"Look, I know this is hard for you. Nobody ever said acting was easy. Look at Brando. Channel your anger into the role. I need you to be the Creature I know you can be."

The Creature doesn't know quite what Jack means by this. He doesn't even know who—or what—he is anymore. Yet he vows to himself that he will try for something more complex than a B-movie monster—to draw not only upon his fury and resentment, but upon his passion for Julie. He vows to do better.

He does, too.

The Creature shows up promptly as requested. He lingers between shots. He tries to make small talk with the crew. But what is there to say, really? He's an eight-foot amphibian, finned and armored in plates of bone. He could eviscerate any one of them with the twitch of a talon. Monster or not, he is a monster to them.

Not to Julie, though, or so he tells himself. Perhaps Karloff is right: set against his natural environment, she seems to recognize his natural grace. Indeed she seems to share it. Unburdened by the clunky scuba tanks the men's roles demand, she glides through the water. And between shots she dispenses with the bathrobe she'd taken to draping herself in on the Universal lot, as if swimming together has drawn them closer. Of all the actors on the set, she alone seems entirely at ease with him. They spend more and more time talking. As he lolls in the shallows, she tells him about her recent divorce and about growing up in Arkansas; she tells him about her first days in Hollywood, working as a secretary and taking voice lessons on the side. Yet she is still capable of blind cruelty.

"You're lucky," she says. "You never had to fight for your dreams."

The Creature hardly knows how to respond. So what if Universal picked him up the minute William Alland laid eyes on him? Unlike Julie, he'll never play another role in his life; all the elocution lessons in the world won't change his inhuman growl. He's not even sure what he aspires to anymore. Stardom? Freedom? A return to the Black Lagoon? In his dreams, he sweeps Julie into his embrace, carries her off to the Amazon, unveils to her the wonders of his vanished life: the splendid isolation of the Lagoon, the sluggish currents of the great river, the mystery of the crepuscular forest.

Maybe this newfound intimacy accounts for the otherworldly beauty of the Wakulla scenes. In the dailies, Julie cuts the surface, her white bathing suit shining down through the gloom like godlight. The Creature stalks her from below, half-hidden among drifting fronds of thalassic flora, rapt by her ethereal beauty. His webbed hands cleave the water. Bubbles erupt skyward with his every kick. As she swims, he glides toward her from below, up, up, up, until he is swimming on his back beneath her and closing fast: a dozen feet, half a dozen, less, his immovable face frozen in an expression of impossible longing. He reaches out a tentative hand to brush her ankle as she treads water—and pulls it away at the last moment, as terrified of her rejection on celluloid as he is terrified of her rejection in life. What one does not risk, one cannot lose; worse yet, he thinks, what one does not risk, one cannot gain. A sense of inconsolable

This Island Earth

despair seizes him. In the images projected on the screen, he sees now how little their worlds can connect. She is a creature of the daylit skin of the planet, he of the shadowy submarine depths.

Jack praises the silent yearning in the Creature's performance.

Yet the whole thing drives the director crazy nonetheless. Frustrated by the task of stitching the haunting underwater scenes together with the mundane L.A footage, he asks the studio for reshoots and is denied. For the first time—the only time—the Creature sees Jack angry, his face a mask of fury. "This could be so much more than another goddamn monster flick," he says in the dim projection trailer, flinging away the 3D glasses perched on his nose. Even this angry gesture drives home the Creature's inhumanity. Alone in the back row, he must pinch his glasses between two delicate claws. His flattened nose provides no bridge to support them. He has no external ears to hook them over. Everything about him is streamlined for his underwater existence.

The Creature grinds his cardboard glasses under one webbed foot. He slams out of the trailer, the door crumpling with a screech of tortured metal as he hurtles into the moonlit night. He is halfway to the water when Julie catches up with him. "Wait," she says, "Wait—"

Her voice hitches in the place where his name ought to be—for of course he has no name, does he? He is the Creature, the Gill Man, nothing more. There has been no one to name him—even the freaks did not name him—and he has never thought to name himself. He would not know how to begin. Fred? John? Earl? Such human names fall leaden on the tongue, inadequate to describe a...a creature, a fiend, an inhuman monster. How will they credit him in the film? *The Creature as the Creature?*

"Wait," Julie says again. "Creature, wa—"

The Creature whirls to face her, one massive hand drawn back to strike.

"Don't," she whispers, and the Creature checks the blow. For an instant, everything hangs balanced on a breath. Then the Creature

THE CREATURE FROM THE BLACK LAGOON

lowers his hand, turns away, and shambles toward the water, his great feet flapping. Something feels broken inside him. Jack's words—

—*another goddamn monster flick*—

—echo inside his head. That's all he is, isn't he? A monster. A monster who in a moment of fury, would have with a single swipe of his claws torn from her shoulders the head of the woman he loved. A monster who would, in the grip of his rage, feed upon her blood. The Creature would cry, but even that simple human solace is denied him. The dark waters beckon.

"Wait," Julie says. "Please."

Almost against his will, the Creature turns to face her. She stands maybe a dozen feet away. In the moonlight, tears glint upon her cheeks. Beyond her, the men—Jack and Dick and Richard Denning, the third lead—stand silhouetted against the golden light pouring through the trailer's shattered door.

"Why?" the Creature says, knowing the doom that will come upon him if he stays.

"Because," Julie says, "because I love you."

So Karloff was right. For a heartbeat, happiness—a great and abiding contentment that no mere human being can plumb—settles over the Creature like a benediction. But what is the depth of love, he wonders, its strange currents and dimensions? What is its price, and is he willing to pay it? And a line from another monster movie comes to him, one that Jack showed him in pre-production: *It was beauty killed the beast.*

This is Hollywood.

It vill fuck you every time.

"I love you, too," he says in his inhuman rasp, and in the same instant, in his heart, he recants that love, refuses and renounces it. For Julie. For himself. He will not be the monster that loves. He will not be the monster that dies. He will not be their freak, their creature. He will not haunt their dreams. They can finish their fucking film with a man in a rubber suit.

This Island Earth

The Creature puts his back to Julie and wades into the water, glimmering with moonlight. It welcomes him home, rising to his shins and thighs before the bottom drops away beneath him, and he dives. He has studied the locations, he has explored the Springs' network of caverns: from here the Wakulla River to the St. Marks and Apalachee Bay, and thence to the Gulf. The Black Lagoon calls out to him across the endless miles, and so the Creature strikes off for home, knowing now how fleeting are the heart's desires, knowing that Julie too would ebb into memory, this perfect moment lost, this happiness receding forever into the past.

S ATURDAY NIGHT AT THE SUBMARINE RACES: a line of cars idle atop Miller's Point, the bluff overlooking Hicksville, Pennsylvania, their windows steamed over and their engines blowing fumes because it's dead center February in the long slog between Christmas and Easter. Me? I'm knocking at the gates of the promised land. Six months of nursing this doll named Betty Moore over chocolate malts at Flanagan's and popcorn at the Gem—six months of puzzling over calculus problems in the school library and passing notes in Old Lady Evanovich's English class—six months of this, and I'm an eighth of an inch from paradise, my hand flat on Betty's bare midriff and my fingertips just brushing the lacy edge of her bra. I'm this close, I tell you—and what happens next is exactly what you'd expect—

Aliens.

Now here's the thing: teenagers had been foiling alien invasions for months by then. There had been a real run on them lately, and who else was going to do it? Adults? Either they were buttoned up inside

This Island Earth

their living rooms watching *Dragnet* or *The Ed Sullivan Show*, or they laughed the whole thing off as another loopy teenage prank.

That's what Arnie Wilson is shouting about, though. Soon as she hears him, Betty wriggles out from underneath me and props herself against the door. She pulls her sweater down and I feel a pang of grief—not to mention annoyance. Arnie's got a reputation as a wise guy for one thing, and for another you never really think an alien invasion will happen to you. But there Arnie is, hammering at the window of my Bel Air and flipping his wig about little green men from Mars. The next thing you know he's scrabbling at the door, and the thing after that he's got ahold of the handle because the door flies open, admitting a blast of Arctic air. It's all I can do to keep Betty from tumbling out of the car. By the time I haul her up and climb over her to the door—there's nothing graceful about this—I'm fighting mad.

I'm on Arnie like a bolt of lightning, twisting up his jacket with my fists and slamming him against the neighboring Plymouth. "What gives, Arn?" I hiss. "Betty and I were having a moment."

I ram him into the Plymouth once again, ignoring the indignant cries from within. Arnie's glasses go flying. He grimaces and lifts his hands in surrender. He can see that he's made a tactical error. I'm the starting fullback for the Hicksville Hawks, 100 yards a game last season, and—I say this with all modesty—I've got the size and speed to prove it. Arnie, on the other hand, specializes in slide rules and pocket protectors. He can't go more than 140 soaking wet and he has the footspeed of a ground sloth.

The Plymouth's window zips down. Todd Bosco pokes his head out. "Hey, lay off—" he starts, and then he sees who he's dealing with. "Sorry, Hank," he says. "Just try not to dent it, all right? This is my old man's tank." And the window zips back up.

Me, I'm getting my hands set to introduce Arnie to Bosco's Plymouth one more time—all I can think about is my fingertips skating the lacy rim of Betty's bra—when Betty herself weighs in behind me.

INVASION OF THE SAUCER-MEN

"You put him down right now, Hank," she says, and I put him down.

Arnie catches his breath. Swallows. Eyes me warily. "I'm sorry, Hank. It's just, I saw that flying saucer and the first thing I think is, I gotta tell Hank. He'll know what to do."

Arn's breath smokes as he says this. The air is utterly still, pristine, so cold that your words practically freeze up the minute they leave your mouth. The sky is clear and moonless. A thousand stars look down.

Bosco steps out of his old man's car.

"What gives, Hank?" he says.

What gives is I'm smoothing the wrinkles out of Arnie's jacket while Betty looks on in disapproval. "Arn here says he saw a flying saucer," I say, giving the Arnster a halfway friendly pat on the cheek. I'm just asking Bosco to hunt up Arnie's specs when Betty hands them over. She's still not happy, I can tell. As for Arnie's glasses? They're a little worse for wear. Cracks spiderweb one lens, and the arm on the other side is bent. I straighten it out as best I can and slide them onto his face. "There you go," I say. "Good as new." And when I catch Betty glaring at me, I add, "Sorry, Arn. I guess things got a little out of hand there." And when she continues to glare, I add even more: "Look, you get those binoculars patched up, I'll pick up the tab, okay?"—which would probably empty my savings account, but it mollifies Betty, and that's what matters to me—because, true confession, when it comes to Betty, I'm more than half over the moon.

By this time, a little crowd has gathered—Bosco and Bosco's girl, Mary Ruth Bennett, and John Peterson and his girl, Nancy O'Dell, and—well, my memory puts us at twelve, including Tom Martin and Linda Jackson and Frank Harris and Janice Williams, but my memory isn't entirely reliable. Time will do that to you, as I expect you know. And then there's Barbara Jones, Arn's steady, a hateful broomstick of a girl with a hooked nose and a set of beady brown peepers, glowering at me from behind a pair of cat's-eye glasses on a

THIS ISLAND EARTH

librarian's chain. This, the whole crowd, standing there with me and Arnie dead in the middle and all of them talking about the flying saucer.

"You aren't just putting us on, are you, Arnie?" I ask, holding up my hand for silence.

Everybody's standing there waiting for Arnie to fess up when Barbara weighs in. "I saw it, too," she says. "We both saw it. It came in low over the ridge. You could see the trees leaning over as it passed." Then, pointing, "It landed on the other side of the hill, where the road cuts down through the pines."

"See?" says Arnie.

"Yeah, I see," I tell him, sighing, because the truth is I don't want anything to do with flying saucers. What I want to do is hop back in the Bel Air and pick up where Betty and I left off.

But what are your options in a situation like that?

When you go 190 and 189 of it is pure muscle, when you average nine yards every time you touch the ball, and when the queen wearing your letter jacket has a truly divine chassis and the kind of face that brought Paris and Menelaus to blows—well you wield a certain authority in high-school hallways. People look to you for leadership. Ask anybody.

Our fathers stormed the beach at Normandy when they weren't much older than we were. Duty's duty, right? If Arnie's right about the aliens, then I guess it's up to us to deal with them. Unfortunately, while I've been running this through my head, the other kids have been getting cold feet.

"Heck, Arnie," Bosco's saying. "It could have been a plane or a meteor or—or, I don't know, any one of a dozen other things, right?"

"Maybe we should call the cops," Tom says.

"And tell them what?" I say. "Some kookie story about a flying saucer? What do you think they're going to say about that? Besides, the nearest phone is down at the Sinclair station, and that's twenty minutes away."

"Well, what do you think we ought to do, Hank?" Janice says.

"That's right, Hank," Barbara says. "What *do* you think?" Yakkety-yak. She was a nasty piece of work, Barb.

"I think we ought to reconnoiter," I say, throwing in a vocabulary word from that old bat Evanovich's class just to show her that I wasn't as stupid as she thought I was.

Barbara pops her gum and shrugs. "So reconnoiter," she says, which is how Bosco, Frank Harris, and I end up walking down Miller's Point Road toward the thicket of pines where Barbara claimed to have seen the flying saucer come to earth.

There was the usual hugger mugger before we got started, some posturing about who was going to go and who was going to stay and "protect the women," and after that the exchange of various embraces, Betty leaning in close against my ear to say, "Be careful, Hank." And then, hesitating, "I love you, you know," which words, often felt—at least on my end—but never spoken, sent so many fireworks rocketing through my brain that it was all I could do to respond in kind. The truth was, I *did* love her, had been in love with her for months by then and had a feeling that I would love her henceforward and forever after, which has turned out to be true in the end.

And it's this particular truth, with all its implications, that I'm thinking about as we set off. The curve with the fringe of pines that Barbara had described was maybe a quarter mile as the crow flies, but nothing is easy on Miller's Point Road, fifteen hair-raising miles of narrow switchbacks and disintegrating pavement, so we end up walking at least a mile, and somewhere along the way this awful fear of losing Betty overwhelms me and I realize what a terrible thing love is—how it can fill you with sorrow at losses yet to come and make you more than half-afraid. There's the aliens for one thing. We're not halfway there, and I'm hoping it *was* a low flying plane—that we'll find nothing on that curve but pinchweed and pinecones. But for another, there's the possibility of some drunken greaser racing uphill, straightening out the curves as he comes, and knocking us right out of our shoes. Walking on Miller's Point Road is like issuing

This Island Earth

invitations to your own funeral, and it's only luck that someone doesn't cash one of them in.

Our luck doesn't hold, though.

Here's the geography: on our right as we descend, the road shears away into a wooded ravine; on our left, a thicket of pine trees hugs the edge of the pavement. Beyond that, who knows? I've driven by the place a hundred times, but it's not like I'd ever pulled over to explore.

"Well, there's nothing here," Frank says in this quavering voice.

"Yeah, we might as well turn back, Hank, don't you think?" Bosco adds, and his voice is pretty shaky, too.

It always falls to the guy like me. People look up to you in a crisis, you have to help them find their better selves—which means you have to be your own best self even when you're afraid. And I was afraid, for foiling a pernicious alien plan never comes without a cost. But I reached down deep inside myself for courage and when I spoke my voice was steady. "I guess we ought to check inside those pines first."

"Those woods might run all the way to Pittsburgh," Frank says.

"Better take a look all the same," I say, and the next thing you know we're off the pavement and into the pines. It was dark outside the thicket. Inside, it's like midnight in the Lost River Caverns. The trees blot out the sky, and down underneath, as we push our way through the undergrowth, unseen branches whip at our hands and faces. "Darn it," Bosco says when one slaps him in the face, and Frank shushes him so loud he might as well be shouting. I could belt them both for being idiots because I'm sure the aliens, if there are any, must hear us thrashing around in here—only I've lost my bearings, and I'm too busy cursing myself for not grabbing the flashlight out of my Bel Air, though you couldn't use a flashlight anyway, because then the aliens would see you. But it doesn't matter in the end. The thicket turns out to be only twenty or thirty yards deep.

Frank nearly stumbles into the meadow on the other side, only I

INVASION OF THE SAUCER—MEN

grab him by the collar with one sap-sticky mitt and pull him down at the last moment. It's a good thing, too, because what we see when we hunker down at the edge of the field and peer out into the starlit night is a flying saucer.

It's aliens, all right.

Six of them by my count, milling around below the ramp from their ship. They're not pretty to look at either. Aliens never are, I guess. These particular specimens stand maybe shoulder high and have giant heads—it's hard to see how they can hold them up; their bodies look like tough little afterthoughts—but beyond that I can't tell much about them. The meadow is a well of shadows.

"You think they have ray guns?" Frank whispers, and I say, "Shhh, you," and bat him in the back of the head. A terrible moment follows in which it seems like one of the little monsters has overheard us. It pauses—it's an ugly bastard, all right—and cocks one of its big pointy ears in our direction.

Two, three, four heartbeats pass before the thing turns its attention away and advances out into the field. It's time for us to go. If there's one thing I know, it's this: when you face an alien invasion, you have to formulate a plan.

I give the nod, and we back slowly into the trees. When we're out of sight, we turn and hightail it for the road. The same unseen branches—one of them slashes at my cheek—claw at us like talons. The bracken clutches our feet. Then—it's a nightmarish moment—some chance tangle of branch and vine seizes me by the ankles. Spinning wildly, I go down hard, as if a linebacker has blindsided me at full speed, smashing me to the field and crushing the breath out of my lungs. In the confusion that ensues—I'm scrabbling at my throat like a dying man—Frank and Bosco try to drag me upright, and Bosco, too, comes crashing to the earth. "Get up, get up," Frank is chanting—I don't think he realizes how loud his voice is—and then, *whoosh*, I can breathe again, great rattling sobs, and for a moment I can't think at all the air is so sweet and good. An instant later we're up and running—or limping anyway—only this time we really *have* gotten turned around, and hurtle thrashing back into the meadow.

Freeze frame, like some cheesy movie down at the Gem:

On one side, Frank, Bosco, and me, battered, bleeding, sap-sticky and weary, our clothes filthy and torn. On the other, the aliens, their big heads turned as one to face us. Full on they're something to see all right, their giant heads like enormous, elongated cabbages mounted atop those sinewy little bodies. And their eyes—their lambent eyes—their great, white, bulging, lambent eyes—have vertical black slits for pupils. Their scrutiny is terrible.

It can't be but a few seconds, but it feels like forever.

Then one of the aliens—the nearest one, it's maybe two dozen feet away—stretches out its hand. A ray gun, I think, only it's not a thought, it's an instinct. And before I've even put the words into thought, I've spoken them aloud—

"*It's got a ray gun!*"

—and we're stumbling full tilt back into the belt of pines. This time there's no getting turned around, and this time nobody gets tripped up. If the branches snapping at our faces leave bloody welts—and they do—sheer adrenaline propels us through the pain. We come crashing out onto Miller's Point Road without even checking to make sure no headlights are sweeping around the curve to run us down, and careen uphill toward the bluff.

The ankle gives out maybe half a mile up—I must have twisted it something terrible—and when I pull up lame, Frank and Bosco pull up beside me. For a breath we stand there, hands on our knees, winded. I glance back to see what might be pursuing us, but of course there's nothing there. The saucer-men are coming, I have no doubt about that, but even with those sturdy little bodies I figure they can't make much speed.

"You okay?" Bosco gasps.

"Yeah. Pretty sure I sprained my ankle." The pain is terrific, and the fear is just about as bad, but I'm calmer now—calm enough to realize that I've got to keep a lid on it. I've got to remember who I am, that I'm the guy who sets the tone. Without me everything falls apart, and then what? Alien domination of the Earth, that's what. So I bottle the fear up deep inside me—so deep that I can almost forget it's there—straighten up, and square my shoulders. "Come on, we've got to make time," I say. "Those...monsters...will be coming soon."

I take a halting step, gasp, take another. Then I steady up some, and settle into it, kind of riding out the pain.

"You sure you can walk?" Bosco says.

"What's it look like I'm doing, Bosco?"

"Well...maybe we can help you a little, that's all I'm saying."

"I've played through worse than this. Now come on, we've got to make time."

We made time. The adrenaline began to taper off, and the cold began to gnaw at us, making the ankle hurt more than ever, but I kept moving. It wouldn't do to let it stiffen up, for one thing, and I had to keep a brave face on, for another—especially when Frank started in.

"What do you think those things were?" he wants to know, his voice all shaky, and I say, "Aliens." He mulls that over for a while, and then he says, "You think that one really had a ray gun?" and I say, "Of course it had a ray gun," and he says, "But—"

"But what? It's an alien, isn't it? You ever hear of an alien that didn't have a ray gun?"

Which is pretty inarguable, you have to admit. So Frank buttons his lip and we limp on in silence, putting another quarter mile behind us—only then *Bosco* weighs in. "Where do you think they come from?" he wants to know, and "What do you think they were doing in that field?" and "Did you see that flying saucer, Hank?"—to which I say, "Mars" and "I don't know" and "Yes, Bosco, I saw it, I'm not blind," and then—just as the road sort of humps up and cuts through a low hill toward the bluff, where the cars are still idling—just as we're coming into earshot of the others and Betty looks up from chewing a nail and smiles and my heart expands within me—just

This Island Earth

then Bosco comes out with the million dollar question, the one we've all been chewing over in silence since Arnie first reported that flying saucer zooming over the ridge.

"What do they want, Hank?" he says.

By then we're standing square in the middle of a cluster of jazzed-up kids. They're all flapping their gums, but no sooner are the words out of Bosco's mouth than every lip falls mute and every eye upon me.

I take a deep breath.

"They want our women," I say.

This is undeniable—what else do aliens ever want?—but stating it right out loud like that sobers everybody into silence. The Barbster is the first to speak up. "No need to get frosted, Hank," she says. "But when did we become 'your women'?" That's Barb for you. You say the issue is "A," she redirects the focus onto "B" without a second thought. And "B" is usually pretty boneheaded.

"Drop dead, Barbara," I say, and by the time Barbara comes back with, "What, and look like you?" everybody else has tuned her out.

They're clamoring for dope on the aliens instead, but I've got other priorities: I want to reacquaint myself with my girl. After all, Mary Ruth's making doe eyes at Bosco and Janice is cooing in Frank's ear about how brave he is—which practically fractures me—so why shouldn't I have a turn? Besides, Betty's hanging on me like a new suit, and who can resist that? She runs the tip of one finger over the welt on my cheek and presses her lips to mine. "I'm so proud of you," she whispers. "Were you scared?"

"Heck no, Betty," I say, and though I wouldn't have thought it possible, she finds a way to press her body even closer to mine. Her sheer presence makes my brain all staticky, like a radio tuned to a dead frequency. "Listen, Betty," I manage—and the words sound fuzzy and distant, like a faraway signal through all that noise—"Listen," I say, "when this is over maybe we can talk about what happens when we graduate." And what I'm thinking in my fuzzed-out way is that we need to lay some plans to punch our tickets out of Hicksville and make a life together. Most kids around here wind up living out their days within twenty miles of the place—the really adventurous ones make it down to Pittsburgh—but there was a whole world I wanted to see, and I wanted to see it with Betty.

Before any of that could happen, though, we had an alien invasion to foil.

Which is why Tom Martin's tugging at my shoulder, saying, "Hank. Listen to me, Hank. We'll have time for the lovey-dovey later."

Anybody else, and they might have gotten a knuckle-sandwich for their trouble. But Tom and I are tight. I could take him if it came to it—I think—but why would I try? Tom's my right tackle and co-captain of the Hicksville Hawks. It works like this: I get the ball, Tom blasts a hole in the defensive line, and I turn on the jets. It's a, what's the word?—symbiotic? It's a symbiotic relationship. On top of which, he's right.

Betty and I share one last lingering kiss. When she pulls away, I'm practically woozy. "Tell them, Hank," she says, but it's all I can do to pull myself together enough to do it. I won't bother you with the repetition, though I'll cop to embellishing a few things and leaving some other things out. Do they really need to hear how we got lost in a belt of woods that couldn't be more than thirty yards wide, for example? And why shouldn't Bosco and Frank come off looking like second-tier heroes? It's the right thing to do. It's like talking about team effort after you've personally busted the opposing defense for 150 yards and three touchdowns. It builds trust and respect, a gesture like that. The lessons you learn on the gridiron will serve you a lifetime, and they certainly come in handy when you face a threat to humanity itself.

Which is what we were facing.

When I wind it up, nobody says a word. You hear about these things, of course, but like I said earlier, you never really think an alien invasion will happen to you. When it does it tends to leave you speechless.

This Island Earth

Finally someone—I think it was John's girl, Nancy O'Dell—says, "What are we going to do, Hank?"

And here's the embarrassing part of my story: you always hear about the ingenious ways teenagers foil alien invasions. The girls use the mirrors inside their compacts to reflect the alien death rays, frying the monsters with their own radioactive weaponry. Or the boys angle their headlights at the night sky, confusing the invading pilots and sending their saucers plunging to fiery destruction. I'd even heard of a teenage genius who used a paper clip and a refrigerator magnet to reverse the polarity of the alien stardrive, stewing the fiends in their ship like fresh vegetables in a *boeuf bourguignon*. But me, I had nothing. My mind just doesn't work that way. I was used to Tom Martin blasting a hole in the line, popping me into the secondary where I had room to run. Who was going to be my lead blocker now?

Barbara Jones, as it turns out. Which was bad enough. What made it worse was the savage little smirk she shot me when she did it. *You think you're so smart, Hank?* that smirk said. *Why don't you get bent?*

But what she says aloud is this: "Let's spin those cars around." And when nobody moves, she points at the crest of the ridge where Miller's Point Road spills down through the cut onto the ice-rutted shelf of the bluff. "C'mon people. Put your fins to the cliff and your high beams on that rise."

Everybody just stares at her.

It's a moment of crisis for me. Like I said, I command a certain authority in the halls of Hicksville High, and it's not easy to take orders from a girl, much less the Wicked Witch of the West. Then Betty touches my hand, and I realize that I have a duty to her—and not only to her, but to our folks and to all the other citizens of Hicksville and to humanity itself.

"You heard her," I say. "Flip those chariots around. Now!"

They hopped to it then, you bet. I slipped inside the Bel Air—jeeze, it was cozy and warm in there—and whipped her around in aces. Not five minutes later, we had the crest of that road blazing like a

INVASION OF THE SAUCER–MEN

kid's face come Christmas morning. When I swung my throbbing ankle out of the car, the Barbster's standing right there. "Tell them to arm up, Hank," she says. "What do you mean?" I say, and she says, "I mean tell them they need weapons." So I tell them, which is how most of the guys wind up wielding tire irons or baseball bats. I favored a bat myself, a white ash Louisville Slugger I'd dubbed Sugar Ray, which still had a bloodstain on the business end from the last time I'd run into Jim Stark, this greaser who'd whistled at Betty in what I considered to be a vile and perverted way. While Betty hadn't much appreciated the wolf whistle, she hadn't much appreciated my defense of her virtue either. Nor did she approve of my decision to store Sugar Ray under the front bench of the Bel Air, pending future engagements.

"You've got a temper, Hank," she said, and when I protested, she asked me to take her home. That had been our first fight—our only fight—and afterward I'd steered clear of the subject of Jim Stark, even though I inwardly vowed to swing for the fences the next time he stepped up to the mound and disrespected Betty.

Some things you just can't let pass.

So I can't help feeling vindicated when Sugar Ray comes into action, and I might even have said so, except Barbara's too busy yakking at me. It seems we have a plan, though it's an inelegant one when you compare it to taking out the invaders with a paperclip and a refrigerator magnet. Anyway, the basic idea is this: Tom and I will conceal ourselves on one side of the hill where the road cuts through to the bluff, Bosco and John will hide on the other side, and Frank and Arnie will take up positions between the cars, invisible behind the glare of the high beams. When the aliens walk down the bluff between us, we'll rush them from three sides. We'll have to move fast to beat their death rays—and I have a bad feeling that we'll take some casualties (my money's on Arnie, who's got a death grip on his tire iron and terror in his eyes). I'm not too much concerned about myself—I've always been quick in the open field—though I'd be lying if the ankle didn't trouble me some.

As for the girls? Safe in the cars, where else?
Except—
"We need bait," Barb tells me.
"Bait?"
"Something to draw them in. A girl."
"But— Who?"
"I could do it," Barb says, "and I'm willing"—
—and here Arnie grimaces—
—"but let's face it," she says, "I'm not exactly the alien type."

Silence follows. Our nerves are frayed by then, because who knows when the bug-eyed freaks are going to show? If they *did* see us in that field—and I keep remembering that outstretched hand—then they'll be in hot pursuit, homing in on the high beams where they converge at the crest of the road. What's more, Bosco, Frank, and I've already wasted too much time getting reacquainted with our girls, which triumph of hormones over intellect strikes me in retrospect as a poor leadership decision. Even a bruiser like Tom could see that.

It's not like we have a lot of time to figure it out, either, which is maybe why Betty says, "I'll do it." And you have to admit, if anybody fits the bill of alien bait, it's Betty Moore. She's—well, I think I've mentioned what a spectacular chassis she had, and I won't say anything more about that. But everyone knows that's what aliens look for in a girl.

Still—

"I can't allow you to do that, Betty," I say.

"I'm sorry, Hank, but you're not in the business of telling me what I can and can't do," she says, and right then I realize that some not-so-subtle balance has shifted between Betty and me. It's hard to know why, exactly, but I sense that Barbara is at the heart of it—that if I'd been able to cobble together some clever weapon involving a tomato stake, a humidor, and a vacuum cleaner, Betty would be climbing into Bosco's tank with the other girls. But now that Barbara was giving the orders, even if she was giving them *sotto voce*, all bets were off. It was a brave new world we were living in.

And I wasn't sure I liked it.

But what are you going to do? You can't just sit by and let aliens take over the world.

Which is how Tom and I end up planting ourselves in the shadows above the road, while Betty stands in plain sight on the bluff below. Despite the cold, she's shucked my letter jacket. Barb wants the aliens to be able to see her clearly, and I'm sure I don't have to explain to you what exactly that means. Suffice to say that in that blaze of headlights, with her dress clinging to her curves like that, Betty looks like a Greek goddess in silhouette, her long shadow stretching out before her. Just looking at her I'm smitten all over again, and I was on the hook pretty hard already. The aliens were going to eat her up, and while I mean that as a figure of speech, with aliens you never know.

So there I am on the hill, hunkered down behind a rock and worrying about my girl. I'm half-numb with cold and my ankle feels like some clown has stuck it in a vise and is giving it a good crank every minute or so—and the Aliens. Do. Not. Come. Which means there's going to be hell to pay, because Betty's going to miss her curfew and her dad's a hardshell ex-Marine with biceps the size of cannonballs, a graying buzzcut, and a take-no-prisoners attitude. So who knows how long it'll be before I get to see her again? And even now the best I can do is cast an eyeball at her from afar, which reminds me of just how close I'd come to paradise before the stupid aliens came along. And the whole time this is going on, I know that Betty must be freezing, too, which makes me want to take her in my arms to keep her warm, which reminds me just how close I'd come to paradise that evening before the stupid aliens intervened, which reminds me that the Aliens. Have. Not. Come, which—well you get the idea. It's a vicious circle is what I'm saying, and after a time, what with the cold and the pain, I drift into this weird reverie in which I'm back in the Bel Air with Betty, my fingertips just stroking the lacy edge of her bra. So when the aliens DO come, I don't even notice until Tom bats me in the back of the head.

This Island Earth

"What'd you do that for?" I start to say, but before I'm even halfway into the first word, Tom clamps one hand over my mouth and jabs a finger at the road below. There they are all right, all six of them, the bug-eyed freaks. They're green, too—you can see that in the glare of the high beams. They're literally little green men, with these ginormous green heads, and these stout little bodies with long arms and big curving talons where their fingers ought to be. They don't seem to be in any hurry either. They're just strolling along, like they're out taking the air of a Sunday afternoon.

Betty? She's a champ. Any other girl would have run screaming into the night. But Betty just stands there. A little wind has swept down off the ridge and her skirt billows behind her, hugging her thighs. She's staring right at the saucer-men. If she's even a little bit afraid, you can't tell it. Just looking at her, I feel a wave of vertigo sweep over me, like even my soul is no longer mine to keep, like it belongs to her for now and ever after, which is what love will do to you.

It's a merciless master, love, and it roots me there atop the cold hillside until the aliens clear the neck of the cut and reach the near end of the bluff. I'd probably still be rooted there if Tom hadn't batted me upside the head again. Then we're running—all of us—converging on the aliens from three sides, only the ankle has stiffened up on me so I'm kind of lurching along, an easy target, and I'm expecting an alien death ray to light me up any second. But it doesn't happen. Nothing like that happens at all. I won't understand what's happened until after it's over. I'm not sure I understand it even now.

All I know is that battle has been joined—and if my eye picks up anything strange about what's happening in front of me, I'm too hopped up on fear and adrenaline to notice it, not on a conscious level anyway. By this time the ankle has loosened up a little. It's shooting pains straight up my leg, sure, like the strongman at a county fair blasting the bell at the top of the post with every blow. But I've got my moves back, that old open field magic, when time itself slows down so much that you can calculate the trajectories of the opposing players without a second's conscious thought. You

INVASION OF THE SAUCER—MEN

could be solving algebra equations or reciting "The Raven" in your head. Your mind isn't even in the game. It's all instinct and muscle memory.

I'm hurtling downslope now, clutching Sugar Ray halfway up the barrel. If the county-fair strong man in my ankle is still ringing his bell I no longer feel it. I'm totally zeroed in on the last of the brutes. It's standing right in front of Betty, its arms lifted to encircle her, its talons outstretched. Betty's screaming. I remember that like it was yesterday. Betty screaming, her hand cupped before her mouth.

Screaming and screaming.

And then I'm upon them.

I lower my shoulder like a cornerback closing on a crossing pattern and bring the fiend down. Coming to my feet on the roll, I take in the naked little ogre with a glance. It's horrible to behold. Instinctive loathing seizes me—animal revulsion at the pulsing arteries that ridge that giant, elongated cabbage of a head, at the bulbous eyes and the downturned slash of the mouth, its obscene red lips frozen in a permanent snarl over jagged ridges of yellowing teeth. And the smell. Even in the freezing air, the smell of the thing is overpowering, a stench of rotting meat, raw sewage, worse.

I have no words to describe what I felt in that moment. I recall only my sense that the thing was an abomination—degenerate, appalling. And it was that as much as anything else, even more than my desire to protect Betty, that galvanized the violence that followed. The bat was an extension of my arms, my arms an extension of my instinctive hatred of the thing. I would have torn it to pieces with my bare hands if I'd had to. The monster—the monster was still on its knees when I brought Sugar Ray to bear, and I can still feel the force of the impact in my shoulders all these years later, still hear Betty screaming as I wind up for another swing.

But my brain has gone all staticky again, and her voice is as faint and thin as the voice of a midnight disc jockey blowing in over the AM waves from some faraway place like Memphis or Shreveport. What she's saying—or if she's saying anything at all—I cannot tell.

This Island Earth

It's just me and the saucer-man down here where the animals live, and the animal with the bat is winning.

The first blow catches the thing square under the chin, driving it back onto the frozen ruts of the bluff. The saucer-man never makes it to its feet again. With a second swing, Sugar Ray shatters the arm the creature has lifted in self-defense. Blind fury follows. Sugar Ray blasts the air out of its hard little paunch. Sugar Ray clubs its legs into kindling. And when the little monster emits a ghastly raptor shriek of terror, Sugar Ray pulverizes its mouth. But even that is not enough. Sugar Ray smashes the light out of the swollen orbs it has for eyes. Batters open those pulsing arteries so that green ichor spews into the air. Crushes the gigantic skull into shards—and keeps crushing, crushing, crushing, until nothing remains but a pulpy soup of tissue and brain matter and broken teeth. Only it's not Sugar Ray that's doing it, it's me, and I might still be there swinging that fucking bat if Betty hadn't wrenched it away and hurled it off into the slaughterhouse night.

I straighten up, the fear and rage and hatred dying away, going back to whatever dark womb fear and rage and hatred are born from. Now there is only silence, and in the silence the sound of Betty weeping. I turn to face her, blinking into the blaze of headlights.

They're all there, standing at her shoulders, these people I call my friends, dumb with the horror of what we have done. But what choice did we have? Adults are locked up inside their private worlds, ossified by misery and time. But still the aliens come, relentless in their determination to destroy us, and so it falls to the young to foil them, by whatever means they can. Sometimes you reverse the polarity of their engines and stew them like vegetables inside their saucers and sometimes you fry them with their own radioactive death rays, and sure, it's cleaner that way, or seems to be, at a safe remove. But a lesser brutality does not equate to mercy. Death is death, violence violence. There are more teenagers than you can count with blood on their hands, or green ichor, anyway.

And what I feel is a vast, roiling resentment.

INVASION OF THE SAUCER—MEN

"What?" I say. "What else could we have done?"—only I'm almost screaming, and I find that I too am weeping. I drag the back of my hand across my mouth to fling the snot away. "They were here to take our women. You think we had any choice?"

Barb alone speaks up to say that she agrees, and even she falls silent when Betty says, "They were friendly."

"Bullshit," I cry. "They were aliens. They were fucking aliens, don't you see?"

Betty's face is cold when she turns her gaze upon me. "It spoke to me," she says.

"And what did it say, huh? What could it possibly have said?"

"We come in peace," she replies, and then nobody says anything at all.

I don't suppose there's much more to tell after that. The rest is just details. We dragged the bodies into the woods to let the elements have their way, and as we walked back to our cars in the dawn just then beginning to pink the horizon, the saucer *whooshed* in low over the bluff and arced up into the deep purple sky where one by one the stars were winking out. We caravanned down Miller's Point Road in the first light of morning. I rode in the Bel Air alone.

I didn't play football the next year—I no longer had the heart for the game—so my free ride out of Hicksville evaporated. And while you would think our shared experience might have bound us together—and maybe it did at some deep unspoken level—those of us on the bluff that night drifted apart in the days and months that followed. In my heart I knew that we were heroes, and I kept faith with that belief, and keep it even now, but I had these dreams all the same—still do. In the dreams, Betty's screaming, only now I can make out what she's saying, and what she's saying is *No, please, stop!* And I take in at last what I had not let myself notice as I hurtled down that hill with Sugar Ray in hand. The other kids have engaged the aliens, but the little freaks aren't fighting back. In the dreams it's not a matter of saving the imperiled Earth. In the dreams it's a fucking massacre.

This Island Earth

Betty went missing the night we graduated—never said a word about it, just shook the dust of Hicksville off her feet and disappeared into the wide blue yonder. I missed her something fierce, but I'd been missing her for more than a year by then. When Arnie Wilson went off that fall to study physics at Penn State, I took up with Barbara, who was too poor to follow. We've been together ever since, Barb and I, but Betty always was my one true love, and Barbara knows it and it pains her.

Yakkety-yak, right?

This was all a long time ago, and the world I knew in those days is irretrievably gone.

But I'm still here, inching my way to paradise.

T HE FIRST ALIENS ARRIVED IN MILLEDGEVILLE, Ohio, when I was still in diapers. By the time I'd graduated into the frilly, pink dresses my mother put me in for elementary school, you saw them around occasionally, strolling down Main Street or picnicking by the bandshell in the park. They'd bought into a rundown neighborhood in the east end of town—primarily Polish and Estonian to that point, though once the aliens began picking up mortgages over there, most people just called it Bug Town. This was lazy thinking because the aliens didn't look anything like bugs, but what are you going to do?

I never really had much personal contact with them until their kids started showing up in my high-school classes. There was grumbling, of course. But who was going to tell a hulking seven-foot alien his kid couldn't come to school? And so I studied *Great Expectations* and Home Economics in the company of creatures not of this Earth. Which sounds more dramatic than it really was. We all got along well enough in class, even if we did keep to our own sides of the lunchroom.

This Island Earth

Which is where it might have ended if it hadn't been for my best friend, Joan Hayden.

The first thing you have to understand about Joan is that she had poor taste in boys. Everybody agreed. First there'd been Luke Jackson, a disaffected former jock who'd been kicked off the football team when he showed up at the Homecoming game half in the bag. After that, she'd taken up with a guy named Jimmy Ford, violating the unspoken divide between the kids in calculus and the ones in shop. That was about the time Joan got clumsy—started slipping in the shower and running into doors—so when she worked up the courage to send Jimmy packing, we all agreed that she was well shut of him.

Which brings us to Johnny Fabriano, where this story really gets underway. Johnny looked like a refugee from *The Wild Ones*—black leather jacket, motorcycle boots, and a greasy DA that looked like it hadn't been washed in a week. He'd dropped out of high school the day he'd turned sixteen and had spent the last five years hanging around Red's Billiards Parlor, cadging cigarettes and hustling pool. He was a dead shot, and, rumor had it, he'd won his car in a hotly contested game of Eight Ball with a gearhead from Brookton. The car itself was the envy of every would-be greaser in town—a chopped '49 Mercury coupé painted a glossy midnight purple with stylized tongues of yellow and red flame licking at the hood and fenders.

Joan had already gotten a reputation for being fast—undeserved, I have to put in, and if anyone knew, I did, because Joan confided everything in me. She'd moved in next door when we were both in second grade, and we'd been joined at the hip ever since, sharing every joy and affliction, from scraped knees to first periods, which when Joan's made its debut, I remember how jealous I was—until mine happened along two months later, inflicting such misery upon me that I have never envied anyone anything ever since, or almost never, anyway.

Joan had grown up in a Pentecostal church, daughter to a strict disciplinarian who saw himself as the earthly agent of the Lord. And

TEENAGERS FROM OUTER SPACE

if at one level Joan rejected all that, at another level she still believed. You never really escape your childhood training, I guess, and it was this division in Joan's personality that ultimately caused all the trouble. For while Johnny Fabriano was a perfect candidate to give her father an apoplexy, he was also a young man with an agenda of his own.

You see where this is going, of course, and it's not a happy place. But when the alien got involved, his good intentions only made everything worse. Good intentions usually do.

My name is Nancy Miller, by the way, and it's nice to meet you, I'm sure. If you haven't already figured it out, this story isn't really mine to tell, but my mother always called me Chatty Cathy, so I suppose it's only natural that it should fall to me in the end. And it's important that you understand that I wasn't always on the scene. Much of what follows is reconstructed from second-hand reports with all the bias and self-interest inherent in such accounts. In short, these are the facts as I understand them. If you want the truth, you'll have to sort it out for yourself. You always do, I guess.

So cast me in a supporting role: plain-faced confidante and collaborator to the beautiful lead. Joan really *was* beautiful, too, which is to say blonde and buxom in the slightly zaftig mold then in fashion. She inspired plenty of interest among the boys at Milledgeville High, but as I've already said, she never returned the affections of the boys who might have brought her happiness, if happiness was even an option for her, and I think it probably wasn't.

Certainly it wasn't with Johnny Fabriano. Like I said, he had an agenda of his own, and if, on Joan's part, he was calculated to infuriate her father, then there's some small irony that had it not been for her father they might never have met in the first place. Sometimes just stopping for gas can change the entire course of your life, and that's exactly what happened when her father decided to swing their old Caddy into Staley's Gulf station one September Sunday after church.

THIS ISLAND EARTH

Gas stations were full service back then—the days of pumping your own fuel were still decades away—and while Mr. Staley fussed with the Caddy's tire pressure, Johnny's '49 Merc roared up to the neighboring pump. Both Joan and her father knew the car, of course—who hadn't seen it around town?—and Joan at least knew its driver by reputation. What she didn't know was what a sweet smile Johnny had. But he did, I can vouch for that myself, and when he turned his head to look at Joan, he passed one to her, like a gift.

Maybe it would have ended there, a shared smile in a gas station parking lot, but Joan's father couldn't help weighing in on the matter. "What a cheap hood," he said, pouring into those two words all the disdain that only those certain of their place in Heaven can summon.

That was enough for Joan, of course. As her father wheeled the car out into the street she smiled back at Johnny.

When she told me about it that night, she was almost incandescent with excitement, so I wasn't surprised when she contrived an excuse to walk by Red's Billiards Parlor after school the next day. Johnny's car was parked at the curb outside and just as we came abreast of the place—I could already see Joan calculating her odds of coaxing me inside—who should appear in the door but Johnny himself, with a cigarette tucked behind his ear and a toothpick in his mouth.

He did a double-take, looked Joan up and down, and granted her another smile. It was like the sun coming out from behind a cloud, that smile. I practically melted myself, and he didn't even know I was there.

"Gas station girl," he said, and Joan said, "I'm surprised you remember."

"Remember?" he said. "How could I forget?"

He did some dexterous little trick with his tongue and passed the toothpick from one side of his mouth to the other. "You got a name, Gas Station Girl?"

So she told him her name, and then she said, "You're Johnny Fabriano. I know you."

You could see it pleased him, her knowing his name like that. The way they were looking at each other, it could only go one way, and nowhere good, so I stepped in front of her and held out my hand, hoping to forestall the inevitable. "I'm Nancy," I said.

He ignored the hand and dipped his chin to acknowledge me. "How you doing, Nancy," he said, and then, taking me by the shoulders, he steered me gently to the side. "Where you girls heading?" he asked, but it was really Joan he was speaking to.

"Just walking."

"Not that way. Not unless you're planning to pay Bug Town a visit." Which was true. We'd already reached the end of the line unless we wanted to stop in for drinks at some dive with sawdust on the floor and "Nobody's Lonesome for Me" on the jukebox. Bug Town lay beyond, and Bug Town was forbidden territory. It had been abandoned to the aliens, and those who *did* work up the spit to visit wouldn't say much except that it was "catching strange." It was the "catching" part of that phrase that concerned our parents, for those who spent much time in Bug Town often became odd themselves. They got a faraway look in their eyes and drifted into silence, as if they were listening to some distant music that no one else could hear. Once in a while you heard about some daring kid making a midnight run through the place, tires screeching, but details were mighty slim on the ground—it was always a friend of a friend of a friend, no one you ever knew—so I figured such afterhours adventures for empty boasts. In short, the aliens walked among us, but we did not walk among the aliens. Which is why, when Johnny asked if we were planning an excursion of our own, I was shocked when Joan shrugged and said, "Sure we are."

Johnny, on the other hand, didn't blink an eye. "Maybe you'd like a ride instead."

"We'll walk," I said, taking Joan's elbow. "Home."

I was wasting my breath.

"Sounds like fun to me," Joan said, prying my fingers loose, and I knew then that it was a lost cause. There was the car, there was the smile, and there was the "cheap hood" himself. Her father already loathed him. So when she said, "You coming, Nance?" I said the only thing I could in response:

"No, Joan, and you shouldn't go either."

Like I said, wasting my breath.

A minute later, Johnny keyed the Merc's engine to life and they roared off down Main Street. This time Joan really had gone too far, I thought as I walked home alone—and at the time I had no idea just how far she'd gone.

They really did go all the way to Bug Town, though I wouldn't learn that until later that night, long after the scene that unfolded at the Haydens' when she got home. Any sane girl would have had Johnny drop her off a couple of blocks from her house and manufactured some plausible excuse for her tardiness—an extra hour at the library, a study session that had run too long. Not Joan. That wouldn't have created the intended effect. I was watching from my open bedroom window—the September air still had the glow of summer—when the Merc rumbled up to the curb. Joan's father was waiting at the door. He couldn't have been home long himself. He hadn't even loosened his tie. He was an insurance salesman, though why a man so devoted to the rewards of the afterlife should take such an interest in the perils of this one, I never could understand. But he certainly took an interest in the perils Johnny Fabriano posed to his daughter's eternal soul.

The Merc thundered away before Joan was halfway up the sidewalk. By the time she reached the front porch, the shouting had begun. It continued for the next hour or so, and while I couldn't make out the words, it didn't take a genius to figure out the tenor of the back and forth between Joan and her father. Her mother was silent, of course. She knew her place in the Biblical hierarchy of the home. Joan, however—well, her father's fury only goaded her to greater histrionics. The entire thing culminated in slammed doors.

He'd locked her into her room, of course. He always did.

It wasn't until after my own dinner that I worked up the courage to call.

"Joan isn't available, Nancy," her father told me, and I could hear the suppressed fury in his voice.

"Thank you, Mr. Hayden," I said. "I guess I'll catch her in school—" But I never got to finish the phrase.

"How much do you know about this Johnny Fabriano, Nancy?" he said.

"Not much, sir."

"Were you with Joan this afternoon?"

I hesitated a moment too long.

"Well, then," he said. "I'm very disappointed in you, Nancy. In fact, I'd like to speak with your father, if he's available."

He was. My mother shook her head in commiseration when I called him over, and my father winked when he took the phone. He listened patiently to Mr. Hayden and made all the right noises in return, but when he finished the conversation, I didn't get much of a scolding. My father wasn't the scolding type, and besides we attended the Disciples of Christ Church, which was about as liberal as you could get in Milledgeville, Ohio, in 1955. He bought his insurance from Mr. Hayden, but he didn't have much in the way of personal respect for him.

"Just be a good friend to her, Nance," he said. "God knows she needs one, living in that house."

Around 1:00 a.m., Joan woke me with a handful of pebbles at my window. This came as no surprise. Sneaking out was routine business to Joan. Just shimmy down the big oak tree outside her window, and clamber back up it whenever she'd accomplished whatever mischief she had to accomplish.

"So what's he like?" I whispered the minute I had her installed in my bedroom, and when she responded, "Dreamy, Nance. He's just dreamy," my heart fell. "Dreamy" was not good. "Dreamy" had the potential for disaster. But what could I do? Discouraging her would merely encourage her, and encouraging her would do the same. It was an impossible hand to play, and I opted then, as I had opted so many times in the past, not to play it at all. I opted for neutrality. It was as close as I could come to fulfilling my father's injunction to be a good friend to Joan.

So what I said was, "Dreamy?"

With conviction: "Dreamy. He's not like other boys, Nancy. He's not like you think."

"What do you mean?"

"Nobody understands him. Everybody thinks he's some—cheap hood"—this last she practically spat—"but he's not at all. Why, did you know he takes care of his mother? His father's dead, and she's not well, and he does just everything for her, and nobody understands what a good heart he has. And he's so gentle and soft-spoken and he wants to know all about me. He's really interested in me, not just in, you know—" She broke off, blushing.

Sure, that's what *you* think, I didn't say. What *I* thought was that Johnny was just smoother than the usual high-school lothario who tried to get his hand—or worse—up Joan's skirt. He was twenty-one. He knew how to play the long game. Like I said, he had an agenda of his own. Have you ever known a man who didn't?

"Did you kiss him?"

"Just once. Right before we pulled up to the house. His lips are so soft. You wouldn't think that, the way he looks, would you?"

I wouldn't. But I didn't say that, either. Instead I asked where they had gone.

Joan looked down. She was quiet for a long time, and when she met my gaze at last, I saw that she was afraid. "We went to Bug Town," she said.

Which brings me back to the aliens—the bugs, as people called them, though as I said at the beginning of this story, that was just lazy thinking, because they didn't really look anything like bugs. And maybe their appearance isn't all you're curious about. Maybe you want to know where they came from and why and what they planned to do here.

But I don't have answers to any of that.

They just started drifting into town by twos and threes and buying up the decaying houses over in the east end. Who can say why? They were aliens, after all, and their motives were as inscrutable as Joan's were self-evident.

Their appearance, on the other hand—there was no mystery about that. They were monstrous things to look at: olive-green seven-foot giants, their squarish heads bifurcated by a big, ropy artery that clove their skulls into disproportionate lobes. It wound down between their lidless, black eyes—shark black, and as empty of expression—and split into frills of bony, close-knit flesh that almost looked like baleen. Their mouths, nestled between those frills, were the most disturbing feature of all: three slavering flaps of tissue that dilated open to reveal jagged, yellow teeth. All this set atop a massive torso armored in bone, with thick arms and legs, and large, three-taloned hands.

And strong.

My freshman year, the first year the aliens showed up at Milledgeville High, Coach Pack recruited three or four of them for the football team. Where he found uniforms to fit them, I have no idea. Perhaps he had them custom made. In any case, the aliens were lethally effective on the gridiron, and we would win the state championship two years running, despite the virulent protests of our rivals. Yet the aliens—I won't call them bugs—were essentially gentle creatures, even shy. They kept to themselves and they listened attentively to our teachers. They contributed to class in moist, lisping whispers. They took copious notes.

Their handwriting was beautiful.

But Bug Town? I knew nothing about Bug Town that I haven't already told you. I was as curious as anybody else about the place—but not curious enough to risk "catching strange," so part of me stood in admiration of Joan for daring to go there in the first place. Another part was furious with her, knowing how much she'd risked to defy her father and her father's god.

THIS ISLAND EARTH

But whatever her motivations, Joan had little to say about Bug Town.

When I asked her about it, her gaze grew distant, as though she were looking straight through me to some faraway horizon, and when she answered me, her voice was a hollow whisper. I knew then that she'd been touched by strangeness, but I did not yet perceive how deep the wound ran or how unbearable its consequences would be—not merely for her and Johnny Fabriano, but for us all.

I began to get an inkling of that—but nothing more—the next day at school.

There were two aliens in our first-period English class. I can't tell you their real names. I can't reproduce their slobbery, whistling language, and certainly not on the page. But when the aliens moved to Milledgeville, they'd taken human names, as well. So you'd see "Jim" at the hardware store, sighting down two-by-fours to make sure they hadn't warped, or "Susan" at the A&P, inquiring about the freshness of the tomatoes. None of them had quite mastered English pronunciation—I expect their weird, dilating mouths precluded mastery—but they could make themselves understood well enough to get along. "Thim" got unbowed two-by-fours, "Thuthan" fresh tomatoes. And the two aliens in our English class, "Eloieth" (Eloise) and "Tham" (Sam—also the star fullback for the Millidgeville Bears), got straight A's. The semester wasn't even two weeks old and they'd already displaced me as Mrs. Guest's favorite student.

Eloieth and Tham—yes I'm going to call them that, not to mock them, but to keep their intrinsic strangeness front and center—were the kind of students who read their assignments days in advance, sat in the front row, and shot their talons up the minute Mrs. Guest asked a question. But Mrs. Guest didn't always call on the kids with their hands up. She had an eye for the doodler and the daydreamer, and just as you were drifting off into some pleasant fantasy or other, she'd bludgeon you with a question—which is what happened to Joan that morning. This in itself wasn't surprising. Joan was an indifferent student at best, if only because her father expected more of her, and she was an inveterate daydreamer. But when Mrs. Guest fired that morning's question in her direction, Joan seemed to have drifted not into some idle fancy, but into a deep hypnotic state.

She didn't respond, didn't so much as stir.

Only when Mrs. Guest repeated the question—pointedly, and at volume—did Joan look up, a puzzled look on her face. "I'm sorry, Mrs. Guest."

"What are you sorry for, Miss Hayden?"

"I didn't hear you, that's all. If you could repeat the question, maybe..." Joan trailed off into silence.

"Yes, why don't I repeat myself? Surely I have nothing better to do. In stanza nine, Keats writes—

And there she lulled me asleep,
And there I dream'd—Ah! woe betide!
The latest dream I ever dreamed
On the cold hill's side.

What do you think he means, Miss Hayden?"

Miss Hayden had no reply on the matter of meaning. The moment stretched. You could hear nothing but the tick of the round schoolroom clock on the wall.

"Miss Hayden?"

But once again, Joan had drifted off.

Tham made some weird whistling sound deep in his throat.

"Please, Sam," Mrs. Guest said. "I think we're all expecting to hear from Miss Hayden."

Silence. People stared at their desktops. Joan, however, seemed unfazed. She'd propped her elbow on her desk, her chin on the heel of her hand.

"Perhaps you need to see the nurse, Miss Hayden?"

A subdued ripple of nervous laughter greeted this not-very-funny witticism. Mrs. Guest silenced it with a glare.

This Island Earth

"Miss Hayden—" she began, but Tham interrupted her, emitting a long, damp series of clicks and whistles. Joan visibly shook herself in response, and a strange expression—half-wonder, half-fear—crossed her face. I saw this, I say; I did not imagine it. She shook herself in response and met Mrs. Guest's gaze with an almost physical force. Mrs. Guest shuddered and recoiled. This, too, I saw; this, too, I did not imagine.

"The knight has been lulled into sleep, Mrs. Guest," Joan said, firmly, as you might speak to a disobedient child. "He has been enchanted into nightmare by a fairy in the guise of a beautiful woman, and though he may wake upon the cold hill's side, he shall never truly wake again, because one does not wake from a fairy's enchantment."

Eloieth let out a long mournful whistle when Joan finished, and then she and Tham both turned away. Silence gripped the classroom. Mrs. Guest swallowed. "I think that's enough for today," she said. "If you'll turn to page 74 and answer the discussion questions, we'll take up 'Ode on a Grecian Urn' tomorrow"—and she retreated to her desk and sat very still and pale until the bell rang for second period.

I didn't see Joan for the rest of the day—English was the only class we had together—but when the final bell rang I gathered my books and ran to meet her for the walk home. She wasn't waiting for me at the picnic tables on the east side of campus—and she'd been waiting there every day as long as we'd been in high school. I didn't stick around. I knew she wouldn't be coming. I knew what had happened even before I really knew it, if that makes sense, so I wasn't surprised when I came around the building and saw her sliding into Johnny's Merc. I called out to her, but she didn't wait. She didn't even turn around.

The shouting match next door went on longer than usual that evening, and though I stayed awake until well after midnight, Joan never showed up at my window. I didn't see her until we walked to school the next morning—and then only briefly, because we hadn't gone a block before Johnny's Merc rolled up to the sidewalk and he reached over to crank down the window.

"Anybody want a ride to school?" he asked.

"I do," Joan said brightly, opening the door. The interior of the car gleamed, every bit as glossy as the exterior—the lavender dash, the chrome-framed gauges on the instrument panel. The radio was pumping out Chuck Berry, "Maybellene." Johnny flashed that reckless grin at Joan. I might as well have been wallpaper. So when Johnny said, "Coming, Nancy?" I shook my head and turned away.

"I'll walk."

"Suit yourself," Johnny said, and Joan wound up the window as they pulled away from the curb. She hadn't even said good-bye.

I put my head down, and hurried on alone.

By the time we'd moved on to *Idylls of the King* in Mrs. Guest's class—we were reading the part where Vivien imprisons Merlin in the tree—that faraway look in Joan's eyes had faded. There were no more weird incidents with Tham. And she had re-dedicated herself to infuriating her father by dating Johnny Fabriano.

That was all anyone could talk about. Five years after his premature departure from high school, tales of Johnny's exploits lingered. Among other things, he was said to have raided the midnight school to steal a carbon copy of Mr. Dunnigan's chem final; fought a legendary bruiser named Otis (now serving time in the state pen) to a blood-spitting draw; and invited Master Sergeant Ashton, the Junior ROTC teacher, who had stormed the beach at Okinawa, to go fuck himself. So every eye was upon her when Joan stepped out of Johnny's flame-bedizened ride. Mr. Hayden soon put a stop to that—he started driving her to school himself—but I knew that Joan was still seeing Johnny on the sly. More than once I woke to the guttural rumble of his car in a neighboring street, and knew that she'd availed herself of her arboreal exit.

This Island Earth

She certainly wasn't using it to visit me, so I didn't see much of Joan for a while. I walked to school and back alone, we couldn't talk during English, and while she still ate lunch at our table, half a dozen other girls did, too. It was hardly the place for confidences. Aside from a chance encounter in the girls' bathroom—and even that was fleeting—we might have been little more than casual acquaintances.

"Do you still think about it?" I asked as we stood in front of the rusty mirrors.

"Think about what?" she said.

"Bug Town."

She didn't answer right away. When she did, she said, "Sometimes it seems like it's the *only* thing I can think about."

Then a gaggle of chattery sophomores burst through the door.

Of course, Joan wasn't the only point of interest that fall. As October deepened, the town turned its attention to high school football. Tham was enjoying a record-breaking season, sometimes piling up more than two hundred yards a game, and his quarterback, an alien kid named Theven (Steven) who ran a little on the small side at 6'10", was throwing the ball with the kind of pinpoint accuracy you didn't usually see outside the NFL. The Bears often bested their opponents by forty points or more, and they could have doubled those numbers if Coach Pack hadn't routinely pulled Tham and Theven out of the game at halftime. It didn't seem sporting to keep running up the score, he told the *Milledgeville Courier*.

The aliens attended every game. The adults kept to sections C and D, but their kids stood in the spirit section and stomped in enthusiasm, occasionally ramming a taloned foot right through the metal risers. And you often ran into them at the concession stand. They were especially fond of chili dogs, ordering them by the dozen—with mustard and onions—and sucking them whole into those flappy mouths, like sucking ping-pong balls into the nozzle of a vacuum cleaner. Their table manners were generally atrocious, though I always assumed that by their own standards they were probably perfectly acceptable. They wore form-fitting knee-length pants—

perhaps out of deference to human sensibilities, perhaps not—but otherwise went naked and barefoot.

Their first few days at Milledgeville High they were constantly being sent home for violating the dress code. But when a delegation of alien parents arrived to ask that the principal exempt their children, he capitulated—maybe because he was sitting across his desk from a party of large, green monsters from outer space, and maybe because modesty wasn't really an issue since no one could tell the male and female aliens apart except by their human names, and even then, who could really say for sure? Maybe they had three sexes, or six, or none at all. They were a weird bunch, taken all together. They were aliens.

But they sure had improved Milledgeville's lousy football team. The Homecoming game—the usual rout—ended around eight. The dance got underway an hour later. Everybody boogied to "Gum Drop," the aliens in a herky-jerky rhythm that seemed to have nothing to do with that of the song, the humans (most of them) on beat; but when the DJ spun "Take Me Back," the alien kids surrendered the floor to their human counterparts. I heard this all second-hand, of course. I wasn't there—plain old Nancy had no date—just as I wasn't there to see what happened in the parking lot outside. I heard Joan's account that night, and I would later hear Johnny Fabriano's version of events. But I never knew Joan to lie, so I'm confident of that part of the story. My understanding of Tham's motives, on the other hand—to the extent that he had motives and they can be understood—is the product of pure conjecture, and it may be that I'm too rooted in a human perspective to speculate with any accuracy.

What I know for sure is that Joan had been forbidden to attend both the game and the dance. But Joan was not going to be denied the night out. She couldn't attend the game. Some Pentecostal ally of her father would betray her. And she couldn't attend the dance because the chaperones wouldn't admit someone Johnny's age (and especially not Johnny himself). But she could make it a special night, and when she slipped out the window around 8:30 that's just what she intended to do. Apparently Johnny had the same idea. His car was idling a block over, and when she slid in beside him, he had a corsage waiting. They were going to celebrate Homecoming on their own, he said, and if his hand lingered when he pinned the flower to her breast she attributed it to his clumsy fingers.

Johnny'd also bought a couple of bottles of sweet wine. Joan had never tasted the stuff, but she wasn't going to decline another opportunity to defy her father. Besides, it turned out she liked the giddy feeling it gave her, the devil-may-care release from the inhibitions that her Pentecostal childhood had instilled within her. She was pleasantly buzzed by the time they pulled into the school parking lot—a destination Joan had insisted on over Johnny's objections. "Let's go to the dance," she'd said, giggling, and when Johnny pointed out that they couldn't go to the dance, she leaned over and planted a lingering kiss on the tender spot just behind his ear. "We can get close," she whispered, an enticingly ambiguous statement, which is how they wound up parked in the darkest corner of the high-school parking lot. The radio was playing the Four Aces, "Melody of Love," when Johnny leaned in to kiss her, and Joan later told me how she remembered the music and the taste of the sweet wine on his lips. It wasn't the first time they had kissed, but it was the first time it really seemed to matter, and she surrendered herself to it.

Johnny slid one hand up Joan's ribs to caress her breast. When she didn't protest, when indeed she seemed to lean into him, he let the other hand drift down to push its way between her thighs.

This wasn't what Joan wanted. It never had been. But Johnny'd been intending to claim this prize for more than a month now, so when Joan protested, murmuring, "No, Johnny," he simply ignored her. He was tugging at her panties when she said it again—

"No, Johnny!"

—and by the time she said it a third time, he'd nearly wormed a finger inside them.

Joan gasped. She tried to thrust Johnny away, but he pushed her back against the seat, bearing down with all his weight. He held her there, panting, and that's when she realized he was fumbling with the buttons on his jeans. That's when she began to scream in earnest.

At the far end of the parking lot, inside the gym, the DJ had just dropped the needle on "See You Later, Alligator." The teenagers from outer space took the floor. Their human peers joined them. The chaperones glanced at their watches—they would be shutting the party down at eleven—and looked out over the dance floor. Nobody was listening for screams from the parking lot, and if they had been, they wouldn't have heard anything over the racket of Bill Haley & His Comets.

Johnny had managed to undo his pants by then.

Joan screamed louder.

And then—this is the part that puzzles me, this the reason that I wish he'd given me his point of view—Tham appeared in the shadows. I still wonder what he was doing out there. None of the aliens smoked, so he hadn't stepped out to sneak a butt. Nor did they drink, so he wasn't outside to sneak one of those either. And he certainly wasn't walking home—Bug Town lay in the opposite direction. Yet there Tham was, and what I keep thinking about, even now, is that time in English when he whistled Joan out of her stupor. Had he communicated the answer to Mrs. Guest's question, as well? It certainly wasn't the kind of answer Joan would have provided on her own, after all. Which makes me wonder if there might have been some connection between them, some conduit for alien...telepathy, for lack of a better word, that had been laid down during Joan's visit to Bug Town. What I wonder is if he knew that Joan was in distress and came to rescue her.

Good intentions, right? And all the damage they can do.

But the damage didn't come till later. In that moment, there in the dark parking lot, those good intentions paid off in a big way. I'm forever thankful to Tham for what he did next. Joan later told me that she was still fighting, still clawing, still screaming. But Johnny was on the verge of overpowering her. He'd just clamped a hand over her mouth to shut her up when Tham's three massive talons, eight inches each, punctured the roof of Johnny's beloved '49 Merc where it curved down to meet the windshield. Johnny cursed and scrambled back against the steering wheel, tugging at his trousers. Joan shoved herself in the other direction and slammed up against the door.

Tham, meanwhile had closed his grip around the metal edge of the roof. He yanked it once, and then a second time, and then—it was like he'd taken hold of the pull-tab on a can of peaches—he just peeled back the top of that Merc and flung it to the pavement. In the crashing instant that followed, Joan told me that she was aware of only three things: Johnny screaming in fury; the pale radiance of the moon filling up the car like water; and the monstrous silhouette of Tham's massive, asymmetrical head peering down at her against a field of stars. She reacted instinctively, shrieking as Tham reached inside the passenger cabin, fished her out, and set her gently on her feet beside the car. Johnny, meanwhile, had exited the driver's side door, the tire iron he kept under the seat in hand. What he saw as he rounded the hood—a seven-foot-tall monster wearing knee-length trousers and a Milledgeville High letter jacket—stopped him cold. The tire iron clanged to the pavement. He stumbled, grappling for the hood of the car to hold himself upright.

By this time Joan had stopped screaming.

In the stillness, she could hear the thump of "Love Bug" from the high-school gym.

Joan reached up and took one of Tham's long talons in her hand.

"This isn't over!" Johnny yelled as they turned away. "This isn't over, you bitch, you hear me!"—but Joan didn't bother looking back. She'd never felt safer in her life. Tham walked her home. Somewhere along the way she unpinned Johnny's crushed corsage and cast it into the shadows beside the sidewalk. And when they reached her house, she marched straight up the walk and rang the bell. Mr. Hayden staggered back into the living room when he opened the door and saw his daughter standing there hand-in-hand with a towering alien from outer space.

"Hello, Daddy," she said sweetly. "I want you to meet my boyfriend—Sam."

Whether Tham thought he was her boyfriend or not is also a matter of conjecture. But from that night on, there was *something* between them, and the consequences of that relationship would eventually ripple outward to engulf us all. But that was later.

The immediate consequences were more predictable.

Mrs. Hayden, who'd walked to the door behind her husband, screamed. And when Mr. Hayden started spewing his typical self-righteous bilge, Joan ignored him. She pushed past him, leading Tham by the talon, and introduced him to her mother. "Nithe to meet you Mthth. Hayden," Tham said, flecking her with viscous extraterrestrial spittle. When Mrs. Hayden just blanched by way of reply, her eyes bulging, Joan took him to the kitchen, poured them both a glass of milk, and served up a platter of her mother's home-made chocolate-chip cookies. They chatted for fifteen minutes—innocuous gossip about schoolmates and teachers—before Tham took his leave. On his way out, he extended his talons to Joan's father (predictably, Mr. Hayden refused to shake) and nodded to her mother. He probably would have smiled if he could have.

"I'm spending the night with Nancy," Joan said, escorting Tham out to the porch, where she kissed him good night.

His kisses were really slobbery, she told me later, and his bony frills posed a considerable challenge. Plus, he ate the cookies by sucking them down whole and he slurped his milk.

Otherwise, Tham was pretty close to perfect.

Mr. Hayden showed up at our front door first thing in the morning, demanding that his daughter come home. My father invited him in and left the two of them alone to talk things out, but talking soon led to bellowing and bellowing to the unmistakable sound of a blow.

This Island Earth

When my father walked back into the room, Joan had one hand to her cheek, but she wasn't crying. She told me later that she was done crying over that man, and as it turned out she was, too. My father quietly suggested that Mr. Hayden might want to go home. Joan was welcome to stay with us until everyone had calmed down, he said.

Mr. Hayden swallowed, but he didn't raise his voice. Mr. Hayden wasn't much more than a bully, and bullies are generally hollow at heart, I think, terrified that the world won't bend to their will. My father certainly wasn't bending. He simply opened the door for Mr. Hayden, who stepped outside. He turned back at the top of the porch steps, seething with humiliation and resentment. His face was white with fury, his fists clenched impotently at his sides.

"I'll have the police here, Dave," he said. "I'll have my daughter home."

"When they arrive I'll be sure to show them that bruise on her face," my father said. "Now get off my porch."

Mr. Hayden walked down the steps and across the yard without looking back. The police never came, though, which is how Joan ended up spending the weekend with us. Come Monday, the bruise had faded to a dull yellow. You had to look close to know it was there at all, and a little blush took care of that. We walked to school together in the bright October morning, chatting amiably about homework and gossiping about the girls at our lunch table. The question of when she would go home did come up in passing ("Never," she said, and she never did). The question of Tham did not.

When the bell rang for first period—we'd moved on to "Goblin Market"—Joan merely smiled at him as she slipped into her desk, and I let myself believe that the "boyfriend" nonsense had passed. Come lunch, I learned that I was wrong.

Joan collected her food and bypassed our table without a word. As she marched toward the corner where the aliens ate, the room gradually grew silent. By the time Tham scooted over to make a place for her at his table, the only sound was the occasional clank of a pot in the kitchen—and then even that stopped, as the staff gathered at the serving window, jaws agape. Joan pulled the whole thing off beautifully, I have to give her that. She never let on that she noticed the silence or the eyes upon her. She just smiled up at Tham and began to eat.

When the final bell rang that afternoon and I walked out to the picnic tables, Joan was waiting. So was Tham. We walked home in companionable silence. Tham carried Joan's books and shortened his stride periodically so that we could keep up. I half-expected to see Johnny's mutilated car idling at some intersection along the way, but if he was there, he hid himself well.

When we reached the house, Joan offered Tham a glass of my mother's lemonade—we'd been neighbors and best friends for so long that she'd practically become a sister, helping herself to whatever she wanted (a privilege I was denied at the Haydens'). Tham declined—

"Thankth, but I thould go," he said.

—and Joan kissed him good-bye right there on the front porch. *She* was on the front porch, anyway. He stood below, to bring their faces into relative proximity. Then he was gone, striding off down the sidewalk while Joan mopped the alien drool off her face with a kitchen towel. Joan's mom watched from her kitchen window. My mom watched, too. I caught the telltale twitch of the living-room curtain from the corner of my eye. But she didn't say a word when we came in, just smiled and offered us some left-over lemon-meringue pie.

Joan and I were puzzling over algebra problems in my room when the phone rang. My mom stuck her head in the door.

"Joan, your mother wants to speak with you."

"I don't have anything to say to her."

"Joan, please, you should—"

Joan looked up. When she spoke she was neither angry nor rude, just matter of fact in a way that brooked no argument. "I'm sorry, Mrs. Miller. We don't have anything to say to each other now. If you want me to leave—"

THIS ISLAND EARTH

"Of course, I don't want you to leave. You're always welcome here, Joan."

Mom gave me a look of mute appeal. But what could I do?

And then Joan said, "Thank you, Mrs. Miller," and turned back to her homework.

But she couldn't stay. We all knew that. Sooner or later—probably sooner—Mr. Hayden really *would* call the police, and in those days there weren't a lot of legal avenues open to a sixteen-year-old girl in conflict with her parents—even if that conflict had culminated in physical abuse. There was much to love about 1955, but like our own or any era, it was anything but perfect. My parents really would have welcomed Joan into our home for the long term. I believe that. But the forces arrayed against them were formidable.

That's what my father said when he came up to my room before dinner.

So I wasn't entirely surprised when Joan didn't come back to my house after school the next day. The problem was, she didn't go home either.

The next day Joan went to Bug Town.

She continued to come to school for a few more days, but she became increasingly distant. She no longer turned in homework, and in class she spent most of her time gazing off into the middle distance, staring at things none of us could see. By the end of the week, she was barely speaking at all. But I don't think I realized how entirely lost to us she had become until I gathered my courage to walk across the lunchroom myself on Friday afternoon. I understood then what strength and courage that must have taken on her part. My footsteps echoed in the silence. I could feel the combined gaze of my peers like a leaden cloak upon my shoulders.

The aliens scooted aside so that I could set my tray down across from her.

"Hi, Joan," I said.

She looked up at me and smiled, and I recognized the smile. It was

TEENAGERS FROM OUTER SPACE

her old, familiar, halfway crooked smile. "Hey, Nance," she said as she might have said if we'd passed in the hall or she'd picked up the phone to find me on the line. It was that natural and spontaneous, and for a moment, looking at her, I felt like nothing had changed. I think that was the most surprising thing. I expected her to be utterly transformed, tuned to a different wavelength, catching strange. And while there was plenty of that there, she was also just Joan, the Joan I loved and remembered, and I missed her.

"When are you coming home, Joan?"

"I'm not."

I didn't want to be rude, so I glanced nervously at the towering alien kids sitting around us, patiently sucking down the school's indifferent fish sticks and fries, before I leaned forward to whisper, as if they wouldn't hear, "But, Joan, they're aliens!"

Joan surveyed the lunchroom. She looked at Luke Jackson, the washed-up jock who'd cared more about booze than he'd cared about her. She looked at Jimmy Ford, who, like her father, had been a bit free with his fists. And if Johnny Fabriano had been there, she would have looked at him, too, I'm sure. She looked at them both, and then she turned back to me with a Mona Lisa smile and said, "No worries, Nance. I'm used to it."

I looked down at my own tray of soggy fish sticks and fries. Joan reached out and put her hand over mine where it lay upon the table. "Bug Town is beautiful, Nance," she said, and a wave of sorrow washed through me. "Come with me," she said. "We can be free."

But she was wrong about that. Mostly, anyway.

Johnny showed up at my doorstep Saturday around six. I heard the unmistakable rumble of the Merc's engine as he pulled up to the curb, and when my father—over my objections—sent me to the door to meet him, I saw the car for myself. It might have been a convertible fresh off the assembly line, that's how neatly the thing had been done, but the car had been mutilated all the same. Shorn of its roof, with its lavender dash laid bare to the October sky and those ridiculous flames licking at the hood and fenders, it had been exposed as a broken toy, the empty vanity of a man who was more boy than man. He didn't even measure up to the title Mr. Hayden had ascribed him. Johnny Fabriano was no cheap hood. No, Johnny Fabriano was a selfish child whose experience of the world didn't extend much beyond Red's Billiards Parlor, and as he walked up the sidewalk to meet me, he seemed every bit as maimed as his car, stripped of whatever aura of menace he had once possessed, like a kid playing dress-up in his brother's leather jacket and motorcycle boots—a kid who hadn't slept in a week, pale and tired (drawn, my mother would have said) with his trademark Duck's Ass in disarray.

"How's your mother?" I asked, before he could even start up the stairs.

"My mother?"

"Yeah. You know your mother. You told Joan about her. How's she doing?"

Johnny hesitated. "She's fine," he said. "I—"

"You what? Hold her hand when she's hurting? Buy her medicine? What?"

Johnny didn't reply.

I sat down on the top step. "I don't doubt that you live with your mother, but I figure the care-taking probably goes in the other direction. She probably gives you spending money. After all, you can't make that much shooting pool." I leaned forward, crossing my arms around my knees. "This is your fault, Johnny. Joan told me what happened in the car."

"Nothing happened," he said. "We were just sitting there talking, and this monster, I don't even know where he comes from, he's just there all of a sudden, and he tears the lid right off the top of my car like that."

"The monster's name is Sam."

"I don't care what his name is. He's a bug, isn't he?" Johnny shrugged. "Maybe he was jealous, or something. Who knows what bugs think. I tried to save her, Nance. I came at him with a tire iron, but he was too quick. He just snatched her up and carried her off into the night."

And maybe he believed this. Maybe he thought he was innocent, courageous, whatever. Maybe he'd convinced himself that his lie was true. People do it all the time. People want to be blameless. People want to be brave.

Still, I couldn't help laughing—a bitter, joyless laugh. "Not the way I heard it, Johnny. You're lucky he didn't wrap that tire iron around your neck." I stood, brushing off my skirt. "This is your fault. You're the one that tried to rape her." He rocked back a little at that, like he'd taken a punch. "You're lucky he didn't kill you. I wish he had. I don't have anything else to say to you."

I was halfway to the door, when he said, "I'm going to Bug Town, Nancy. I'm going to go get her."

I kept my back to him. "Let Mr. Hayden handle it."

Johnny snorted. "That old bastard's not going to do anything."

He was right, of course. Mr. Hayden was done with Joan. She'd spent a week away from home by then—nights a man of his mind could interpret in only one way. As far as he was concerned, Joan had sacrificed her virtue—and when it came to women, virtue was all that mattered. Joan had shamed him, and if there was anything Frank Hayden would not abide, it was being shamed. She might as well have been dead.

"And what are you going to do with her, bring her home?"

"No, Nancy," he said. "You are."

And God help me, I turned around.

I missed her, that's all. She'd been my closest friend—my only real friend—for almost a decade, and I didn't know how I was going to go on without her. Aside from my parents, Joan was the only person I had ever loved. And so, without even talking to my father, I followed Johnny Fabriano down the walk to his mangled car. I went to Bug Town with good intentions. I went with love in my heart. And that was our undoing.

This Island Earth

Passing through the outskirts of Bug Town was like passing through any other dying neighborhood. Worse maybe. A few human families lingered, but most of the houses stood untenanted, their paint peeling, weathered *For Sale* signs jutting up from their unkempt lawns. But as we drove on, the signs dwindled and we began to see evidence of renovations in progress—skeletal networks of scaffolding, stacks of lumber and cinderblock in dusty lawns. Though still recognizably human, the houses troubled the eye. At first glance, you couldn't quite say why. At second, you realized that everything was subtly out of proportion. The lintels of the doors had been jacked up to accommodate seven-foot frames, the rise of each porch stair modified for a lengthier alien stride. Even the angles were almost imperceptibly—disturbingly—out of true. The houses seemed to lean toward the street with an all but sentient vigilance.

We began to see dusky yellow ground cover that you might have mistaken for knee-high weeds had each meaty stalk not sprung to alertness as we passed, and turned watchfully to the street. Pale, violet shrubs choked out the familiar autumnal trees, their sinuous branches drifting like seaweed in the still air. Squat, plump cylinders of washed-out orange quickened with breath. Aliens began to appear, striding down sidewalks or rocking in the shade of front porches as the October evening set in. They turned their heads to watch us as we crept by.

With each passing block, the streets became increasingly unearthly. Entire homes had been buried under thick, undulating vines, succulent and smooth. They coiled around windows and doors, and slithered out across the lawns to envelop street signs and lampposts. Fleshy, tentacled trees—I have no other word—shouldered up to the sidewalk and intertwined their limbs in a dense, rippling canopy that blocked out the sky. And in that swimming underwater dim, everything pulsed with soft colors—pinks and pale yellows and blues—as if a single heartbeat throbbed in every living molecule. And everything smelled ripe and rich as gardenias just before they go to rot. And everything sang.

I sometimes hear it still, that soft, arrhythmic music, ethereal, and eerie as the tones of a theremin. It got under my skin somehow. It got inside my head, like an itch I couldn't reach to scratch. There was something beautiful about it, and something peaceful, and something utterly cruel. If you listened to it too long, I thought, you might never want to hear anything else again. I wondered if this was what Joan meant when she told me that we could be free, because it didn't sound like freedom to me. It sounded like the worst kind of bondage. It sounded like slavery.

"How come it didn't get you, too?" I asked.

Johnny shook his head. "I turned on the radio. I kept my eyes on the road."

"And Joan?"

"Joan looked."

I reached over and switched on the radio, turned it up loud, so I couldn't hear that music chiming in my head.

"How are we going to find her?"

"I have no idea," he said.

But in the end it didn't matter. She found us.

She was waiting on the porch of a house—or what had been a house—midway down the next street over. She stood tall and unafraid at the top step, the one unmoving point in that undulant landscape, her face softly illumined by the slow-pulsing colors. Her hair hung loose around her shoulders, and those succulent vines twined around her calves, like snakes tasting of the air. She looked serene, like a goddess or a saint, indifferent to mere human affairs. Yet she smiled when the Merc coasted to a stop at the curb. She smiled when she saw me, and the smile was her old smile, welcoming and warm and faintly mischievous. Just looking at it, I felt a surge of hope that she might yet be saved.

Then Johnny silenced the radio.

That strange, cruel music rang once again inside my head.

"Go get her, Nancy," he said, and when I didn't move, too

mesmerized by the terrible beauty of Bug Town, he reached past me to the glove box and took out a revolver. I gasped—I'd never seen one, not in real life—and I thought once again that he was nothing but a fraud, a child playacting at something he could never be. But the next thing he did made me realize that it was infinitely worse than that. He shoved the muzzle of the gun into my ribs, hissing, "The fucking bug can't have her. Not after what he did to my car," and I saw that Johnny Fabriano was crazy.

Maybe he always had been. Or maybe it was the mutilation of his car that drove him to it—the humiliation of the thing, the exposure of his cowardice, and the consequent fear, jealousy, and fury. Or maybe it was Bug Town itself. Maybe it affected different people in different ways. I can't know for sure. But when he dug the business end of the pistol into my ribs for the second time, I stepped out of the car, and started up the walk.

It was the single most terrifying moment of my life. The fleshy yellow stalks of grass bent their attention upon me, and I saw that each one terminated in a black unblinking eye. The snaky vines coiled around my ankles. I felt the gentle susurration of the tentacled trees upon my face.

The car door slammed as Johnny scooted out to follow me. When I looked back, he was maybe five feet behind me, pacing me, the pistol extended in one shaking hand. His face was strained and pale, and his eyes were terrified, and as that alien music sang out inside my head, I felt the full peril of the moment bear down upon us all.

Then Joan started down the stairs. We met halfway down the walk, embraced, and stepped away.

"How did you know we were coming?" I asked.

"The music," she said. "Everything sings, and everything speaks. We all knew you were coming. Don't you feel it?"

And I did. It was like she'd flipped a switch at the base of my brain. My nerve endings shot out the tips of my fingers, all the way to the limits of Bug Town, where those first stalks of yellow grass sprang up from the October earth. A torrent of unfiltered imagery swept me under. I caught flashes of aliens nailing up studs in those half-renovated houses, of aliens sweeping off porches and taking dinner out of the oven and changing the oil in their cars, of aliens—of Eloieth!—bending to their homework and tossing frisbees in the dusk. Panic seized me. For a single flailing moment, I thought I would drown, and then—

"Breathe, Nancy," Joan said.

—I got it. It was a matter of focusing the attention, of surfing the wave—and once I mastered it, I came crashing back into my own moment with a new 360° clarity. I saw Johnny at my back, brandishing his pistol, saw Joan smiling before me, saw Tham descending the porch steps behind her. He strode down the walk to stand at her shoulder. The central artery that clove his skull pulsed with color, pink and blue and yellow, each in turn. "Hello, Nanthy," he said.

"Hi, Sam," I said. "I came to see if Joan wanted to come home."

"Thath up to Joan."

Joan didn't even hesitate. "No, Nancy," she said. "This is my home now. I'm free here."

And what I saw then was the most terrible thing of all: Joan had not been seduced by the aliens. She had chosen them.

Chosen them. Bug Town might have been catching strange, but our teenage neighbors from outer space had not ensnared her. The era itself had induced her to seek another path. I understand that now. The '50s weren't an ideal time to be a woman (has there ever been one?). Factor in an abusive father and an oppressive religion, and lots of alternatives might seem preferable. She had made a choice when she'd taken Tham home and introduced him as her boyfriend, when she'd allowed him to walk her back to my house from school, when she'd kissed him good-bye there on my porch. She had chosen Bug Town, and given her particular set of circumstances who wouldn't have? In striving to escape everything her father represented, she'd run straight into the teeth of a decade that was almost as bad.

This Island Earth

Wasn't Bug Town a better option? Wasn't Tham a better man? Who else would have left her to decide her own fate? Not even my father, and he was the most loving man I've ever known. In the end, he'd have returned Joan to her father's keeping.

"Stay with me," Joan said.

"We would welcome you, Nanthy," Tham said. "Come with uth. Everyone ith welcome." Then, looking at Johnny: "Put athide your weapon. Join uth."

"Never," Johnny said.

"Nanthy?"

Oh, I was tempted. The world had little use for a plain girl like me, even if she did make good grades. What future lay before me? A career as a nurse or a teacher? Or, God help me, a homemaker, fate worse than death?

But there was that music in my skull, that maddening itch that I could not scratch, that flood of images to be processed. Maybe I'd have gotten used to it in time. I don't know. But in that moment I could not abide that sentient, serpentine world, endlessly interconnected. I was me. I was Nancy and no one else and didn't want to be. I would face whatever was to come alone, no matter the cost.

I was free.

"I can't, Joan," I said.

She nodded. "I'll miss you," she said, reaching out to squeeze my hands.

I never got a chance to reply.

"You can't have her!" Johnny screamed. I staggered away from her, tapping into that network one last time. I saw everything that followed with that same 360° clarity, languorous and slow. I saw it all. Saw Johnny swing the gun toward Tham, his hands still shaking. Saw his finger white upon the trigger, saw the hammer fall, and the cylinder turn in its casing. I heard the concussion of the shot.

Tham lifted his hand too late. Joan had already hurled herself in front of him. She took the bullet in the stomach. I saw that too. Saw the force of it carry her backward. Saw the blood. There was so much blood.

Tham caught her in one arm. In the same instant, the ropy artery that wound down between his eyes flared red, and a bolt of crimson light erupted from the outstretched talons of his other hand. Johnny never had a chance. A burst of flame engulfed him. The stench of charred flesh filled the air. His blasted bones tumbled to the ground.

Then time kicked back into gear.

Tham had already swung Joan up into his arms. He cradled her like a man carrying his bride across the threshold. "Lath chanth, Nanthy," he said.

I shook my head and stumbled backward toward the car. Tham carried Joan up the porch stairs and through the door of the slithery, vine-grown house. I never saw either one of them again.

The rest of that night is hazy in my memory. I stumbled back to the Merc, I know that, and scrambled across the bench to the wheel. Johnny'd left the key in the ignition, and when I twisted it, the engine roared to life. Johnny—or more likely the Brookton gearhead he'd won the car from—must have modified the engine, because I barely touched the gas and the car lunged forward, like all the furies of the earth propelled it.

I nearly lost control on the first corner. On the second one, I did. The car veered across the oncoming lane and careened over the sidewalk. I can still see the fleshy tree it struck. It was stouter than it looked, that tree. The hood of the car folded up like an accordion when I smashed into it. The steering wheel hurtled up to meet me. I remember nothing of the blackness that followed.

When I woke, Bug Town was dying. The slithery vines lashed around as if in agony, and the tentacled trees had begun to droop. When I crawled out of the car, the stalky yellow grass barely turned to look at me. And in the slow, dimming pulse of colors, I could see that their shark-black eyes had begun to film over.

This Island Earth

As for the music, it had died away altogether. There was a profound relief in the silence, and a sadness, too, I guess, though the sadness wouldn't really hit until I understood fully the magnitude of our loss. Joan was gone—maybe dead—and the aliens had disappeared. The high-school football team's run at the state title had been derailed. The lunchroom seemed strangely empty.

That was later, of course. In the moment, I gave this no thought at all. My brow was tacky with blood, and my head felt as if someone had split it with an ax. It was all I could do to lurch off toward home. I made it maybe half a block before I collapsed in the street. I was still there when the police found me the next morning.

I spent the following night in the hospital, and the morning after that I really was home, headachy and exhausted. My parents couldn't seem to decide whether to baby me or scold me, so they did both by turns, but the babying predominated. Privately, my father even told me that I'd acquitted myself admirably, though I couldn't see much to admire about my complicity, however unintended, in Johnny Fabriano's madness and all the damage it had wrought.

Good intentions, right?

A few days later I felt well enough to go back to school. Everyone was bursting with questions—for a week or so, I was suddenly the most popular girl at Milledgeville High—but Chatty Cathy had fallen silent at last. My grades plummeted that semester. I groped through a fog of guilt and sorrow. The solicitous looks of my teachers were almost unbearable. The last thing I wanted was kindness. I thought of almost nothing but Joan as I had seen her last, cradled in Tham's arms, those strange lights playing on her face. And the blood. So much blood

I made a comeback in the spring. The fog began to lift, my grades to improve. But Bug Town never recovered. I suppose the bank wrote off the unpaid mortgages. The neighborhood itself fell into ruin.

My father drove me through it—at my insistence and over my mother's objections—a week or so after I went back to school. The place was no longer catching strange. It was hard to believe it ever had been. The yellow stalks of grass lay wilted on the earth, and the ropy vines had withered, leaving houses bearded in brown streamers. In places, the streets were virtually impassable. The meaty trees had begun to collapse. We wound through them, crushing limp tentacles beneath our tires. We slipped in silence by the wreckage of Johnny's treasured Merc, its nose crumpled, adding to the indignity Tham had already inflicted upon it. I guess the police must have towed it out of there eventually. I never heard. I *did* hear that all they ever found of Johnny was his bones. His funeral was sparsely attended. I was there. His mother—though she didn't speak to me—looked perfectly healthy.

In retrospect, I suppose that the aliens must have opened some kind of portal from their home world, and that the things that grew there were seeping slowly out into ours. People don't talk about it much these days, but occasionally you'll hear someone speculate that Bug Town was the vanguard of a slow invasion and that its transformation presaged that of the entire planet—that Johnny was a hero who'd saved humanity from the ascension of triumphant alien overlords.

But Johnny Fabriano was no hero. I have no doubt that the aliens were fundamentally benign. I think they'd come to Milledgeville in search of a better life, that in transforming Bug Town they were simply making the neighborhood feel a little more like home. Maybe I'm naive, but I just can't bring myself to believe that you shop at the A&P, picnic in the park, and send your kids to the local high school when you are bent on genocide. If they'd had any interest in crushing us they could have done so without a second thought. They could open doorways between stars, tear the roofs off cars barehanded, and shoot death rays out of their fingers. Why mess around by taking out mortgages and renovating old houses?

In the end, I believe, they retreated in the face of Johnny's madness. When they slammed that interstellar doorway shut behind them, they choked off the source of all that catching strange and Bug Town died.

I miss them. Miss Eloieth and Theven and all the rest of them. I miss Tham, whose good intentions came to naught in the end. I miss Joan most of all. Not a day passes that I don't wonder what happened to her.

I like to think they saved her. I like to think she's free.

THE GHOUL GOES WEST

"BUT NOW, SINCE I PLAY DRACULA, I AM THE BOGEYMAN"

MY BROTHER DENNY DIED when I was twenty-six.

I got the call at 1:13 in the afternoon—which made it 10:13 in Los Angeles. I know this so precisely because I'd been at my manuscript all morning, lost in a dream of old Hollywood, and when the phone startled me out of my reverie, I glanced at my watch, as you do when you have been surprised awake. I was in my apartment, at my desk, the merciless August sunlight of east Tennessee molten in my windows. Denny and I had both fled the grim wastes of western Pennsylvania, seeking warmer climes. As soon as he'd collected his high school diploma, Denny had gone west, to California. Two years later, when I collected my own, I'd headed south. I sometimes thought he'd made the better choice, but that morning, when I picked up the phone, I was reminded otherwise.

The man on the other end asked if I was Benjamin Clarke.

"Ben," I said.

The man paused as if the intimacy was unwelcome. When he spoke again—"Mr. Clarke," he said—I recognized the flat,

This Island Earth

impersonal sympathy affected by all officialdom, from priests to principals, when bad news was to be delivered. I braced my hand against the desk, and when he started to introduce himself as Officer Something or Other I interrupted him.

"It's Dennis, isn't it?" I said.

It was, of course. I'd known it from the minute I'd heard that tone in the officer's voice. He went on to describe the circumstances, but he needn't have bothered. Heroin might have been the proximate cause. But it was Hollywood that killed him.

The way Hollywood had of grinding up its postulants was much on my mind at the time. For the better part of a year, I'd been working on my thesis, a study of Ed Wood and his bizarre entourage, Vampira and the Amazing Criswell, Tor Johnson and Bunny Breckinridge, the whole gang of oddballs and misfits, Bela Lugosi among them. In one way or another, Hollywood destroyed them all, but it was Lugosi's doom that particularly interested me, then and now. It was Lugosi who had drawn me to study film in the first place. It was Lugosi who had drawn Denny to Hollywood.

Sometimes I think Lugosi must have dreamed the place into being before he even knew it existed—just as it was itself a dream, roused out of the slumbering dust by men who dared to seize life and pin it still breathing to a screen. It ate its history, and it feasted on hope. In Hollywood, even then, you were only ever as good as your last picture.

Lugosi came there in 1928. Already 46 years old, he'd fled his father's fists more than two decades before. Fled the cobbled streets of Lugos, where Hungary and Romania kissed. Fled most of all the profession that had been chosen for him. He did not want to be a banker, did not want even to be himself. He wanted to be no one at all. He wanted to be everyone. He wanted to be a star.

He'd worked his way to New York in the bowels of a merchant steamer. Broadway brought him fame, but even that fell short of his ambitions. So he took flight yet again, lured on by the glittering

THE GHOUL GOES WEST

promise of the west. He fled until there was nowhere left to flee. He fled to Hollywood, and the sea.

Lugosi's story is unique only in its particulars. In its broad strokes it's the story of a legion of dreamers just like him: behind them some provincial misery, before them the promise of another self, waiting to be born. It's Denny's story in a nutshell, and I guess it's mine as well—but in the winter of 1969, when our version of the universal tragedy really began, Bela Lugosi served as midwife to our aspirations. Denny turned fourteen that year—I was two years behind him—and though Vietnam was in full swing, Nixon had just taken office, and the Steelers were still reeling from a 1-13 season, what mattered most to us that February was a TV personality named Gabriella Ghoul. Pittsburgh's bodice-bursting answer to Vampira, Gabriella Ghoul had a starring role in both our onanistic fantasies and the local late-night creature-feature showcase.

Our mother disapproved of Gabriella and the creature features both, but Denny and I watched them anyway, sitting mesmerized on the threadbare carpet before the old black-and-white Zenith that we'd inherited from my grandparents when they upgraded to color. The movies Gabriella Ghoul introduced varied wildly in quality. If you got *The Bride of Frankenstein* one Saturday, you would get *The She-Wolf of London* the next. But Lugosi's *Dracula*—the only *Dracula* that really matters—stood apart from both the gold and the dross, sui generis.

It is in many ways not a great film. Dwight Frye's effete, lisping turn as Renfield has not aged well and the visual grammar of the movie is static and stagy, with little in the way of camera movement. I can still remember our disappointment in the opening scenes that cold February night. We had been snowbound all day and had hoped for something really good—a rerun of *The Beast from 20,000 Fathoms* or *The Creature from the Black Lagoon*—to alleviate our boredom. Instead we got this flat, hammy antique.

We were on the verge of turning the movie off and going up to bed when Lugosi made his first appearance, creeping down the vast, cobweb-shrouded steps of Castle Dracula, candle in hand. The powerful impression Lugosi made then renews itself every time I watch the film. I am twelve years old again, seeing for the first time his slow, deliberate gestures, listening anew to the broken cadence of his line readings, that inimitable accent, the timbre of his voice. Lugosi's performance is broad—he never escaped his theatrical training; he was always playing to the back of the house—but his onscreen charisma is undeniable. His presence dominates every frame thereafter, and one leaves the movie thinking it is better than it actually is. Lugosi didn't just play Dracula; Lugosi *was* Dracula.

I remember tearing myself away from the TV to look over at Denny. He looked gaunt and gray in the flickering blue radiance of the screen, his eyes deeply shadowed. He looked like he was already dead. In some sense, I suppose, he was.

Such were my thoughts as I boarded the plane at McGhee Tyson the following morning. I was routed through Atlanta and I managed to hold thoughts of Denny at bay until the long haul from Hartsfield to LAX. As the plane shuddered and wrenched itself free of the planet, it broke upon me that I was now entirely alone in the world. Our father had died in a mining accident when I was five and our mother had succumbed to cancer almost six years ago, not long after Denny left to chase his screenwriting dreams. I'd been seeing a girl in Knoxville, but both of us were pretty half-hearted about it. I'd left a message on her machine saying that I'd be out of town for a while, I'd give her a call when I got back, though I didn't expect I'd really do so and in fact never did.

I don't mean by this to suggest that Denny and I were close. We weren't. Even before our mother's death, our dispositions divided us. Denny was reckless and I was not. He had some minor trouble with drugs in high school, and a few brushes with the law, also minor. I was always cleaning up his messes: shoving his laundry into the hamper, dragging him out of parties when he'd had too much to drink, and once, memorably, helping him bundle a half-naked

The Ghoul Goes West

cheerleader out his bedroom window. By the time he graduated high school, movies were the only thing holding us together—and even there our impulses differed. Mine were academic, his creative. I liked to tease scenes apart; he liked to storyboard new ones. When he left for L.A., we were already drifting into separate orbits. Mom's death finished the job.

We talked two or three times a year after that, twenty minutes at most. Denny would share some hair-raising story or other, I would describe my latest academic enthusiasm, and then we'd sign off, fraternal duties fulfilled for another four or five months. We never talked about anything real. I had vague intimations that he'd hit some rough patches in Hollywood, but he never shared the details. He was more forthcoming about his fleeting moment of success, churning out scripts for a sitcom that never found its legs.

"It's not a bad show," he told me a few days after he landed the job. "Have you seen it?"

I had not.

"You should," he said. "See what your older brother's up to out here in Tinsel Town."

So I watched a couple of episodes, more out of curiosity than any kind of sibling loyalty. The thing was called *Girl's Best Friend*. It was about a twelve-year-old girl and a talking dachshund—really an alien in disguise, dispatched from his home planet to study earthlings. The dog was constantly getting into binds because it didn't understand human customs. Or how to be a dog. People overheard it talking every other episode, initiating your standard slapstick brouhaha. The talking was accomplished by bad puppetry. You can imagine.

It was beneath my brother's talents.

"It's just a way to make ends meet until something better comes along," he told me when I pointed this out. "The money's great. I'm going to be making almost a thousand dollars a week."

In 1980 this was big money indeed. But a TV writer's job is perilous. When *Girl's Best Friend* got its cancellation notice—it would come two years later—Denny would be unemployed again.

This Island Earth

"I hope you're planning to bank some of it," I said.

Denny just laughed and changed the subject. That was the way it went.

The last time we talked, I told him my thesis was on Ed Wood. He was incredulous.

"Ed Wood?" he said.

My thesis director had asked the same question, in the same tone. At the time, *Plan 9 from Outer Space* was simply one of the worst films ever made. It had not yet begun to generate the cult of camp affection it enjoys today. My director felt that the project was a waste of my talents, and it was only with great reluctance that she'd signed off on the idea. But I was interested in the tragedy of Lugosi's final years, and by then his fate had been inextricably bound up with Wood's.

"Poor Bela," Denny said when I explained this. The phrase had been Boris Karloff's, or so the story went, and over the years it had become a kind of countersign, code for all the things that lay unspoken between us. Poor, poor Bela. Thinking of it now, as I winged my way across the country to untangle the mystery of my brother's death, I felt something catch in my chest, and for a moment it was hard to breathe.

"Hey, you okay, buddy?" asked my seatmate, an older guy who'd been drinking gin and hogging the armrest for the last two hours.

"I'm fine," I said. I wasn't, though, and the question didn't help.

It was the same question I'd asked Denny at the end of that final conversation. "Poor Bela," he'd said, and there was something troubling in his voice. I couldn't put my finger on it. Sadness maybe, or bitterness, or sorrow.

"You okay, Denny?" I asked.

"Fuck you, Ben," he said. Six months later he was dead.

In his waning years, when he struggled to make ends meet in low-budget farces such as *Bela Lugosi Meets a Brooklyn Gorilla*, Lugosi often spoke of suicide. If this talk at first elicited sympathy and concern from Ed Wood and his band of happy misfits, they soon became tiresome exercises in self-pity. You can only cry wolf so many times.

This tension came to a head one evening in 1956 when Lugosi found himself in San Francisco, tub-thumping for *The Black Sleep*, his first role in a major studio film in eight years. Yet even this modest comeback was a humiliation: once famous for his voice, Lugosi had been reduced to playing the mute valet of Basil Rathbone's mad scientist. It was this, more than anything else, that led to his suicidal rumblings that night in the fourth-floor hotel room he shared with Tor Johnson, the behemoth former wrestling star who'd once billed himself as the Super Swedish Angel.

As the story goes, the Angel, tiring of Lugosi's musings, knotted one meaty fist in the back of the old man's Dracula cape. Gripping Lugosi's belt with the other hand, Johnson thrust him out the open window. I sometimes imagined what the experience must have been like for Lugosi, looking down between his feet at the busy street below. The pedestrians on the sidewalk could not have suspected that only the Angel's mighty hands, the strained seams of a cheap Dracula costume, and a stifled hiccup kept a drunken Hungarian from crashing down on them.

Picture it, if you can: the Angel crying in vexation, "Is this what you want, you damn hunkie?" and Lugosi swallowing, sobered. Inside, he'd pined audibly for an end to his sorrows; his new post outside the window must have imparted an altogether different perspective. The neck of his cape would have felt like a noose; when the Angel gave him a shake, the sidewalk would have wheeled far beneath him.

"Well?" the Angel is said to have bellowed.

"I think I vould like to come back in," Lugosi reportedly said, and so the Angel hauled him back inside to face, once again, his reduced circumstances.

What a precipitous decline it had been. There had been a time when Lugosi's name had been on every lip, when Universal had been inundated with fan mail for their new matinee idol. He'd had money,

This Island Earth

a sumptuous estate in the Hollywood Hills, a Buick Straight 8 Deluxe. In short, he had been a star. Biographers have sometimes wondered why a man of his stature ever took up with such crackpot scrabblers after Hollywood glory as Ed Wood and Tor Johnson. Most of them have concluded that he was driven by financial exigency. But I wonder if there wasn't more to it, if Lugosi hadn't been seduced by the myth of his own stardom, and if they hadn't fed his need to fulfill that myth—for among Wood and his troupe of lunatic aspirants, Lugosi would have retained the sheen of Hollywood celebrity. If they represented the nadir of Lugosi's career, he represented the zenith of theirs. The Super Swedish Angel must have admired him. Perhaps he regretted his fit of pique. Perhaps he told Lugosi that he stood at the threshold of a career renaissance that would lift them all to the giddy heights of fame.

"Why, you've got the lead in Eddie's new film. He's just got to raise the money," he might have said. "You'll see. Eddie will come through."

"Bah," Lugosi would have said, shaking his head. He loved Eddie. Eddie had been good to him. But when, in all the years Lugosi had known him, had Eddie Wood come through?

This is all a reconstruction, of course, colored by my own affection for Lugosi. There are multiple versions of the story; only in a few of them does the Angel actually dangle Lugosi out the window. In some, there are others in the room, men who were trying (and no doubt failing) to keep Lugosi sober for his next PR appearance. In one version, Lugosi's rant occasions a desperate call back to Los Angeles, to Hope Lininger, Lugosi's fifth wife.

"He's threatening to jump," the caller cried down the line.

"Then for God's sake, open the window," Hope is said to have replied.

I rented a Chevy Cavalier from Avis, threw my bags in the trunk, and caught the 105 east out of LAX. By the time I'd found my way to the 101 and the iconic Hollywood sign hove into view, my muscles were tense from negotiating the heavy Los Angeles traffic. But I still felt a thrill at seeing those nine letters strung across the slope of Mount Lee. Hollywood had always been more idea to me than geographical reality: a liminal threshold between what was and what could be willed into being, where Norma Jeane Mortenson could become Marilyn Monroe, Archibald Leach Cary Grant, and Marion Morrison John Wayne. Hollywood was a place where an impoverished Hungarian immigrant named Béla Blaskó could become Bela Lugosi.

In the end, of course, Hollywood had destroyed Monroe and Lugosi both—but it had also granted them a golden moment of stardom. The vast multitude of dreamers who washed up there weren't even that lucky. They came in search of the selves they might become; they died in obscurity—or worse. In 1932, an aspiring actress named Peg Entwistle hurled herself to her death from the top of the Hollywood sign, a metaphor too obvious even for the silver screen.

Movies change lives.

That's the fundamental axiom of my faith.

Unfortunately, they don't always change them for the better.

I found Officer Something or Other—his name turned out to be Grant—at the Hollywood Station of the LAPD, a low brick building on Wilcox. He was gruff and gray, but not unkind. When I asked if I could see Denny's case file, he sighed. "You don't want to see that," he said, and when I averred that I did, he shook his head and set me up in an empty interview room: one-way glass, green and white tile on the floor, an ammoniac smell of Pine-Sol. I sat at the battered table, and looked down at the file, a manila folder labeled with my brother's name and a case number.

"Let me fill you in, instead," Grant said from the door. "Some photos in there, you see them you can't unsee them, you know what I'm saying. Maybe you don't want to remember your brother that way."

This Island Earth

"I think I have to look," I said.

Grant nodded. "If you say so." He closed the door, and I was alone with the file. I hesitated, tempted suddenly to push it aside, to stand up and let myself out of the room, to catch the next flight back to Knoxville. Denny was dead. What more was there to know or do? I'd spent the first decade and a half of my life cleaning up his messes. Why not let someone else take care of this one?

Who knows why we do the things we do?

That's one thing the movies always get wrong: the complexity of human motivations.

I opened the folder.

The police report was straightforward. A woman had called it in. She refused to give her name, and by the time the police had arrived at Denny's apartment, she was gone. Denny had been dead for a while. The cause seemed obvious enough. He was on the sofa. The needle was on the floor at his feet. Grant had already told me they were just waiting for the toxicology report to confirm it.

I thumbed through the pictures. Maybe they wouldn't have been so bad if I could have pretended that Denny was asleep. It wasn't easy to do, though. There was something missing in the set of his face, some vital essence. I couldn't put my finger on it then, and I can't now. He was dead, that's all. You didn't have to look twice to know it.

I tapped the photos into alignment, slid them in behind the thin sheaf of papers and closed the folder. I found Grant in the squad room. He tucked the file away in a drawer. I took the seat beside his desk.

"You okay?" he asked.

That question again. I laughed without humor. "Sure. I guess so."

Grant studied me in silence. A buzz of activity filled the room, low and electric: men talking quietly into phones, the hum of a photocopier, laughter from a counter by the coffee urn.

Grant had tracked my gaze. "Can I get you a cup?"

"No."

"Good. Stuff tastes like battery acid," he said. He said, "Is there anything else I can do for you, Mr. Clarke?"

"Did he suffer?"

"Just went to sleep, that's all."

I thought about that for a while. There was suffering and there was suffering. I figured you didn't stick a needle in your arm unless things were pretty bad.

"I'd like to see his apartment," I said at last. "Am I allowed to do that?"

"Have to ask the property manager. We're done there. I can call ahead, if you want."

I said that I'd like that. Thanked him. Stood.

"Mr. Clarke."

I turned to face him.

"How long has it been since you've seen your brother?"

"Two years."

"You were close?"

"No."

He nodded. "No use chasing ghosts," he said.

But I didn't have any other choice, did I? How else could I lay them down to rest?

By the time I wheeled the rental into the lot of Denny's apartment complex, the buttery California light was melting into the arms of an enveloping blue dark. The shadows softened the utilitarian lines of the building, a repurposed motel, rundown and graffiti scrawled, the windows barred. An overflowing dumpster leavened the cool air with its reek. According to the sign out front, this was the Paradise Arms—the master stroke, perhaps, of an accomplished ironist.

I caught the manager as she was closing up for the day. She was weary and heavy set, sixtysomething, kind. "I'm sorry for your loss," she said as she led me to Denny's apartment. "It's an awful tragedy."

She unlocked the door and turned on the light.

The place was a not unpleasant contrast to the squalor outside.

THIS ISLAND EARTH

The kitchenette, behind a waist-high dividing wall, was spotless, the living space clean and spare, without luxury aside from the TV, a 32-inch Panasonic with a matching VCR. The other furnishings had seen better days. A card table piled with books looked like it might any moment collapse. The chairs were mismatched. The sofa sagged. A half-dozen video tapes in clear rental boxes stood atop a coffee table that could have been fished out of the dumpster outside. From the far wall, where Denny had taped up a poster of Dracula, Lugosi leveled his menacing gaze. Bela had brought Denny to Hollywood. It was fitting, I suppose, that when he died there, Denny had died under the failed Hungarian's watchful eye.

"You'll want to go through his things," the manager said. Then, apologetically: "Sooner is better, of course."

"Yes."

"You could start in the morning—"

"Why not tonight?"

She glanced at her watch. "It's nearly six. You'll want to get to your hotel."

"Perhaps I could stay here."

I could see her thinking it through.

"Is the rent paid?" I asked.

The manager hesitated. "Through the end of the month," she said. In divulging this, of course, she had already conceded. Five minutes later she pressed the key into my hand, and a moment after that I was alone in the apartment where my brother had died.

But it was Lugosi, as much as Denny, that I found myself thinking about that night as I sat sleepless in his living room, wired with jet lag. Denny had lost his battle with drugs; Lugosi had won his. In 1955, shortly before the debut of *Bride of the Monster*, his second feature with Ed Wood, Lugosi checked himself into Metropolitan State Hospital for morphine addiction. He was by then poverty stricken, emaciated by alcohol and drug abuse, despairing. Wood had pledged the premiere's proceeds to defraying Lugosi's medical

The Ghoul Goes West

expenses, but the opening-night profits, if any, must have been negligible—certainly inadequate to cover even a fraction of Lugosi's costs. Despite Wood's ambitions as an auteur, he had no talent or even competence as a filmmaker, and his posthumous fame as a camp icon was then inconceivable. It is one of the tragedies of Lugosi's career that critics routinely rank his films with Wood among the worst movies ever made.

Nevertheless, Wood was a good friend to the former star, paying him regular visits at the hospital long after Hollywood had written him off, and promising him the lead in his next opus when there were no other parts to be had. Perhaps the scripts Wood showered him with provided Lugosi some comfort during the harrowing three months that followed. He later described his withdrawal from morphine as a nightmare of painful extremes: scalding fever one moment, glacial cold the next. At times, he could not bring himself to move. At others, his limbs spasmed violently. He gnawed his blankets to fight the pain. He shat himself, a hot, reeking gruel down the back of his thighs, and he wept in shame as the nurses cleaned him up. Afterward, he struggled to the chair, humiliated, and watched them change his sheets with business-like efficiency. "I want to die," he moaned, and it was true: in that moment, he longed for nothing more than annihilation.

Yet he recovered, and when he left the hospital, he exited with one of Ed Wood's screenplays in hand. "I'm looking forward to work again," he told a reporter on the steps of the sanitarium. "I have an assignment playing the star part in Eddie Wood's *The Ghoul Goes West.*"

But Wood could not get the financing to shoot the picture. Lugosi had played his final starring role. A little more than a year later, he died of cardiac arrest while taking an afternoon nap. Hope Lininger found him clutching a copy of Ed Wood's unproduced screenplay. Hollywood had killed him a decade before. The heart attack merely made it official.

Poor Bela, Denny would have said. Poor, poor Bela.

THIS ISLAND EARTH

But Denny, too, had died in thrall to the bitch goddess of the screen. He'd sacrificed everything to her: his ambition, his family, and finally his life. When Mom fell ill, I took a sabbatical from school and returned to Pennsylvania to take care of her. I hadn't been home a week before the doctor told us she had six months if she was lucky. I called Denny with the news. "Come home," I said.

"I will," he promised, but the sitcom deal was just coming together, and he kept putting it off—one week and then two. The weeks piled up and turned into a month.

"You need to come, Denny," I said. "She's dying."

"One more week," he said, but there were no more weeks to be had. She died three days later.

Denny didn't come home for the funeral, either. He'd been in the writers' room of *Girl's Best Friend* for less than a week and didn't want to risk making a bad impression. Mom would have understood, he told me, and maybe she would have. But I spent the rest of the fall at home alone, seeing the will through probate, getting the house ready to put on the market, attending to the life insurance and a thousand other details. When all was said and done, the estate came to just over $80,000. I mailed Denny a cashier's check for his half, and included Mom's engagement ring as a keepsake—something to remember her by, since he seemed to have forgotten.

I talked with Susan Mazur, Denny's agent, the next afternoon. She had an immaculate second-floor office in an old building two blocks off Wilshire. I'd expected something altogether different: a high-powered Hollywood super-lawyer in a glass box downtown. William Morris maybe, or CAA. But of course Denny didn't move in those circles. It had been three years since *Girl's Best Friend*, and as I've said, that had been a middling success at best, commensurate neither with his ambitions nor his ability, which had apparently been considerable. He was good—"really good," according to Mazur. "Hell, that was part of his problem," she told me. "He thought he was *too* good for this town."

"What do you mean?"

"I mean that show, the dog from space thing. I worked hard to get him in that room, and he blew it."

"How?"

"The kid was a wreck. All he could talk about was you and your mother. It was a tough thing for him, losing your mom. After he quit—"

I sat back. "I thought the show was canceled."

"That was later. He lasted a couple months at most." She gave me an appraising look. "He didn't tell you?"

"No, I—He never mentioned it." I'd always assumed that he'd lasted for the entire run. "What happened?"

"He decided talking dogs were beneath him. He should have stuck it out, saved the money against a dry spell, but—" She shrugged, sighed. "It's hard to take in, isn't it? What a terrible goddamn waste."

"When did you see him last?"

"A month ago, maybe? Not long. He had this script he wanted me to look at," she said. "Some kind of crazy biopic about Bela Lugosi. Not a commercial project. I have it around here somewhere."

"Can I see it?"

"Why not," she said. "Let me see if I can dig it up."

She showed me to the door ten minutes later, still shaking her head in disbelief. And then I was outside, Denny's screenplay in hand. I tossed it on the passenger seat of the Cavalier. I couldn't bring myself to look at it. What kept coming back to me was how furious I had been when Mom had died and he'd decided to stay in California. What kept coming back to me was the conversation where I'd told him that talking dogs were beneath him. Now, I wondered why I'd found it necessary to share that insight. He surely didn't need me to point out that he'd fallen short of everything he'd hoped to be.

In the months after my mother died, when the house seemed to echo around me, I probably saw two or three movies a week—virtually every film that showed up in the small town where Denny and I grew

This Island Earth

up. I felt something unclench inside me the minute I walked into the theater lobby. The ushers and projectionists soon knew me by name; the staff at the concession stand had my order waiting by the time I stepped up to the counter. But the really comforting moment came when the lights went down and I fell away from myself, lost in whatever dream flickered to life on screen. I watched without discrimination. I might see *Piranha* one night and *The Deer Hunter* the next, and both were fine by me. It didn't matter what world the movie carried me off to, as long as it carried me away from that pinched and narrow Pennsylvania town—from the stark fact of my mother's death, and my resentment of Denny for leaving me to tie off the loose ends of her life alone.

And even when I wasn't at the movies, I was tuning in to them at home. There were still lots of films on network TV in those days: Johnny Weissmuller on Saturday afternoons and Shirley Temple on Sundays, and all sorts of made-for-TV movies, from *The President's Mistress* to *The Time Machine*. And though Gabriella Ghoul was long gone, you could always count on catching a Hammer horror film after the late local news on Saturday night.

Movies, then. Movies to the last.

And it was a movie I needed when I returned to Denny's apartment that night. I sat at the card table, eating takeout Thai and studying the books piled up around me. Most of them looked like research for the Lugosi screenplay: the standard biographies (Lennig, Bojarski, Cremer), plus a study of the classic Universal monster movies, two or three histories of Hollywood's Golden Age, and a coffee table book featuring photos of Los Angeles in the thirties. But just then I didn't want to read about movies. I wanted to lose myself in one. So after I put my leftovers in the fridge, I sat down to look at the videos on the coffee table.

I was halfway through the stack when I realized that the movie I was holding didn't exist.

None of them did.

The Ghoul Goes West

As far as I've been able to determine, Lugosi never met Gene Autry, the famed Singing Cowboy of the '30s and '40s. But during the last year of his life he was scheduled to star opposite Autry in *The Ghoul Goes West*, the Ed Wood film he'd mentioned on the steps of the sanitarium. This is not as implausible as it seems. Wood's former roommate, Alex Gordon, who'd grown close to Autry, could well have brokered an introduction. And Autry might have welcomed the opportunity to work again. By 1956, his career was on a downward trajectory. He hadn't appeared on screen in three years. He'd gained weight. He was drinking heavily. Hollywood had been extraordinarily good to him—he'd made 93 films between 1934 and 1953—but in the end she withdrew her favors. The proposed film never came about. Wood couldn't get the financing. Autry backed out. Lugosi died, leaving Wood with a handful of test footage he recycled into *Plan 9 from Outer Space*, the camp classic that would cement his reputation as the worst filmmaker ever to square up a shot.

The entire episode earns only a single dismissive sentence in Lennig's otherwise comprehensive Lugosi biography. It doesn't even merit that in Autry's 1978 memoir.

Yet the film I was holding—a commercially produced VHS tape—was clearly labeled *The Ghoul Goes West*. And it was not alone. A second glance through the stack confirmed that the other films were similarly impossible. They shouldn't exist. They didn't exist. They had never been shot. They'd been abandoned. But here they were. Here was the Orson Welles adaptation of *Heart of Darkness*. Here was *Something's Got to Give*, Marilyn Monroe's final film, left unfinished at her death. Here were Hitchcock's *Kaleidoscope*, Clouzot's *Inferno*, von Sternberg's *I, Claudius*. A prank, surely. Someone had pasted fake labels onto the tapes—but why? To what purpose?

Retrieving *The Ghoul Goes West*, I glanced at the sticker on the case: Dimension Video. Then I turned on the television and slotted the tape into the VCR. The film opened with a black-and-white shot of the Amazing Creswell seated behind a desk, delivering a bizarre

This Island Earth

monologue about "the mysteries of the past which even today grip the throat of the present to throttle it." The speech was portentous and theatrical, overcooked, the framing static. Then the image faded, to be replaced by a flat desert landscape with a saguaro cactus, obviously fake, on the right side of the frame. The credits came up on the left, each new name preceded by the sound of a pistol shot. Autry had first billing, Lugosi second, both of them above the title. The rest of the cast followed, among them Vampira and Paul Marco and Tor Johnson, Wood's usual suspects. My only thought as the attribution credit came up—

WRITTEN DIRECTED PRODUCED
BY
EDWARD D. WOOD, JR.

—was that I was looking at some kind of bizarre forgery. Then Lugosi, in full Dracula garb, appeared on screen, rising from a casket in a dim crypt that looked like a suburban garage. It was unmistakably him. By that point in my thesis research, I'd seen virtually every movie Lugosi had made three or four times. I knew the shape of his face almost as well as I knew my own. I recognized the trademark gesture as he turned to face the camera and swept his cape around to cover his mouth. A stroke of lightning split the screen. It illuminated a gothic castle set implausibly atop a desert butte— clearly a painted flat, executed with about as much expertise as you'd expect in a third grader's school play. Another cut, and here was a posse of cowboys gathered around a campfire. In the shot that followed, Gene Autry showed up, stout and out of shape, possibly drunk. He was strumming a guitar and belting out "Back in the Saddle Again"—or trying to belt it out; his once-pleasant tenor was shot, and he was slurring his words.

I won't try to describe the film that followed. It involved Lugosi, his vampire wife (Vampira, of course), and his mutant servant (Tor Johnson) menacing some rancher's daughter, whom they wanted to impregnate (!) with their atomic ray (!). Autry and company rode to the rescue. It didn't make much sense. But it wasn't a forgery. Lugosi was undeniably Lugosi, Autry was unquestionably Autry. And the production was signature Ed Wood. The writing was incoherent, possibly the product of insanity. The production values were appalling.

Once I'd settled into the film—once I'd gotten past the fact that it could not exist—the whole enterprise saddened me. This was Hollywood. Its most fervent acolytes were mired in delusion. Its fading stars clung to their former celebrity. If passion alone had been enough, Ed Wood would have been an auteur on the order of Orson Welles (though Hollywood destroyed Welles, too); if hunger were sufficient, Lugosi and Autry would have held the spotlight until they died. Mesmerized, I watched the film straight through to the end, rewound it, and watched it again.

After that I watched the other films. By the time I finished the last one, *Inferno*, it was nearly four. I rewound the tape, ejected it, and put it away, examining for the second or third time the plastic box. Beyond the name of the store, there was no information to be had there—no address, no phone number, nothing. The videos might have come from anywhere. They might have come from nowhere at all.

Denny's alarm roused me, grainy eyed and exhausted, just past nine. I had one of those moments of psychic dislocation that you sometimes experience when you wake up unrested in a strange bed. For a breath, I wasn't sure where I was or how I'd ended up there or why, and when it all came flooding back—Denny's death and the long cross-country trek and the stack of movies that did not, that could not, exist—the whole series of events felt like some unfathomable dream. I sat on the edge of the bed for a long time. When I finally pulled things together enough to stand, I had to nerve myself up to face the movies in the next room. I was afraid they'd be there. I was afraid they'd be gone.

They were there.

This Island Earth

I resisted the impulse to sit down and watch them through again immediately. Instead, I breakfasted on leftover Thai, standing in front of the open refrigerator and eating drunken noodles straight out of the box. After a shower, I felt almost human again. Human enough anyway to sit through the first fifteen minutes of *Ghoul*, to see if I could pick up anything I'd missed the first two times around. This was futile. There aren't many nuances in an Ed Wood film. What you see is what you get. So I rewound the tape, ejected it, loaded it back into its box—and then, seized by some excess of anxiety or paranoia, hid it away behind an old blanket on the upper shelf in Denny's closet. Grabbing the video of *Something's Got to Give*, I went looking for the manager in the old motel office.

She stood behind the counter when she saw me come in. She wanted to know how I was doing, if I was making any progress on Denny's apartment. I lied on both counts, held up the video, said, "Do you have any idea where Dimension Video is?"

She pondered that, said the word Dimension aloud, as if that would help her remember. At last, uncertainly, she said, "I don't know about Dimension. There's a Video Hut a block over, by the laundromat."

A Video Hut was useless to me, of course. I asked to see her phone book. Sitting on a plastic chair in the lobby, I checked it and checked it again, white pages and yellow pages, under both movie rental and video rental. Nothing, nothing, and nothing. If Dimension Video existed, it wasn't trying very hard to get the word out. I sighed and handed the book back across the counter.

"You find what you're looking for?"

The answer was no, in senses both literal and existential. I took a chance on the Video Hut. Maybe they'd bought the stock of a defunct store.

"I don't think so," the ponytailed kid behind the counter said. He squinted at the label on the box, then handed it back to me. "Sorry I can't help. Maybe you should talk to the lady owns the place. Lou. I could take a message."

THE GHOUL GOES WEST

"I'll check back another time."

"Your call," he said. "Have a good day."

I promised that I would try.

It was a fruitless endeavor, though. I dropped the video off at the apartment, climbed into the Cavalier, and spent the rest of the day touring L.A. I visited Lugosi's star on Hollywood Boulevard. Had he lived to see it, Lugosi would have been thrilled at this affirmation of his achievements. But Hollywood took him to its bosom too late. He died mostly forgotten in a small apartment on Harold Way—the last stop on my swing through the city. I stood outside in the cool California evening, gazing at that apartment for a long time. I'd already tracked down Lugosi's other homes, following the ascension of his star from the Ambassador Hotel to his mansion on Outpost Drive, where he lived at the apex of his fame in the mid-'30s, and through its long decline in a variety of ever smaller accommodations during the '40s and '50s. But the Harold Way location struck me most powerfully. How could a man who had once commanded the adoration of millions wind up in such straitened circumstances, I wondered, and as I stood there in the blue twilight, watching the streetlights come on one by one to shed down their soft refulgence, it seemed to me that the air filled with the inconsolable longing and desire of a city full of disappointed dreamers.

Denny's screenplay was no biopic, because the Bela Lugosi it depicted never existed.

Bela Lugosi died in August 1956.

He did not shoot a film called *The Ghoul Goes West* in the spring of 1957.

He died clean. Despite all his faults, despite a failed career, despite his manifest deficits as a father and a husband, despite his despair, he never relapsed, and part of me despised Denny for depriving Lugosi of the one battle he had in reality won. Perhaps the first star to submit himself—publicly—to drug treatment, Lugosi left the hospital a changed man.

THIS ISLAND EARTH

The Lugosi in Denny's screenplay did not die in '56. The Lugosi in Denny's screenplay relapsed when Hope Lininger finally reached the limit of her endurance and abandoned him—which also never happened. In Denny's screenplay, Lugosi, desperate for a fix and no longer able to find a doctor who would cooperate, turned to Tor Johnson. The Super Swedish Angel, who suffered from bad knees after his years in the ring, had no trouble getting a prescription. But he was a tormented man. Out of dog-like devotion, he procured Lugosi's drugs; out of love, he begged Lugosi not to use them. Lugosi did, of course, and by the time *The Ghoul Goes West* went before the cameras, he was dosing himself regularly, sneaking away during breaks on the set to shoot up in the rundown studio's lavatory—a filthy closet with a hollow-core door and a broken privacy lock.

It was in that lavatory that one of the key turning points in the screenplay occurred—a brief scene, but an important one: Lugosi is fumbling with a syringe when Gene Autry knocks at the door, saying, "Hey, is anyone in here?" Bela, startled, drops the loaded needle. It fetches up under the sink.

"If it will please you," Bela says, "I will be just one min—"

But the Singing Cowboy has already barged into the bathroom, cradling a pint of bourbon. He's pressing a drink on Lugosi—"Breakfast of champions," he says—when he notices the syringe. He retrieves it, holds it up to the fly-specked light. "Hell, Bela," he says, "I thought they got you off this stuff."

"Yes," Lugosi says, helping himself to a slug of the breakfast of champions. "So did I."

Sitting there at the card table in Denny's apartment, I sipped at a beer and turned the pages of the screenplay. The scenes sprang to life before me—Gene Autry's discovery that his director is a transvestite ("Hell, son," he says, "is that a skirt?") and Lugosi's developing conflict with his co-star. Bela, despite the morphine, is always the consummate professional. Autry, on the other hand, is a sloppy drunk. He forgets his lines; he misses his marks. Matters come to a head when they're shooting the campfire scene that will introduce Autry's character.

"Eddie," Lugosi says to Wood, "horror picture is perhaps no place for singing 'Back in the Saddle Again.'"

"But he's the Singing Cowboy," Wood protests.

Lugosi, too focused to notice that Autry has walked up behind him, says, "His voice, Eddie, it is not so good anymore."

Eddie's eyes widen. "Bela—" he says.

Too late.

Autry's hand closes over Lugosi's shoulder. When he turns, Autry's face looms into his field of vision like a small moon, blotchy and cratered with pores.

"Why you son of a bitch," he says. "You junkie, you ghoul."

And then he punches Lugosi in the face.

Gene Autry's Cowboy Code, a set of ten rules by which the Singing Cowboy's young fans were to live their lives, expressly forbade socking 74-year-old men in the jaw. "The cowboy must be gentle with children, the elderly, and animals," Rule Number 4 read. I know this because Denny inserted the entire code as a title card into his screenplay. In the scene immediately following, he imagined a reconciliation between the two men. The slug line placed the action in the Cameo Club, the bar Lugosi—the real Lugosi—frequented in the final year or two of his life. To my knowledge no pictures of the place survive, but I have always imagined it much as Denny described it: dim and cool, with scuffed barstools and booths of buttoned red leather: an old man's bar, quiet, little frequented, Lugosi nursing his bruised jaw with a cheap scotch when Autry sits down beside him.

"Have you come to punch me again?" Lugosi inquires.

"No." Autry sighs. "Eddie said I might find you here."

"I do not wish to be found." Lugosi stands, dropping a handful of bills on the bar. "Good evening, Mr. Autry."

"Stay a while, why don't you?" Autry says, touching Lugosi's elbow. "I'll buy you a drink. Hell, I'll buy you a dozen, if you like."

This Island Earth

"Please not to touch me," Lugosi says, but he slides back onto the stool.

Drinks are ordered: bourbon, a top-shelf scotch.

Autry sighs, lifts his glass in toast. "It's a slippery goddamn slope, isn't it, Bela? One day you take a drink, the next you take two, and suddenly you can't get through the day without the stuff." He snorts. "You know what I mean?"

A bit of stage business follows. Lugosi takes out a lighter and lights one of his reeking cigars. He takes his time getting it going, turning the cigar in the flame until he has it burning evenly. He puts the lighter on the bar. "Bourbon, morphine," he says. "It is the same. Sometimes, I think it would be better if I—" He shakes his head, draws on the cigar, expels a stream of noxious smoke.

"Sometimes what?"

"It does not matter. I am too much a coward." Lugosi meets Autry's gaze. "And you, Mr. Autry. What is it that you fear?"

Autry looks down. He turns his glass on the bar. "You know, Bela, I went to serve my country in the war. Flew C-109s over the Hump, and I was never afraid. But when I came back, Roy Rogers had taken over as the number one singing cowboy in America." He shakes his head. "Irrelevance. I guess that's what I fear the most."

"You are a young man yet."

"I'm forty-nine years old."

"I was forty-nine when I played Dracula," Lugosi says. "You have many lives yet. Me, I am an old man. Finished, as you Americans say."

Autry laughs. "You Americans, huh? How long have you been in America, Bela?"

"A long time," Bela says, and though Denny's screenplay makes no such note—though one of the limitations of cinema is that it has no access to its characters' inner lives—I imagine Bela suddenly stricken with nostalgia for his native land. He had forever been a stranger to his adopted one. "Listen to my voice," he says. "I am neither American nor Hungarian. I am always in between, a failure, a nothing."

The Ghoul Goes West

When Autry protests—"Now, Bela," he begins—Lugosi waves him off. "You are a cowboy," he says. "You are more than American, Mr. Autry. You *are* America. Me," he says, "I am hunkie. I am failure. I am, as you say, a ghoul."

I didn't finish Denny's screenplay—not then, not right away. I couldn't bring myself to do it. Instead, I snagged another beer from the refrigerator, retrieved *The Ghoul Goes West* from its hiding place in Denny's closet, and plugged the tape into the VCR. I couldn't really concentrate, though. My mind kept drifting back to Denny. I wondered where he'd found the thing. I wondered what he'd thought of it.

I think that's what I missed most after Denny disappeared into Hollywood: just chewing over old movies with him, finding out what he thought about them. He was the only person I'd ever known who could talk about the films I wanted to talk about. Don't misunderstand me. My classmates in the master's program were cinema geeks, too. But they wanted to discuss Buñel and Visconti. Denny and I were more interested in O'Brien and Harryhausen. They read *Film Quarterly*. We subscribed to *Famous Monsters of Filmland*.

The last movie we saw together was Henry Hathaway's 1947 film noir, *Kiss of Death*. Mom had been gone two years by then. I had just finished college with a more-or-less useless degree in English and had taken the year off to contemplate pursuing a still more useless degree in Film Studies. In the meantime, I was working in a video store and conducting a scattershot survey of film history, skipping around in the store's collection at whim. I was in my blaxploitation phase when Denny called to say he was coming to visit.

"Why?" I remember asking.

"Just thought I'd catch up with my baby brother," he told me. "That okay with you, Ben?"

"Sure," I said. "Why not?"

Which is how he ended up in Knoxville a month later, crowding into my run-down apartment in Fort Sanders. In the week that

THIS ISLAND EARTH

followed, he slept late while I put in my hours at the store. After I clocked out, we ate delivery pizza, drank beer, and watched whatever we'd selected from the shelves for the evening. And talked movies, of course—what we'd seen, what we wanted to see, what we should see. Directors and leading men. Starlets and scream queens. The night before he left, we wandered up and down the aisles, looking for something to watch. I pushed for *Darktown Strutters*. Denny made a case for *Run Silent, Run Deep*. We compromised on *Kiss of Death*, though we'd both seen it before. It had Victor Mature in one of his best roles, and we both loved Richard Widmark's star-making turn as an unhinged, giggling psychopath named Tommy Udo. And of course it also had perennial heavy Brian Donlevy, cast against type as an assistant district attorney.

Donlevy had his own connection to Lugosi.

In 1952, after Lugosi fell on hard times, his then-wife, Lillian Arch, went to work as an assistant on Donlevy's TV program, *Dangerous Assignment*. Donlevy and Lillian soon became close. At one point Lugosi, drunk and stricken with jealousy, called the *Dangerous Assignment* production office, and demanded to speak with Donlevy. "That man is destroying my marriage," he raved. Sober, he regretted his loss of composure, the latest in a series of self-inflicted humiliations, both personal and professional. The final blow came when Lillian left him less than a year later. Donlevy must have played a role in her decision—she would marry him in 1966, ten years after Lugosi's death—but I think she loved Lugosi all the same. She'd stayed with him through two difficult decades, watching helplessly as he spiraled into morphine addiction, alcoholism, and poverty. Though he couldn't see it, Bela was the one destroying the marriage, not Donlevy. He'd just worn Lillian out.

Denny disagreed. "It wasn't Bela's fault, not the way you mean. Those were symptoms, not the problem. If he'd made different decisions—"

"Like accepting the Karloff role in *Frankenstein*, I guess." This line of reasoning was nothing new. Lugosi had famously declined the role. He didn't want to endure hours in make-up every day. He didn't want a part without lines. He didn't want to be typecast as America's bogeyman—though of course it was already too late for that. He was too old to be the leading man he'd hoped to become. His accent was too thick, the impression he'd made as Dracula too indelible.

Karloff, on the other hand, had accepted the role—had embraced it, and turned in a performance still stunning in its pathos. *Frankenstein* elevated him to stardom, and he made all the right choices thereafter. He embraced his role as the bogeyman, held out for good parts, and went on to enduring success.

Lugosi became Karloff's shadow other self, Karloff what Lugosi might have been.

But Denny had another perspective. Turning down the role had been a life-changing mistake, sure—assuming he could have turned in a performance of Karloff's caliber. But Bela had even then had it within his power to save himself.

"How?"

Stardom is a tricky thing, Denny told me. An illusion. Gossamer and moonlight. "You have to act the part," he said. "No matter how dire the circumstances, you hang on to the fancy cars, you make yourself seen at the best restaurants, you date the most beautiful women. You project the illusion long enough, you become it."

"The man was bankrupt in 1932," I objected.

"The man was too proud to call in his markers."

"What markers?"

"Bela was huge in 1932. He should have traded on that celebrity. All he needed to do was hang on for the right part. Instead, he sold himself short for the first thing that came along. He looked desperate. And desperation is fatal."

"Whatever you say, Denny," I said. "Come on—early day tomorrow."

It was, too. We were up before dawn, off to the airport. It was raining lightly, and as the oncoming cars hissed by, shadows streamed across Denny's face. He was quiet, pensive.

THIS ISLAND EARTH

"What's on your mind?" I asked.

Denny studied the strip malls as they slipped past. "I haven't been entirely honest with you."

"Okay."

"I need money, Ben."

"Money? Jesus, Denny, Mom left you forty thousand dollars."

"You don't under—"

"What about your talking dog? You made plenty of cash then, didn't you?"

He sighed.

"Didn't you?"

"Ben—"

"Answer me."

"It's gone," he said. Then, gazing out at the line of mountains in the distance, dark against the brightening sky, he said, "It's all gone."

"What happened to it?"

"It's like I said last night," he replied. "You have to look the part, okay? You have to be the thing you want to become. After a while, I just couldn't maintain the lifestyle. I kept waiting for the next break." He laughed. "You saying you don't have the money, Ben?"

"I work in a video store."

"That's not what I asked."

"Yeah, I have it." I hit the ramp for the airport exit too fast, and braked hard, the car leaning into the curve. "I need the money, Denny. I'm going back to school."

"Right. Okay, then."

A jet roared in overhead. I pulled to the curb at Departures. Traffic was just beginning to heat up. Taxis and shuttle buses, people smoking on the sidewalks. I got out and walked around the car and heaved Denny's bag out of the trunk.

"You should come with me," he said.

"You know that wouldn't work." I held out my hand. "Take care of yourself, okay?"

Denny ignored my hand. He pulled me into a hug. "You, too, Ben," he said. And then, reaching for his bag: "But I guess I don't have to worry about that, do I?"

He nodded and started off down the sidewalk. I watched him all the way through the sliding doors. He didn't look back.

I never saw him alive again.

I kept knocking back beers until everything grew fuzzy and my vision narrowed to a dim tunnel. At some point I stumbled off to bed. I woke up after noon, hungover, my memory of the night before an oily void shot through with stark eidetic flashes—rewinding *Ghoul* for yet another viewing, trying to concentrate on Lugosi's performance, though my focus slipped for seconds, minutes, half an hour at a time; sitting at the card table, staring blindly at Denny's screenplay, as if the title page alone could reveal some truth or explanation that I had not noticed before. But if any truth was there I could not discern it, or discerning it, I could not in the light of morning recall it.

I got up, scrubbed the moss off my teeth, and washed down a couple of Tylenol from the medicine cabinet. In the living room, I ejected *Ghoul* and returned it to its case. I swept a dozen beer cans off the kitchen counter. When I carried the garbage bag out to the dumpster, I saw that I'd parked the Cavalier halfway up on the sidewalk. I had a vague memory of going out for more beer. I was lucky I hadn't killed someone.

I stashed *Ghoul* in its hiding place in Denny's closet, and headed back out to the car. I spent the next couple of hours at a nearby mortuary, chosen for its proximity to the apartment as much as anything else. The undertaker was professionally solicitous. He expressed his condolences, asked about a burial plot, tried to sell me a casket and set up a service. I nixed the service and opted for cremation instead. I was out of there in less than two hours, but the experience brought Denny's death home to me with a raw finality that transcended even that of the photos in the case file. I kept thinking about the way we'd been when we were kids, before we drifted apart—before Lugosi and the doom he'd brought down upon us.

I passed a park, and pulled over. The air was warm, but not oppressive, as it would have been in Knoxville. The foliage was in riotous bloom. I found a bench and turned my face to the sun, letting the warmth burn away the hangover. Denny's words came back to me, paradoxical: to become the self you aspire to be, you must inhabit that self from the moment you imagine it into being. Maybe that had been the difference between us. I'd always been more or less content being me. Denny, for whatever reason, had longed to be someone else, had sacrificed everything on the altar of that dream. I wondered if he might have achieved it if I had given him the money he'd asked for. I'd been frugal with my half of Mom's inheritance. It was true that I had planned to go back to school—had indeed done so—but it was also true that I could have spared at least enough to keep him going for a while. What might have happened then? What might he have become? And underneath these questions, others, troubling in different ways. How had he acquired movies that did not—that could not—exist? And having come into possession of them myself, what was I to do with them?

Where was Dimension Video?

I had a small epiphany then: I'd never intended to return the movies, not really. How could I relinquish them? But I was desperate to see the rest of the store's collection. Denny would have felt the same way, of course. For him, the desire might have been more pressing still. After a decade in Hollywood, he'd never seen a single word he'd written appear onscreen. But what if—

The question was absurd. Impossible. But, then, the whole thing was impossible.

I tried to puzzle out some sense or logic in it, some explanation for the entire episode, but by the time I returned to my car—hours later—no answers had presented themselves. I stopped for a sandwich on the way back to Denny's apartment. Afterward—by impulse—I swung the car into the lot of the Video Hut. Maybe the owner was in."

She was.

The guy behind the counter directed me to an office at the back of the store. She stood when I introduced myself: a tall, angular woman in her thirties with a cap of close-shorn blonde hair, not pretty exactly, but you wouldn't soon forget her. Her name was Louise Roth—"but everyone calls me Lou," she said, settling me in the molded plastic chair opposite her desk. She listened attentively as I explained my dilemma: my brother had left some rental tapes I'd like to return, but the rental boxes had no address or phone number—just a name, Dimension Video.

"Dimension Video, huh?"

"That's right."

"I'd let it go," she said. "No one's going to come looking for them. Lost tapes are the price of doing business. I'm sure you have bigger fish to fry with your brother's death. What was his name? Danny?"

"Denny."

"Right. Tall guy, dark hair, lived down at the Paradise Arms, is that right?"

"You knew him."

"Not really. I remember him, though. He used to come in and pick up a movie once in a while. He had good taste."

"What do you mean?"

"Most people, they want the new releases or the adult films. Your brother went a little deeper—he was always hunting up some obscure movie or other. Mostly we didn't have what he was looking for. But he stuck around to talk once in a while. We both had a fondness for old horror movies. Not a lot of people want to talk about *I Was a Teenage Frankenstein*, you know what I'm saying?"

I laughed. "That was Denny, all right."

"Funny thing is," she said, "he came in not too long ago asking about Dimension Video himself."

"Well, he seems to have found it."

"Finding it wasn't the problem," she said. "Finding it again was another thing. He was looking to return the videos he'd rented there, and the place had just evaporated. So he said, anyway."

"That doesn't make sense. If he'd rented the movies there in the first place—"

"Exactly." She leaned back in her chair, steepled her hands under her chin. "He said it specialized in hard to find stuff. Really hard to find. That true of the movies he left behind?"

"You could say that."

"Care to tell me what you have?"

I hesitated. "You ever hear of an old Marilyn Monroe flick, *Something's Got to Give*?"

"Doesn't exist. Not the whole film, anyway. She died and they never finished it."

"I know," I said, and after that neither of us said anything at all. Finally, I stood. I thanked her for her time.

She accompanied me out through the store. The evening rush was just beginning, the aisles filling up with nine-to-fivers looking for something light to kill the evening. I wondered what they'd think if they knew that somewhere out there a store called Dimension Video was renting out movies that didn't exist. I suspected they wouldn't much care. Lou, on the other hand—Lou walked me all the way out to the Cavalier.

"I'm sorry about your brother," she said as I slid behind the wheel. "I don't know what he was into—or what he's gotten you into—but if that movie did exist..." She shook her head. "Well, I would give a lot to see it."

"Thanks again," I said. "Really."

She stepped back. I closed the door, started the car, and pulled away. I glanced in the rearview mirror when I got to the light at the end of the block. She was still there, watching me.

There was a girl in Denny's apartment.

I heard her when I swung open the door: a rustle in the gloom, a silence that felt like waiting. I switched on the light. Everything was as it had been: the books and the mismatched chairs, the TV, the video tapes stacked on the table. Imagination, nothing more, I thought, but I checked the bedroom all the same.

She was cowering on the other side of the bed—a slender blonde. I put her in her mid-twenties. In that light it was hard to be sure.

"Don't hurt me," she said.

She said, "You look like Denny."

She said, "I miss him."

"I miss him, too," I said, and the statement struck me with the force of revelation: I'd been missing Denny for years. I hadn't even known it.

We ate at a diner down the street—Luke's, a place that didn't look much more promising than the Paradise Arms. Booths of torn green vinyl. Chipped plates and peeling laminate on the tables, a dead fly on the window seal. Fluorescent tubes buzzed overhead. In the flickering yellow glare, she looked weary and brittle, older than I'd thought she was, haunted by the ghost of her own beauty, which was utterly conventional. At home in Wisconsin, she'd have been a stunner. In Hollywood, she was just another pretty girl—and that was before time and care had begun to take their toll. Her blue eyes were dull, bracketed by fine lines, her lips pale, compressed by weariness. She was too thin in a town where it was impossible to be too thin.

Her name was Julie and she'd come to L.A. to be a star. She'd become a hostess at a steak house instead, making the round of open-call auditions for more than five years, in which time she had scored only one part—if you could call a single line ("Is that a dachshund?") on *Girl's Best Friend* a part. The only positive in the whole experience, she told me, had been meeting Denny, and even that was debatable. "He quit the show two weeks later," she told me. "He said writing lines for a talking dog was beneath him."

So there went that chance—for both of them.

She kept up with the auditions. He kept tinkering with screenplays. Eventually, they moved in together. I never knew anything about it, of course. So much of Denny's life had been hidden from me. Another secret didn't seem to matter.

"Was he using drugs?" I asked.

She shrugged. The shrug was eloquent. This was Hollywood. Weed, coke, pills, you name it: one thing led to another. Nancy Reagan could have predicted it. It hadn't happened overnight, but when the money began to run out, they'd broken up. She wasn't cut out for the Paradise Arms. She didn't like heroin. She moved in with a girlfriend from the restaurant. She didn't see Denny much after that. But she missed him constantly. She worried. She checked in two or three times a week.

"You were the one that found him, weren't you?" I said. "You called it in."

She sighed. "Don't tell, okay," she said. "Please. I don't need the trouble."

"How'd you happen to be there?"

"He called me. Said he wanted to say good-bye. I asked him what he meant, but he didn't say. He just told me he loved me. He'd never said that before. Never. It scared me, so..." Another eloquent shrug. "I had a key. Just in case, he used to say. You never know. And when I let myself in..."

"He was gone?"

"Yeah."

"So you're saying it was intentional. Suicide."

She pushed food around on her plate.

"Here's the thing," she said. "He was always leery of the stuff. He used clean needles. He was careful about dosing."

"But why would he do it?"

"Why does anyone do it? You come here with all these plans, and you wind up seating tourists in a shitty restaurant instead. And the thing is, you can't go home. Because you didn't make it, right, and that's the last thing you want anyone to know. This place is supposed to be paradise, but it feels more like purgatory to me. Everybody drifting around in limbo. I should have gone to college, become a nurse or whatever. An accountant."

"It's not too late." This from the professional student.

"Sure it is," she said, pushing her plate aside. "Listen, thanks for dinner, but..."

"Julie, why'd you come back to the apartment?"

She looked down. "There's this ring," she said. "He used to let me wear it on special occasions. It was like a thing between us."

"You find it?"

She hesitated. And then, meeting my gaze, she dug into her pocket and laid it on the table between us. My mother's engagement ring. "I'm sorry," she said. "I just... I wanted a keepsake, something of Denny's, you know."

"Yeah," I said. "I understand."

I didn't say anything after that, and she didn't either. The clamor of the diner filled the air around us: the clink of silverware and the muted hum of conversation and someone calling out an order in the kitchen. I thought about Denny, all I didn't know about him, all I never would. He'd told this absolute stranger to me—he'd told Julie—that he loved her. He'd called her at the end to say goodbye.

Our exchange at the airport came back to me. *Take care of yourself*, I'd said.

You too, Ben, he'd responded. *But I guess I don't have to worry about that.*

I slid the ring across the table to her.

"Are you sure?" she asked.

"He'd have wanted you to have it," I said, and I wondered if it was true.

Outside the diner, I asked her about the video tapes. She laughed. "You, too, huh?"

"What do you mean?"

"The last time I saw him, we had lunch. That's all he could talk about. These movies he'd gotten ahold of. What's so special about them, anyway?"

I pondered how to tell her that they were impossible, they didn't exist. "They're pretty rare," I said. "Do you know where he found them?"

"*He* didn't know where he'd found them."

"What do you mean?"

"He said he rented them from this place near West 65th and Broadway. But he must have gotten the address wrong, because when we drove down there he couldn't find the place."

"He wanted to return the tapes."

"I don't think so," she said. "I think he wanted more of them." Then: "Listen, I have to run, okay. Like I said, thanks for dinner."

"You mind giving me your number?" I asked.

She thought about it for a minute, and then she scrawled it out on the back of a receipt she dug out of her purse. She thrust it into my hand, wished me luck, and started off down the sidewalk in the opposite direction. When I called her a few days later, the number was out of service. I never saw her again, either.

We expect our movies—and I'm not talking about experimental films here, I'm talking about movies, I'm talking about Hollywood, I'm talking about stars—we expect our movies, we *want* our movies, to resolve themselves, perhaps because life so rarely does. Plot threads should be neatly tied off, character arcs completed. Consider the case of William Faulkner, who came to Hollywood in 1932 and returned, intermittently, for the next two decades. Faulkner turned out to have a genius for the movies. He received screen credit for just six pictures, but he put his stamp on many others. His single most famous movie, however—an adaptation of Raymond Chandler's *The Big Sleep*—achieved its notoriety in part because it doesn't come together as neatly as we'd like it to. No one could ever figure out who killed the chauffeur—not Faulkner or his collaborators on the screenplay, not the director, not Chandler himself ("They sent me a wire asking me," he later wrote, "and dammit, I didn't know either").

I include this anecdote because the conclusion of my own story—Denny's story, and the story of the impossible movies that he left behind—is a lot messier than I would like it to be. The morning after I ate dinner with Julie, I drove down to West 65th and Broadway. Dimension Video wasn't there. As far as I have been able to determine, it was never there. No one I've talked to recalls it. It does not appear in municipal archives. No business license exists. There are no tax records. I hunted for the place for weeks, broadening my search street by street. Nothing. It simply wasn't there.

By the time I gave up, I realized that I'd given up on my thesis, as well. The Ed Wood I was writing about no longer seemed entirely real to me. There was another Ed Wood—a ghostly doppelgänger who'd directed a ghost of a film starring the ghost of a man who'd died of a heart attack a year before *The Ghoul Goes West* ever went into production. I couldn't sort out who was real and who wasn't. All I know is that I camped out in Denny's apartment so long that I ended up taking over the lease. A month passed, and then another. I ate takeout pizza. I ate Chinese. I ate at Luke's. I drank too much beer. I drank until I was sick of myself, and then I woke up hungover one day and poured all the booze in the apartment down the sink. I showered, ate a slice of cold pizza, and walked to the Video Hut. Lou was in her office.

"I have some movies I think you ought to see," I told her.

We watched them that night on the sofa where my brother died. She gazed at the flickering images in rapt silence. "Where did these come from?" she asked at one point, never taking her eyes from the screen. "I don't know," I said. After that, Lou and I took up the search for Dimension Video together. Somewhere along the way we started seeing each other. I suppose it was only a matter of time. We have a lot in common—almost as much as Denny and I did.

Which brings me back to Denny. Denny and Lugosi.

In the final scenes of Denny's screenplay, Ed Wood wraps *The*

This Island Earth

Ghoul Goes West and the cast retires to the Cameo Club to celebrate. Autry buys rounds for everyone—"I have plenty of money, anyway," he tells Lugosi—but is otherwise morose. Bela shares his dolor. "I have not even that solace," he says, and though the screenplay doesn't describe his thoughts, one can easily imagine him ruminating about the cramped apartment on Harold Way. Awash in morphine and Autry's top-shelf scotch, he might have drifted for a time, lost between Hungary and Hollywood, the career he'd had and the career he could have had, scraps of old dialogue straying through his mind: *Listen to them, the children of the night, what music they make* and *I never drink wine* and, most of all, *I am Dracula*, the phrase that had made him a star. Perhaps he would have recalled a fragment of his monologue from *Bride of the Monster*, the previous picture he'd made with Eddie Wood. "Home?" he might have said. "I have no home. Hunted, despised, living like an animal! The jungle is my home. But I will show the world that I can be its master!"

Except he couldn't, of course. The world mastered him. Denny's screenplay ends with Lugosi's death—not from the heart attack that killed him in reality, but from a deliberate morphine overdose. He'd found fame as Dracula, but his success never reached the height of his ambition and he spent the rest of his life watching it slip away.

Denny wasn't even that lucky. He squandered his moment. He would write no talking dogs. Hollywood killed him as surely as it had killed Lugosi before him.

And me?

Ten years further on, and I'm still here. I work behind the counter at the Video Hut these days. Lou and I do what we can to steer our clientele to the films that matter most to us, but it's the new releases and the adult videos that keep the lights on.

And I guess that's the end—except for the matter of Denny's ashes. They came back to me in a cardboard box the size of a shoebox. I opened it up one time, expecting, I suppose, a fine gray powder. It was coarse and granular instead, with whitish-gray fragments that could only be bone. They would have made a fine prop for a Bela

Lugosi movie. *Irony: it's good for the blood*, Gabriella Ghoul would have said. And with that I closed up the box again. It sat on the chest in Denny's bedroom for several months before I drove it down to Holy Cross Cemetery in Culver City, where Lugosi is buried in the Dracula cape he could never seem to shrug off in life. I scattered a handful of ashes there. The rest I scattered at the base of the Hollywood sign during a midnight expedition up Mount Lee. The sign isn't as impressive as you think it will be when you see it close up—but nothing ever is, is it?

When I was done, I thought about Peg Entwistle and I thought about Lugosi and I thought about the movies that couldn't possibly exist back home in my apartment. But they *did* exist. Somewhere, in some other place than this, those movies were made. Somehow they wound up in Denny's possession, and that's enough to give me hope. I like to imagine that there's a place where Peg Entwistle became a star, where Bela Lugosi became the leading man he'd aspired to become, and where my brother Denny still survives, living up to the measure of his dreams.

Acknowledgements

BRINGING A STORY TO FRUITION is a difficult task at the best of times. It may be especially difficult when you're trying to take seriously the premises implied in such titles as "Teenagers from Outer Space" and "I Married a Monster from Outer Space." Faith can falter. Mine did. Without the support and encouragement of three very good friends—Nathan Ballingrud, Jack Slay, Jr., and Durant Haire—I might never have finished many of these stories at all. I am grateful for their generosity, their kindness, and their wisdom.

Nathan was always there to talk me through the rough patches. Jack and Durant gave each story their concentrated attention, tirelessly reading—and re-reading—each story, providing nuanced and helpful commentary through multiple drafts. Jack has a knack for discerning what I'm trying to achieve before I've quite sorted it out myself. Durant is that rare and useful critic who tells you what you don't want to hear. My colleague Julie Voss also read many of these pieces, with her usual care and insight. Participants in the annual Sycamore Hill Writers Workshop provided me with helpful commentary on "Night Caller from Outer Space" and "The Ghoul Goes West." Because these readers took the stories seriously, I was able to, as well.

Others also helped. I drew throughout these stories upon my uncle Mike Pennington's seemingly comprehensive knowledge of classic cars from the 1950s. In "Night Caller from Outer Space," I leaned

Acknowledgements

heavily upon the expertise of my colleague Bill Richter, who shared his experiences as an AM radio DJ in the early 1960s, and upon the knowledge and memory of my father-in-law, Wayne Singley, who grew up in and around Moulton, Iowa, in the 1940s and 1950s. In some cases, the needs of the story outweighed the obligation to accuracy. But the usual caveats apply: any errors here are my own.

I am also indebted to the editors who first bought these stories and turned upon them a keen editorial eye: John Joseph Adams, Neil Clarke, Ellen Datlow, Wendy Wagner, and Sheila Williams. My agent, Matt Bialer, helped this book find a home. Nicky Crowther and Neil Snowdon at PS Publishing gave it one.

Finally, I my owe my deepest gratitude to my daughter, Carson, and my wife, the lovely and talented Jean Singley Bailey. They did not begrudge my endless hours of distraction; they endured my habit of reading passages of these stories aloud; they never doubted, even when I did. It would not be hyperbole to say that Jean saved my life. Without her selfless love, boundless forgiveness, and unstinting kindness, I would likely never have found the courage to write these stories in the first place.

ABOUT THE AUTHOR

D ALE BAILEY IS THE AUTHOR of eight previous books, including *In the Night Wood*, *The End of the End of Everything*, and *The Subterranean Season*. His story "Death and Suffrage" was adapted for Showtime's *Masters of Horror* television series. His short fiction has been frequently reprinted in best-of-the-year anthologies, including *The Best American Science Fiction and Fantasy*, *The Best Horror of the Year*, and *The Year's Best Weird Fiction*. He has won the Shirley Jackson Award and the International Horror Guild Award, and has been a finalist for the World Fantasy, Nebula, Locus, and Bram Stoker awards. He lives in North Carolina with his family.

Publication Credits

"I Married a Monster from Outer Space" was originally published in *Asimov's Science Fiction* (March 2016). It won the *Asimov's* Annual Readers' Poll Award for Best Novelette of 2016.

"I Was a Teenage Werewolf" first appeared in *Nightmare Magazine* (December 2016; Issue 51). It was reprinted in *The Best American Science Fiction & Fantasy: 2017* and *The Year's Best Weird Fiction, Vol. 4*.

"The Horror of Party Beach" was published in *Lightspeed Magazine* (October 2018; Issue 101).

"Night Caller from Outer Space" is original to this collection.

"Creature from the Black Lagoon" debuted (as "The Creature Recants") in *Clarkesworld Magazine* (October 2013); it was reprinted in *The Year's Best Dark Fantasy and Horror 2014*.

"Invasion of the Saucer-Men" first appeared in *Asimov's Science Fiction* (March/April 2017).

"Teenagers from Outer Space" was published in *Clarkesworld Magazine* (August 2016); it was reprinted in *The Best American Science Fiction & Fantasy: 2017*.

"The Ghoul Goes West" originally appeared at *Tor.com* (January 17, 2018).